Expecting Magic

JC BLAKE

Published by Redbegga Publishing, 2022.

This is a work of fiction. Similarities to real people, places, or events are entirely coincidental.

EXPECTING MAGIC

First edition. December 20, 2022.

Copyright © 2022 JC BLAKE.

Written by JC BLAKE.

To my family.

Chapter One

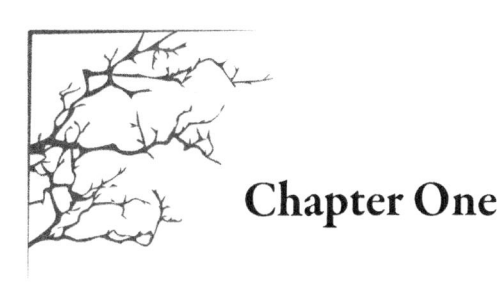

Flames licked at the beaded silk dress, eating into the lacy fabric, and trimming the blackened edges with volcanic orange. Cathy took another swig from the bottle of Prosecco and threw the bouquet she'd spent months designing, and even longer imagining, onto the fire.

"He's a shit! A no good, lying, thieving, treacherous shit!" she shouted into the night.

An upstairs window slammed shut next door as Lexi's arm slipped across her shoulders. "Cathy, you're gonna be alright," her best friend, and number one bridesmaid, soothed. The bonfire crackled, and embers eddied in the hot air, volcanic specks dancing in the night.

Another tear slipped over her lashes. "Sure," Cathy replied, the word laced with bitterness. The pain of being jilted at the altar, left standing alone and rejected in front of her entire family, most of her friends, and some of her work colleagues, stung, badly.

The day had started out beautifully in the hotel suite. Surrounded by bridesmaids curling their hair, applying makeup, chatting excitedly, and sipping delicious champagne from crystal flutes, it had been the morning she had dreamed of. The makeup artist had done an amazing job of making her forty plus face look young and radiant, and the hairstylist had curled and pinned her hair into a frothy mass in an up-do sparkling with diamante. The vintage lace veil, with silver tiara that glittered in the sun as it shone through the hotel window, had completed the look. With tears in her eyes her mother had said, 'Your dad would have been so proud,' then quaffed another mouthful of champagne, her cheeks already flushed with alcohol.

Arriving at the church, Cathy had been met by a fretful Uncle Keith. 'He hasn't arrived,' he'd said. 'Take another turn around the block. I'm sure he'll be here soon.'

One turn had turned into two then three. On the fourth, Uncle Keith wasn't at the gate, her signal to enter the church. But Uncle Keith wasn't at the entrance waiting to take her arm either and the church hushed to silence as she stood in the doorway. Her uneasiness relaxed as she saw Dan at the altar, his back to her. She faltered, unsure of what to do, but the organist began the wedding march and she decided to go it alone and walk down the aisle. Whispers followed her and it wasn't until she had nearly reached the altar that Dan turned around.

Only, it wasn't Dan.

Behind her footsteps clattered, and she turned, sure it would be Dan, flustered and apologetic, to see Uncle Keith, breathless, his cheeks ruddy. From the look in his eyes she knew something terrible had happened and dread sank through her. 'Where is he?' she'd asked, now certain Dan had been in an accident. 'He's not coming, love," Uncle Keith whispered as he'd reached her side. "I'm sorry.'

The whispers grew to a cacophony as the guests realised she'd been jilted. If the tombstone-slabbed aisle had opened to the very yawning mouth of hell, she would have been grateful. She took another swig of champagne, head buzzing as the alcohol suffused her blood.

Lexi gave her shoulders another comforting, pity-filled squeeze. "Things will get better. You're not the first bride to be jilted at the altar." She handed her another tissue. "And you won't be the last."

Leaning her head against Lexi's shoulder, the champagne numbing her pain, Cathy watched as the bouquet of battered pink roses and wilting peonies, sizzled then disappeared into the flames.

"Listen, I've been talking to the girls. We can cast a hex, go for the jugular, and shrink his balls—if you like?"

Choking as laughter bubbled, Prosecco spurted from her nose. "If they get any smaller, they'll disappear!"

Lexi laughed. "Then there's your silver lining! You've had a lucky escape. You do *not* want to spend the rest of your life with a man with small balls!"

Lexi spoke with such sincerity that Cathy managed a laugh. "I guess," she replied.

"It's true, and he's probably a Jaffa anyway."

"Jaffa?"

"Seedless."

Pain seared her heart; at forty-three, her chances of having the baby she had put off for so long and now so desperately wanted, had just gone from slim to none. Another sob rose. Lexi gave her shoulders another squeeze.

"There'll be other men. It's not too late."

Lexi, mother of three beautiful girls, knew Cathy's pain; they'd spoken about it over the years, and knew how she'd struggled with the choice of starting a family versus advancing her career. 'Once I've got this promotion,' she'd say, 'then we can start trying for a baby. Dan's cool with that.'

But Dan hadn't been 'cool' with that, not really.

He'd wanted kids from the beginning, was ready to get married and settle down a few years after they met, but she was mid-career and it was about to skyrocket, or so she thought.

Throwing another flower into the fire, she watched it sizzle as the flames enveloped it. She'd hit the glass-ceiling and no amount of working way past home time, or busting a gut on the next project, or wooing the next client, could break through it. That was until Steve, her boss, had died suddenly. He had issues – heart inflammation caused by some experimental medication he'd been taking – but death hadn't seemed a possibility. He was one of those invincible guys, a larger-than-life character who had climbed the greasy pole with ease and managed to make friends along the way. Plus, he was a runner and lean with it, so his sudden death was a shock to them all. But despite the grief, his departure to the Ever After was a new opportunity, at least that's how Cathy sold it to Dan; there was a real chance of promotion this time, and Steve's salary was pretty much double hers, their lives would be set. So, she'd doubled down on efforts at work, staying even later at the office, working harder on more projects, organising even more meetings, networking with the colleagues that could make a difference when it came time to choose Steve's replacement. She had really pushed the boat out; that promotion was going to be hers.

Dan had been pissed to say the least, but she knew he'd come round.

Only, he hadn't.

"Why did he do it this way?" She wiped another tear from her cheek. "Why did he have to humiliate me?" Another self-pitying sob overwhelmed her.

Lexi sighed. "He's a coward, Cathy."

Cathy picked up the exquisite veil that had cost a small fortune.

"Are you sure you want to do that?" Lexi asked, holding her hand back from the flames. "It's so beautiful, vintage lace."

"I'm not going to save it for next time! This *was* my only chance."

"Oh, Cathy! That's not true, and someone else may want it. Sell it. At least get some of your money back."

"Dan paid for it," she said. "And anyway, it's bad luck. I'll jinx whoever buys it. A jilted bride is the last person they want to buy a wedding veil from."

Wrapping the veil around her hand, she screwed it into a ball and threw it onto the fire then took another swig from the bottle as the fabric began to crackle and burn. The past week, since Dan had been a no show at the altar, had been a blur of self-pity, ignoring calls from her mother, and drinking her way through the crates of Prosecco she'd bought for the wedding breakfast.

"I'm supposed to be in Barbados right now!" she sobbed as another wave of self-pity crashed over her.

Lexi remained quiet.

"It was my dream honeymoon. Ever since I was a kid I wanted to go on honeymoon to Barbados. It was perfect. I should have gone, even if I was on my own," she sighed.

When Lexi didn't respond, Cathy knew her friend had something to say and when she stared into the fire and poked it with a stick, her suspicion was confirmed. "What is it?" she asked. Lexi pursed her lips in response but didn't reply. "You know something ... don't you."

The deep sigh Lexi took before beginning to speak made Cathy's stomach lurch in queasy anticipation. "Don't you think I should have gone anyway?" she asked.

Lexi shook her head. "Cathy ... Dan is in Barbados."

"What!"

"And ... he's not alone."

A wave of cold rolled over Cathy, roiling in her stomach, the sensation of sinking intense. "How ... No! It's not true. He was just fed up with me working such long hours. He wanted kids. This new promotion was just the last straw-"

Lexi shook her head. "I don't know how long it has been going on ... and I swear to you that I didn't know anything until yesterday, but he's there with Alice."

Alice was one of their friends, one of their close friends, she'd often join her and Dan for dinner. Nubile, curvaceous, ready to settle down and breed, Alice. Ten years younger than Cathy, Alice.

"Alice!"

Lexi nodded. "Yes, Alice."

"But ... but she's just giving him moral support."

Lexi pulled out her mobile phone, scrolled for a moment, then passed it over. The screen held an image of a couple in swimwear walking along a fabulous beach with white sand and a brilliant blue sky. The very beach Cathy had seen a hundred times on her screen and imagined walking along with Dan after their wedding. The next one was a selfie showing Alice and Dan kissing beneath the palm leaf roof of a beachside bar. Tongues were involved and Alice's eyes seemed to be throwing out a challenge. He's mine now, they said.

Despite the fire, Cathy turned cold. "The bitch! She ... and he ... he is a lying, cheating ... shit!"

"It gets worse."

"Worse! How could it get worse?"

"Scroll down," Lexi said.

Cathy scrolled past several more posts until she came to one picturing a woman's hand. The distinctive rings marked it as Alice's. She was holding a pregnancy test and it was positive. Her heart, already beating hard, grew painful and, from deep within her core, rage surged. The fire sputtered, blazed then died, embers blackening in an instant.

"Woah!" declared Lexi with a glance to the fire. "Steady on. You're gonna be alright, just hang on to that thought." Lexi knew just how chaotic Cathy's magick could be.

"She's pregnant," Cathy managed. Jumbled thoughts whirled but made no sense. "It's never going to be alright."

"Then revenge it is," Lexi declared. "Do we cast the spell to shrink his balls tonight or tomorrow? I've got the girls on speed dial."

Chapter Two

After Lexi left, Cathy continued drinking. Head buzzing, and now more than a little unsteady, she sat on the sofa, unable to sleep. Thoughts of Dan and Alice plagued her. How long had it been going on? Why hadn't she noticed?

You were working eighty hours a week?
You've barely seen the guy for the past few months.

Sure, but ten years, they'd been together for ten years! Surely, she would have noticed something.

Ten years of putting off getting married. Ten years of saying no to trying for a baby ... just wait another year!

She went through the past months as though on a film reel, picking out the moments when Alice and Dan had been together. They were friendly, but Alice was just that type—touchy-feely. She'd stand beside him, hand on his shoulder as he peeled the spuds for Sunday dinner, laughing at another of his ridiculous, adorable, jokes, whilst Cathy carried on working at the table, laptop open, glad of the cups of coffee Alice supplied her with. They'd be chatting and laughing in the kitchen whilst Cathy worked out the minutiae of another quote to reel in another client, making herself indispensable to the company, the one who brought in the big fish.

Looking back there *had* been signs. Dan hadn't touched her for ... months! There had been a time when they couldn't keep their hands off of each other, but recently ... recently she'd been too tired, or too stressed. When Dan and Alice had gone out to meet up with some of their other friends for meals or a night at the pub Cathy had been relieved; it had taken the pressure off as she'd doubled down on nailing the promotion Steve's death had opened up for her.

She groaned, head thumping; Alice had taken her man, but she'd handed him to her like a box of open chocolates—*here take one, they're delicious!*

Another wave of self-pity washed over her. Another tear welled over her lashes and dropped onto her cheeks.

Her mother had carped on about it being her fault, and it was!

Cathy had lost her man and with him any chance of having the baby she now so desperately wanted. She was forty-three, forty-four in a few months, what chance did she have of finding the right guy to have a baby with before her ovaries shrivelled and died? None!

As she took another slug of wine a buzz from her phone alerted her to an email. Even through the last week, when she was supposed to be on honeymoon, and despite her misery, she'd kept in touch with work. Cathy fumbled for the phone on the coffee table and opened the screen. It was from Kelly in HR. The heading read, 'Termination of Contract'.

"What the hell does that mean?" Befuddled with alcohol, she could only think that a contract had been lost so opened the message. She read it with barely focused eyes then read it aloud, trying to make sense of it.

"Gross misconduct ... contract terminated ... arrangements have been made for you to collect your belongings at ten am." The words still didn't make sense.

She was fired?

What!

"What the hell!"

Scrolling through her list of contacts she clicked on 'Glynnis Douglas', her closest colleague. They weren't great friends but had worked on the same team for the past two years and Glynnis would be sure to know what was going on—she always did. Cathy pressed 'Call' without checking the time.

Glynnis answered after several rings. "Cathy? What's wrong? It's late."

"I've been fired!" Cathy blurted, the words slurred even to her ears.

"Fired?"

"Kelly in HR ... I got an email. They've fired me."

Silence followed as she waited for a response, then Glynnis sighed down the line. "Cathy, I know this is going to be hard to hear, but they've found a replacement for Steve."

Suddenly sober, she sat up. "What? Who?"

"Martin Shaw, he's already in position," Glynnis explained.

"What?" If Cathy had an enemy, Martin Shaw was that man. They had spent years trying to outcompete one another and she knew that he was after Steve's job too. "But he's ... That job was mine! I've worked so hard."

"I overheard him talking, Cathy, sounds like Steve had already singled him out to replace him; they went to the same university, their wives are friends—you know how these guys stick together."

The glass ceiling!

Steve had betrayed her too and there was a tone to Glynnis' voice she didn't like, as though she were enjoying telling her the bad news.

"You were his office wife, hun, not his heir." Cathy could hear the smirk in her words.

"But they've accused me of gross misconduct—what the hell is that about?"

"... There's a box on your desk waiting for your stuff. I'll see you at ten. Maybe we can go out for coffee sometime, commiserate. I'm sure you'll find another job." Her tone was sickly sweet, and completely disingenuous.

"But ... this is ridiculous!"

"Honey, when you're caught passing on company information to the competition ... Play stupid games, win stupid prizes," Glynnis gloated. "Now, it's late, and I've got a meeting first thing. Night."

The phone went dead. Cathy was dismissed, forgotten before she had even left. Accused of a crime she didn't commit—a tactic she had seen played out before but never imagined would be used against her. It was over. There was no point in even trying to clear her name.

"The conniving ... lying ... lying bastards!" Rage erupted and she threw her phone across the room. It fell on a chair and landed with a thud, undamaged, on the carpet.

It was over. Her life was over. What was the point of going on?

"There is no point!" she shouted. "No point at all!" Staggering from the sofa, overwhelmed with humiliation, she made her way to the bathroom and the medicine cabinet. "No point at all," she whispered. The pain of hurt and grief filled every cell in her body.

Alcohol hadn't brought oblivion, but she knew what would.

She reached for the pills, pain killers that would shut down her mind, shut down her body, if she took enough.

"I'll take the lot," she slurred, "then they'll be sorry. Sod you, Dan. Dan the man and his perfect wife. Dan the man and his perfect kids." It was childish, but she didn't care, all she wanted was for the pain to stop.

Grabbing the pack of pills, she made her way back to the living room, and grabbed another bottle from the crate. The corkscrew slipped a couple of times, and she dropped the bottle when the cork popped, but managed to fill up a glass and chug half of it before flopping back on the sofa. She didn't count the pills, just popped them out of the packet until a big enough pile sat on the coffee table. She took another slurp of wine and grabbed a handful.

"This is it," she said. "Goodbye Dan. Hope you rot!"

Her hand trembled as she cupped it towards her mouth.

Just do it! No one wants you. You're a washed-up old bag and you won't even be able to get another job once the word gets out, never mind a man! Just a dried-up old hag, left on the shelf to shrivel.

Another wave of self-pity overwhelmed her, and she emptied the pills into her mouth. They sat on her tongue, their coating beginning to dissolve.

Just take another glug of wine. End it now. The pain will be gone.

Reaching for her glass, she held it against her lips.

"No! It's not the way."

Startled by the voice, she twisted in her seat to search for the intruder and then began to choke as the pills were thrown to the back of her throat. She coughed, boked, then sprayed them across the carpet.

On all fours, gasping for breath, she spat out the remaining pills. Head throbbing, it took a few minutes before she realised someone was knocking at the front door. After pulling herself to an unsteady stand, she staggered to the door and flung it open, leaning against the frame for support.

A cloaked figure, hidden by the shadows of his hood stood on her doorstep. "Good evening, Mistress Earnshaw."

"Smidnight," she managed, barely able to focus. "Whassit?"

"I'm here on behalf of your late aunt, Mistress Hyldreth Earnshaw."

"Late?"

"Yes, sadly, your aunt passed to the Ever After several months ago, but she has sent ... she left a will, and I am very pleased to inform you that you are a recipient of her largesse."

The words barely penetrated her understanding. "Largesh?"

He held out a large wrap of manilla paper tied with black ribbon and sealed with red wax.

She took the envelope, pushed the door, then sank to her knees and blacked out.

Chapter Three

Heath opened his eyes, the half-empty glass threatening to spill from his hand, as he woke from sleep. The fire, lit by Argenon, burned low in the hearth, taking the chill that had descended upon the room as night grew deep.

He ignored the chitter at his shoulder, barely conscious of the creature as it flittered to the mantlepiece and sat with the others as they watched.

"Argenon, why do you let these damnable creatures pester me!" he growled, noticing the throng of tiny creatures along the mantle. "Get rid of them!"

Disgruntled chitters filled the air and several of the creatures rose with a buzzing of wings. Little bigger than hummingbirds, the fairies, with their mass of dandelion seed-like hair, swooped across the fireplace before returning to their place.

"They have become uncommonly annoying these past days."

"Forgive them, Lord. They're picking up on the changing energies within the house. It senses her return. As do you."

Heath gave a disgruntled huff. "Fine lot of good it will do." He drained the last of the whisky, enjoying the sensation of the fiery liquid, the glass ridiculous in his massive hand. "Another," he demanded.

Argenon filled the glass.

"Mistress Earnshaw believed it would."

"Has the letter been delivered?"

"Yes, Lord. I delivered it myself."

"And she took it?"

"... Well, yes, although ... the lady was indisposed at the time. I have instructed Mercurio to remain and ensure that the letter is read."

Heath sensed an obfuscation of the truth. "Indisposed?"

"... Tired after a long day's work, I presume. From her demeanour I assumed that she had enjoyed a glass of wine prior to my visit."

"Drunk?"

"Tired is how I'd describe it, Lord."

Heath shook his head, a band of pain beginning to tighten across his forehead.

"Lord, I feel certain that your wait is nearly over-"

Heath grunted.

Argenon replaced the decanter on the table then placed another log on the fire. "I read the runes, last night," he said as he placed a second log beside the first.

Heath watched the elderly man with interest, scanning his face for signs of deceit. "And what did they tell you?"

"Promising, my Lord. Very promising," he replied with a reassuring smile and stepped away from the fire and into the shadows.

"Fie on it! Just tell me."

"They foretold fertility ..."

"Good!"

"But-"

"But!" Heath snapped. "There is always a 'but'! Spit it out man!"

"But also of adversity ..."

Heath groaned.

"... and deception."

Too agitated to remain seated, Heath stood, his massive frame blocking the fire's glow, casting Argenon in deeper shadow. Catching his own reflection in the mirror, he scowled. Staring back at him was the face of sin punished; bones contorted by a curse so strong that it had held him in its grip for centuries. His dark brow furrowed, pulling down above eyes filled with anger and a deep, abiding loathing. "The Curse will win then," he said, considering the corrupted visage that stared back. Canines protruded from a jaw too broad and elongated to be considered anything but ugly.

"We will overcome it this time," soothed Argenon.

"Like the last time and the one before that?" The faces of previous brides swam in his memory, the hope they brought crushed as the Curse destroyed any chance of escape from his centuries' old purgatory.

"This time will be different, Lord. I feel it in my bones-"

"Hah!"

"And the runes predicted fertility."

"Yes, but will it bring forth a live birth?"

Argenon remained silent.

"See! Even you, so full of hope, do not believe it will."

Argenon sighed. "I promise you, on my oath, that I will do everything in my power to see that it does."

Heath sat back down in the chair, sinking into its deep leather frame, almost hidden by the wings. "There is a chance … if she arrives before the Harvest moon."

"I'm hoping that she will arrive within the next few days, Lord."

Heath nodded, though his free hand gripped the arm of the chair. The Curse had bedevilled him for centuries and, along with the hope for release that came with each new bride, so did the fear of crushing disappointment and failure. This time it had to work. This time, if he failed, he would take steps to end his miserable life for good.

The fire crackled, sending sparks from the burning logs. The fairies chittered, rising from the mantle as they sensed the danger of his temper. Heath swatted at them with lacklustre effort as they climbed to the ceiling then swooped as though in a frenetic murmuration. "Argenon! Rid me of these terrors," he said before downing the half-glass of whiskey. "Before I break them with these claws and crush them underfoot," he growled, holding out a taloned and massive hand.

The chittering became a cacophony of overly excited shrieks before Argenon stepped forward, held out his arm for the swarm to land upon, and carried the creatures from the room, tutting about 'behaving in the master's presence' before closing the heavy door with a soft thud.

Chapter Four

Cathy woke to grey light, the front door ajar, drizzle spattering her face, and the black and beady eye of a crow staring down at her.

The crow cawed in a disapproving way as their eyes locked then stepped forward and pecked at the outstretched hand still clutching the unopened envelope. Too numbed by alcohol, and unsure whether she was awake or still in the uncomfortable depths of last night's dreams, she didn't respond. It cawed again, a little louder, then pecked again, a lot harder. This time she flinched and, if birds could look satisfied, it did.

Laying at the open entrance to her house being pecked at by a bird for all the world to see, or at least the nosey neighbours in her quiet, pensioner-infested cul-de-sac, simultaneous waves of nausea and heat swirled in her belly and surged over her skin. With a low groan, she shuffled back from the entrance and closed the door, shutting out the insistent bird.

The effect of the past days' drinking were taking their toll and, mouth furred, skin clammy, head pounding, she made her way to the kitchen for a drink, desperate for water. Passing the scattered pills and upturned wine glass, she threw the envelope onto the sofa as she remembered last night's efforts at self-destruction and then the email from work.

Sagging against the sink, memories flooded her thoughts. She had been terminated! Terminal velocity had been reached and her life had been obliterated. "None of this is real. This cannot be my life," she rasped as her fuddled brain struggled to comprehend what had happened.

"You've got the voice of a forty-a-day chain smoker. That's real."

Searching for the voice, head thumping, she spun to an empty space. There was no one in the room. But it had seemed so real!

You've been drinking—a lot. You've frazzled your brain and now you've got the DT's. Delirium tremens. You're so full of booze that you're hallucinating.

"Open the letter then!"

The voice came from directly behind and this time when she turned, she saw it—the nagging crow from the doorstep. Beady eyes watched her, its glossy feathers gleaming despite the early morning greyness of the room.

"How the hell did you get in here?" she asked with a glance to the closed door.

It eyed her with disdain from its perch on the back of her sofa.

It had to be an hallucination. Birds did not speak, no matter how much she and her coven sisters had hoped and fantasised about being able to communicate with animals. No amount of witchery had ever helped, and none of them had the familiars that witches were supposed to have. Even her mother, who had 'the gift', even if it was erratic, couldn't talk to animals and definitely didn't have a familiar.

Keeping one eye on the bird before she opened the door in the hope it would head for the light and fly out, she filled a large glass with water and swallowed the lot. Her stomach rolled with queasy disgust.

"I'm waiting." The bird's beak opened and closed in time with the words.

"You did not just speak to me!" It had to be an hallucination. "Birds don't talk. You are not real. This is all part of a dream—no, a nightmare. I'm still asleep. I have to be."

The bird cocked its head and closed its eyes. "Yawn!" Its tone was disparaging. "Here we go again!" it said with resignation. "I am real. I am not a figment of your underutilized imagination or your alcohol-sodden brain."

"This is ... wow ... this is intense," Cathy said, regretting every mouthful of wine swallowed since being jilted. She had fried her brain and sunk into some sort of psychotic episode. Lexi had told her to take it steady; she should have listened.

The bird groaned. "What do they teach witches these days? Nothing useful, obviously." Hopping down from the back of the sofa, the bird pecked at the manilla envelope. "Open it!" it insisted. "Then we can get on with things. I do not have all day."

As Cathy stepped forward, the bird raised a black and glossy wing. "On second thoughts, go and brush your teeth first. You stink. I can smell your breath from here."

Despite being a figment of her imagination the bird wasn't wrong; her mouth felt like a herd of pigs had trampled through it. She made her way to the bathroom.

The events of last night were unclear, and she had no recollection of the letter being delivered, or getting the pills, or how she had come to be half in, half out of her front door that morning.

"Never again!" she sighed

"Do hurry up and stop with the self-pity. It's quite disgusting; shows a low and weak mind. And where you're going ... you'll need to toughen up."

Insistent *and* rude. Her imagination sure knew how to throw out the most annoying types of hallucination.

After brushing her teeth, her mouth now minty fresh, she returned to the living room, stepping over the pile of pills to avoid the wet patch on the carpet where the remains of her wine had spilled from the glass.

"It stinks like a whore's boudoir after an orgy in here," the crow quipped.

Startled, she could only stare at the bird but despite her shock, she laughed. "You may not be real, but you are the rudest bird I have ever met."

"I advise opening a window, fresh air does wonders." The glossy bird sighed then shook its head. "And anyway, I doubt you've met any birds before or spoken to them, it's obvious to me that you are a highly inferior practitioner of the arts, and I am shocked that I've been put into this situation. It is an insult to my station."

"Rude and arrogant," she said and reached for the envelope, keeping her distance from the bird, real or not.

"Open it then!" it nagged.

"Give me a minute!" The imaginary bird was becoming annoying.

Half-drawn curtains made the room dingey but outside the morning sun had begun to brighten to a lighter grey. She pulled the curtains back, then sat at the table, and opened the envelope.

Despite her suspicion that the bird was a figment of her imagination, the envelope, with its thick manilla paper, felt real. The wax seal was imprinted with what looked like a dragon at its centre and lettering circled the edge. Intrigued, and not wanting to break the seal, she prized it off with a knife then pulled the ribbon free. The envelope opened to a square, revealing inner leaves filled with writing in a rounded script that reminded her of the medieval manuscripts Lexi was so in love with. "Insular," she said, remembering the name of the Anglo-Saxon script.

"Well done! You've managed to impress me. Now read it."

Cathy threw the bird a withering glance. It stared back with defiance.

"Fine. I will," she replied, then read, "'Thyse is the last Will & Testament of Hyldreth Earnshawe. I beinge of sounde mynde and memorye and body do herebye make and declare the following to be mye Last Will and Testament, hereby revoking all other Wills by me heretofore made.

I herebye direct that all my worldly possessions and monies be given in totality to Catherine Earnshaw, daughter of Sybil Earnshaw nee Yikkar of Pendle and Caleb Earnshaw of Penrith.'"

At the bottom, it was signed 'Hyldreth Earnshaw' in a shaky though elaborate copperplate hand.

"She left the house to me!"

"Read the Codicil."

Cathy scanned the will. Written in a smaller, though matching script, was written:

'Take Note - All lands, buildings, and monies shall pass to Miss Catherine Earnshaw upon her marriage to the Tenant of Witherwood Hall and the resultant production of an heir until which time she will take on the role of Housekeeper, managing the estate and taking care and control of its current inhabitants.'

A frown creased her brow. "What does this mean, production of an heir? And who the hell is the Tenant of Witherwood Hall?"

Care and control?

"Tsk! You are to marry the tenant and produce a child, or you get nothing. Well, not quite nothing. You get a job and a house and access to the money to run the estate, but only when you marry and give birth to a child will the property and its income become yours in perpetuity."

Cathy remained silent, her mind failing to process the craziness of the words.

"In order to inherit the house and its money, you must have a baby."

"Baby?"

The bird sighed. "Married first, though, of course."

"Married?"

He shook his head. "Whatever were they thinking," he muttered. "Very well, my job is done. I shall see you at the Hall."

A waft of energy pushed at Cathy's shoulder and then the bird disappeared.

Chapter Five

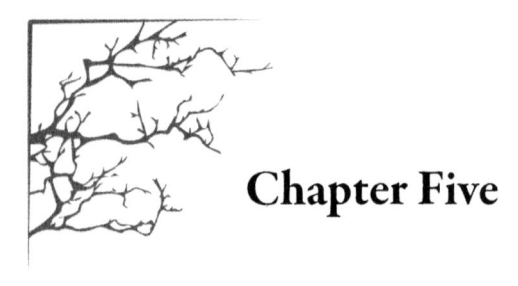

"No way!" Lexi took the Will from her hand and read it aloud. It sounded just as crazy as the first time she'd read it. "This is mad."

Cathy took another sip of coffee as they sat on the patio whilst Lexi's kids played on a lawn littered with brightly coloured plastic tractors, bicycles, balls, and pull-along toys. The two older children jumped on the trampoline, hemmed in by safety net. Her youngest, Josh, sat shovelling sand into his brother's shoe. Lexi smiled and waved as they called for her to watch.

"It is crazy. Last night was weird, but this morning was surreal." Cathy leant forward. "There was a bird staring at me when I woke up and it was bloody rude!" she said remembering the crow's disparaging comments.

Lexi threw her a questioning frown above the paper. "Rude?"

She nodded. "Bloody rude," she repeated. "Like 'you stink and why am I here talking to this idiot' kind of rude."

"It spoke to you?"

Again, Cathy nodded. "I know! I know how it sounds, but the damned bird talked to me. I thought I was hallucinating at first but … but it was like a messenger, I think."

"It delivered the envelope?"

"No, it was a weird guy who brought that. I was drunk. I don't remember much."

"So drunk you passed out and woke up with your door open! Cathy! That is so dangerous-"

"Sure, I know, and I won't do it again, but-"

"So maybe the bird was there but you just imagined it talking."

"Lexi! You're a witch, for heaven's sake. We practice magic. We cast spells. We get results. The damned bird talked to me. I'm sure."

"Okay, okay," she said in a quieter tone with a glance across to her kids. "I believe you. This," she held up the will, "this is what's unbelievable."

"I know! But it's there, in black and white."

"And you have an Aunt Hyldreth?"

Cathy nodded. "I do. We used to visit on the holidays—Solstice, Yule—when I was a kid, until dad died."

"You can't do it," she said. "It's like an ... an arranged marriage."

"They work, sometimes, I guess. Millions of people do it."

"Mail order bride!"

Cathy laughed. "I guess, plus, I get the house and *all* of Aunt Hyldreth's money."

Lexi shook her head. "You'll be signing your life away," she said. "You can't do it."

"That's easy for you to say, Lexi," Cathy said with a glance across the lawn to the children. "You've already got everything—a beautiful house, fantastic kids, a gorgeous and loving husband."

Pity filled Lexi's eyes. "I'm fortunate, I admit it."

"Fortunate! I'd give everything to have what you've got."

"I love you, Cathy, but you could have had it all, Dan-"

"Don't talk to me about Dan!"

"He waited-"

She held up a hand. "I know. It's all my fault. I've already had this from my mother!"

"Okay, I won't say another word."

"So," Cathy said in a calmer tone, "this could be my last chance. Last night ... last night I realised just how stupid I've been. Putting my poxy career before what really counted. I pushed Dan into Alice's arms—I know that—and I've left it too late to start again. Lexi, I'm forty-four this year. I haven't got many fertile years left."

"You could always have some eggs frozen?"

"What and be the oldest mum in the playground?"

"I'm one of the eldest," Lexi replied with a shrug of her shoulders.

"Sure, and you're five years younger than me. What if I'm fifty before I meet the right man? I'll be practically decrepit. The kid will think I'm his grandma."

"I get it, but-"

"I've made up my mind, Lexi. I'm going to Witherwood Hall."

"Let's put it past the girls first. What do you say?"

"Sure," Cathy said, determined that they wouldn't change her mind. "And I've got business I want some help with."

"Oh?"

"Martin Shaw. He stole my job, and I'm not letting him get away with it."

A smile grew at the corner of Lexi's mouth, and she held up her mobile. "I'm sure we can do something to help."

Within minutes Lexi had convened an emergency coven meeting for that evening and the 'girls', as she affectionately called the eccentric collection of women that belonged to the group, arrived at the house with a mixture of breathless excitement and wide-eyed curiosity.

With Lexi's children in bed, they gathered in the garden, sitting themselves around the large circular fire pit she joked was her cauldron. Logs crackled as flames leapt within the metal bowl, bright against the backdrop of a darkening sky. Cathy popped the cork of another bottle of the Prosecco she had bought for her wedding and offered it to Naomi. The woman took it and began to fill the glasses offered up then filled her own to the top. "I'm not driving. I'm getting a taxi home," she said before taking sips from the overfilled glass.

Sasha, a younger woman who had just passed her exams to become a solicitor, looked at her with concern. "Don't get tipsy before we cast," she warned. "Your energies will be blocked.

Naomi batted a hand at her and laughed. "Alcohol lets my energies flow. My spells are always more powerful."

"It's the opposite for me," Sasha said. "I get all fuddled. I need a clear head."

"That's because you're a novice," Naomi replied then took another sip of the bubbling wine.

Cathy watched the exchange with interest, noting the frisson of tension between the women. Sasha was young, that was true, but she had studied the craft as diligently as she had studied for her exams. That Naomi was jealous of her knowledge had become obvious during previous meetings. Naomi had powers but claimed that she preferred to allow the magic to flow through her intuitively. Secretly, Cathy believed that Naomi could be a much more powerful witch if she would study the craft rather than pick things up in an ad hoc fashion. "It helps me channel the energies," Naomi said glancing at Sasha over the rim of the glass. "I can cast from within here," she said tapping at her belly, "and not here." She tapped a finger to her temple and took another sip of her drink.

"Ooh! What are we casting?" asked Judy, an older woman with a mass of greying hair held up in a messy bun. She sipped her wine, then eased back in the balloon back wicker chair. One of two that she always claimed when the coven met at Lexi's.

"We're avenging Cathy!" Carole said, twirling a finger around a long curl of her bright blonde hair. Several years younger than Lexi, Carole worked as a triage nurse at a local practice. Like Lexi, she had three young children, and a husband who adored her. It wasn't hard to see why. She was petite but curvaceous and always ready with a smile, and when she spoke to you, she had that knack of making you feel special, as if you were important to her. In return she loved her husband and thrilled at being a homemaker and mother. In the past Cathy had pitied her for her part-time job, lack of 'real' prospects, and ambition. Her job was nothing compared to Cathy's career. Now she felt a sense of shame for being so condescending. She had been a fool. Carole was happy and content with her life—she was the successful one, not Cathy.

Cathy's meandering thoughts refocused as Abby, the youngest woman, and the most recent addition to the coven asked, "Are we casting against Alice then?"

Carole shook her head whilst throwing Abby a frown after a quick glance at Cathy.

The mention of Alice prodded at Cathy's pain, but she pushed the sensation away. Talking about Alice and Dan was too raw. "Nope!" she said with a forced but kindly smile at Abby, "I'm after a different cheating rat. Martin Shaw. He's a work colleague and he stole my job."

This revelation was followed by a series of sympathetic murmurs and the women grew quiet as Cathy described how hard she'd worked to get the promotion that she knew was rightfully hers only to be stabbed in the back by Martin Shaw and unceremoniously fired from the company.

"He lied about me!" she said remembering the accusations of giving away sensitive information to the competition that had been laid against her.

"That's terrible!"

"He really stitched you up," commiserated Carole.

"He did," agreed Cathy, "and I want him punished."

Abby clapped her hands. "This is going to be fun."

"I suggest the pox," Naomi said. "I know Martin Shaw and he's a total creep."

"Ooh, tell us how you know him, Naomi," Abby said.

"He used to work for my company. He was notorious for working his way through the office and leaving a trail of broken hearts in his wake."

"A lothario," said Judy.

"A what?"

"A lothario," Judy repeated. "An unscrupulous seducer of women."

"If you say so," laughed Abby. "He sounds like a rat to me."

"He is," Cathy agreed. "He's ruthless and doesn't care who he hurts as long as he gets what he wants."

"So, what are we going to do then?"

"Syphilis," suggested Carole. "Or gonorrhoea. That's really nasty. You should see the fellas we have come in at work." Carole shuddered. "It goes all green and slimy ... down there."

"Gross!"

Cathy laughed. "I like the way you're thinking, sisters. I was planning on something that would make him itch and bring him out in a nasty rash."

"The pox," suggested Judy.

"Plague?"

"We've got to do this properly," counselled Naomi. "He has to suffer. Giving him a few spots and making him itch a bit won't be enough punishment for what he's done to our sister."

Murmurs of agreement passed among them.

"Okay, what about halitosis. And I mean a really stinking, mouth full of dead fish kind of halitosis."

Abby giggled. "Or make him blow wind."

"I wanted to do that to Alice," admitted Cathy. "I imagined what spells I would cast against her, although she's pregnant so I wouldn't do it yet. I know she's squeamish about it so I wanted to cast a spell that would make her fart every time Dan tried to kiss her."

Laughter erupted. "That would be hilarious."

"I don't know why you're being so soft," said Naomi. "You should make them suffer for what they've done to you."

Cathy sighed. "I know, but ... I just haven't got the energy to hold onto that much bitterness."

"Being offered a house and husband is one way to get over it," Judy said.

Cathy smiled. "I think it has helped. I don't feel so ... so torn up about it all now. Life seems kind of exciting to be honest."

"Some people have all the luck," Naomi said then took another sip of wine.

"Not sure it's luck," said Lexi. "Cathy's been through hell these past weeks."

"And it's wonderful that she has fallen on her feet," replied Naomi.

"It's amazing," Abby agreed. "Are you going to go through with it?"

Cathy nodded. "I am. I'm travelling up there once I've collected my things from the office."

"And cast your magic against Martin Shaw."

"Yes, and I want to see him squirm."

"Then the pox it is."

"But not the real pox," Carole said. "I mean, that's contagious isn't it? Is that what killed all of those people in the Middle Ages."

"No," replied Lexi, "that was the Black Death. Bubonic plague."

"We can't cast a hex to give him that!" Abby said. "It's dangerous."

"Of course we can't, but we can cast a hex that gives him something that imitates it."

"Just a little bit of pox, for an hour or so," Judy laughed.

"Exactly," Cathy said. "But I want it to be something that everyone will see."

"Are we all agreed. Martin Shaw shall receive a dose of super pox."

"Yes."

"Aye!"

"If it makes him itch like mad, then yes," said Cathy. "And I want pustules, great big gooey pustules."

"Gross!"

"You are wicked, Cathy," Abby laughed.

"It's not going to be real, not a real contagious disease though, right?" said Carole.

"That's right," said Cathy. "But it will make him itch for real. And the pustules will ooze."

"Got it."

"I feel queasy," said Abby, wrinkling her nose.

"I want to be there to see it," Naomi said.

"I'll video it for you," promised Cathy.

"And then send it to Dan," suggested Naomi, "so that he knows what you did."

Cathy shook her head. "No. Let Dan have his perfect life."

Lexi slipped an arm around her shoulder. "Aw, hun. You'll be happy again one day soon, I promise."

"I hope so," Cathy said.

"You will. You'll see."

"Seeing those pustules ooze down Martin's neck will definitely make me happy," Cathy laughed shrugging off the intense sensation of despair that had wafted across her at the mention of Dan.

"Then let's to it sisters." Lexi stabbed a finger to a page in her grimoire. "I think I have the perfect hex, but we'll need something that belongs to him, hair, something like that."

"Will nail clippings do?" Cathy asked.

"You have not got nail clippings!"

"Already?"

Cathy nodded. "I've never trusted him, so I collected them as insurance."

Carole snorted. "How did you get hold of his nail clippings?"

"He's got a horrible habit of clipping his nails at his desk. I just snuck into his office one evening and emptied his trash."

"Sneaky!"

"Well, I prefer to think of it as being prepared," Cathy said with a smile and a glance to the gathered women.

Chapter Six

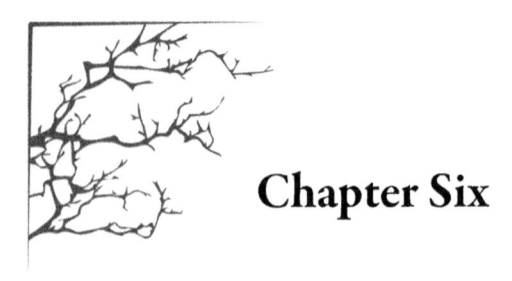

With the spell cast, Cathy returned home and spent the rest of the evening packing. Now that she had decided to go to Witherwood Hall, she was going all in. At work, she was known for her ruthless efficiency, and she applied those skills to sorting out her house. Discovering that Dan was to become a father had killed her self-pity, now she was angry, and she turned that energy to good use.

The following day, she arranged for a professional packing company to come to her house, pack up all of her belongings, and place them in storage. She contacted an estate agent to value the property in the morning and a solicitor to deal with the conveyancing and Dan.

The prospect of living at Witherwood Hall had grown in appeal as had the idea of an arranged marriage. Aunt Hyldreth had been a little eccentric but kind and thoughtful too and Cathy had reasoned that she would choose a suitable husband for her only niece.

With most of her belongings packed, Cathy put the remaining champagne up for sale on social media, then settled down for the evening, imagining her new life as Housekeeper, and meeting the tenant of Witherwood Hall for the first time. She'd already idealised him. He'd be tall, with a beard, have dark hair, and look at her with lustful eyes

EXPECTING MAGIC

the very first time they met. Imagining him any other way opened the flood gates of doubt, so she fixated on that image. She was going through with the marriage, and that was that. Witherwood Hall, its inhabitants, and its tenant, were her future, of that she was certain.

The booze sold within the hour, and she went to bed early, sober, and determined to keep a clear mind intact for the coming days. Plus, she wanted to keep the visit to the office when she had arranged to go in and collect her things sharp in her mind. There was nothing at her desk she was particularly attached to, so the visit wasn't really necessary, but she wanted to see the outcome of the spell the coven had cast for herself. In the past they had practiced a little light magic, some of the less dangerous spells her mother had passed down to her; causing a flash of acne, a runny tummy, hiding things, just stuff to take a bit of vengeance on people, usually colleagues who'd got on their nerves—nothing major. Martin's punishment was their most adventurous and advanced effort yet.

On the morning of the meeting, after showering, and packing the last few items in her suitcases, she locked the house, deposited the keys with the estate agents, and made her way to the office.

It felt odd to turn up in jeans and a casual top, and instead of pushing open the doors with a mobile in one hand, already discussing issues with clients, anxiety high on the scale, she walked with an easy stride through the lobby and called the lift in excited anticipation. Although a little nervous about the scathing looks that would be thrown her way from her now ex-colleagues her curiosity at seeing the evidence of the hex they'd cast against him trumped the anxiety.

She reached the floor that housed the company's offices and made her way to the reception desk, knowing that her card to the main work area wouldn't work. Mary, the receptionist, gave her a pitying look but remained professional. "Good morning, Miss Earnshaw. If you wait here, I'll fetch security."

"Security? But I'm just here to collect my things."

"It's just procedure," she said with an apologetic tone. "Try not to take it personally."

"I understand," Cathy said with a tight smile, trying not to let her annoyance shine through; Mary was only doing her job.

She sat in the waiting area until two paunchy guards arrived. Neither smiled.

"This way, Miss."

"Sure," she said and rose to follow them. As she passed various co-workers they offered tight smiles, pitying glances, or ignored her by staring at their screens. The sensation of being watched was intense and she was glad to reach her own office, but the relief was suffused with bitter disappointment; Martin's office, next to hers, was empty.

She turned her attention to the sparse collection of personal items on her desk, noticing that her hard drive had already been removed along with the files stacked on the shelves opposite.

"Laptop please, miss," the larger guard said, holding out his hand. She passed him the device in its protective case. Her access to any company files had preceded the text and when she'd tried to log in to her emails afterwards, the account had been blocked. Handing the laptop over to the guard removed any doubt that her time at the company was over.

She began to pack her personal items, picking up a silver frame. It held a photograph of her and Dan just after he'd proposed – the happy couple stared back at her. The moment, captured forever, seemed a lifetime away. "Seven years," she murmured remembering that Dan had proposed seven years ago. Seven years of putting him off naming the day. Seven years where she'd wriggled out of having the son or daughter he so desperately wanted. Her mother was right; she was a fool. A lot of men, she'd said, were more upset than happy when their girlfriends or wives told them they were with child. Judy had confided that her husband had suggested she 'get rid' of theirs each time she'd become pregnant. She grabbed the photo and dumped it in the box. It could go in the trash with the rest of her past life later.

With the box filled, and the guards watching her every move, she turned to leave. Martin Shaw stood in the doorway, complete with gloating smile.

"Well, well, if it isn't our very own spy."

She threw Martin a scowl whilst checking for any sign of red blotches on his face. "Whatever you think I'm guilty of, I'm not," Cathy replied, disappointed that there was no evidence of pus-filled boils. "This is all a misunderstanding." She'd been framed, and he knew it. He probably also knew that she suspected he was the one behind it.

"Sure, Cathy, but your emails say different," he smirked.

Liar! She pressed her lips together, forcing herself not to retaliate, and instead recited the pustule-inducing hex in the hope of giving it a boost.

Box in arms, she took a step towards the door. He scratched the top of his thigh, close to his groin, and it was with intense joy that she noticed a frown pass over his face as he began to itch the side of his face.

Cathy repeated the last line of the hex, her focus entirely on the power of its words. Martin's frown deepened as he scratched the top of his lip.

"Anyway, condolences," he said as she passed.

"For?"

"Well, I heard Dan had finally realised what a mistake he was making."

She threw him a glare noticing, as she narrowed her eyes, that several red spots had appeared above his collar. They seemed to swell as she watched. "Life's going to be good for me, Martin," she replied as several more spots bulged close to his mouth. He rolled his shoulders as though in discomfort then scratched at his hand.

"You're itching," she stated, fascinated by the way he scratted at one spot then immediately itched another. "Fleas?" she questioned as he scratched beneath his chin.

"Don't be stupid. It's probably a reaction to something I've eaten."

He began to scratch an area close to his groin.

"Crabs?"

The guard beside her snorted.

Martin scowled at the man. "Of course not."

"Well I think you've got fleas then," Cathy goaded. Both guards took a step back.

"I have not got fleas! I don't even own a dog, or a cat."

"If he's not been bitten by fleas, it could be some disease," one of the guards said. "Those spots look nasty."

"They do," Cathy agreed. "He's covered in them. And they do look like bites although ..." She winced as she noticed the spots around his mouth begin to bubble, the centre darkening.

The guard to her left grunted. "Perhaps we should leave," he said.

"Could be an allergic reaction," the other suggested. "I suppose."

"Could be," agreed the other one without conviction, "but I've not seen anything like it before. Allergic reactions are usually lumps, not white heads, aren't they?"

"And it's spreading. They're all around his mouth now."

Martin's face contorted as the spots on his face began to swell. He itched an area close to an enlarging pustule.

"I wouldn't touch that, mate, not if I were you," cautioned the guard. "Looks like you've got some nasty blebs coming up on your face."

"You need a doctor, Mr. Shaw" said the second guard.

Cathy watched in fascination as Martin touched his face with tentative fingers, his eyes widening in alarm as they felt the rising blisters. He itched his groin once more. "What the hell is it?"

"Syphilis," Cathy said with a touch of malice. "Or gonorrhoea."

The guards sniggered. "Nah, that just makes your willy go green and slimy."

"Looks like chicken pox, but worse" said the first guard. "Jesus! Look at the size of those blisters!"

Martin itched whilst the men spoke and one of the pustules, now grown to the size of a pea split and began to leak a pus-like fluid. The tallest guard gagged.

"He needs a doctor. What if it's contagious?"

"Could be an outbreak," the shorter guard said, a grimace pulling at his face as the fluid oozed from the pustule.

Several more blisters expanded, filling with yellowish fluid. The hex was working far more spectacularly than Cathy had anticipated and, as another pustule erupted with a definite 'pop!', she almost regretted giving it the extra boost.

"He needs to be in quarantine!" the taller guard said with a grimace. "What if it's that monkeypox? That's contagious."

"Only in close contact."

"Well, we're pretty close to him," the guard said taking a step back.

"Not that kind of contact. I mean *real* close contact, like you know ..."

"It's sexually transmitted," Cathy explained. "Like syphilis."

"It's not syphilis!" Martin said with irritation.

"Could be monkeypox though," the guard replied.

"It's not monkeypox!" Martin shouted as he continued to itch.

"Could be," the guard retaliated.

"It's not!"

"Whatever it is, I'm not going near him."

"Me neither."

"Should we take him to a hospital?"

"Nah," replied the guard. "Let's just get him into his office."

"I'm not touching him! If it's contagious we should evacuate the building."

"Who made you the health police?"

"I'm not, I'm just saying, if it's contagious, maybe we should contain it in the building."

"Jesus, Gary, we're not in some apocalypse movie. If it's a sex thing, it's not going to be that kind of contagious is it," the guard explained.

"It's not a sexually transmitted disease," Martin insisted. "I've eaten something."

Gary snorted. "Yeah, and I do not want to know what *that* is." He turned to the other guard. "Listen, Tim, there's no way I'm getting trapped in here with this weasel if it is contagious. Let's get him locked up in his office."

Tim nodded his agreement, and both turned to Martin.

"Right, Mr Shaw, we're going to have to ask you to go back to your own office."

Martin's shouts had drawn a crowd and curiosity quickly turned to disgust as more pustules erupted and oozed pus down his face.

"Jesus! What is it?"

"The pox or something," said Cathy, enjoying the scene. "I think it's an STD."

"Gross! Look at ... it's going to pop."

"Is it that monkeypox?"

"Looks like it could be."

"I think I'm going home."

"Me too. Have you got any wipes?"

"Sure, they're in the top drawer of my desk."

The chatter among the staff continued and as Cathy reached the outer door, Glynnis greeted her with a disingenuous smile. It quickly dropped as she noticed the commotion. "What's happening?"

"Martin's got some hideous sexually transmitted disease, looks like the pox."

Glynnis' face drained of colour. "Pox?"

"Yeah, and it looks contagious. He's covered in massive, oozing sores. They just come up like pimples and explode."

Glynnis stared across the open-plan office, one hand on her neck, and began to itch.

"Don't worry," Cathy soothed with malice barely hidden. "You'll be alright as long as you haven't been in close contact with him recently."

Glynnis caught her eye and made a small gasp.

"You haven't, have you?"

The flicker in her eyes confirmed the rumours to be true; Glynnis had been having an affair with Martin. In that moment Cathy felt victorious. Martin didn't really have the pox and the hex would soon wear off, but there was enormous satisfaction in humiliating the man and the fear in Glynnis' eyes only added to it. "Play stupid games, win stupid prizes," Cathy said and pushed her way past Glynnis.

Chapter Seven

With the box of personal items thrown on the backseat of the car, Cathy pushed the gear into reverse, checked the rearview mirror then realised she didn't have the address for Witherwood Hall. With the engine humming, she typed 'Witherwood Hall' into the satnav. When it failed to locate the property, she searched on her mobile but could find nothing that gave her the exact address. She scanned her memories for the journeys she'd taken with her family as a child. She knew the general area of the country in which it was situated, and even remembered some of the route, but that was all. Eager to reach the Hall, and leave the office, her house, and Dan behind, she set off, deciding to ask for directions once she drew close.

After driving for an hour, too on edge to listen to the radio and its incessant chatter, relentless adverts, and fearmongering news reports, she pulled over to a service station. Travelling further, without a clearer idea of direction could result in taking the wrong junction and leading her miles off course, she realised.

Once inside the station, coffee steaming, she sat beside an enormous plate glass window. She rested for several minutes, sipping the coffee, and watching the cars filled with families on their way to or back from holiday, or businessmen and women in suits, pull in and out.

"So," she murmured, mobile in hand, "let's find you." She typed Witherwood Hall into the search bar again. When the search failed to provide her with useful information, she widened to less specific terms, typing just 'Witherwood' in the search bar. Again, there was nothing to give a specific location, but there were a number of intriguing articles reporting the myths and legends of the area. One that caught her attention was 'The Witches of Witherwood and their Pagan origins' and another intriguing one was titled, 'The Beast of Witherwood: Urban Myth or Legend?' There were also a number of newspaper articles reporting strange events in the area. She scanned the articles for any information about the location of the Hall, but the only mention she could find was one referring to the property as derelict and dating back to the sixteenth century. Interestingly, it mentioned that the Hall had been built over a much older wooden structure and archaeological finds in the local area suggested neolithic settlement. "Derelict?" she said as she scrolled back up through the article. "It wasn't derelict when I visited." She tried a different tactic and typed 'Witherwood Hall' into a route planner. No route was offered for the Hall, but it did offer directions to Witherwood. The map beside the directions pinpointed the woodlands, showing it to be in the county of Northumberland close to the Scottish border. "So far!" she said as the app calculated that she had another two hundred miles to go and a journey time of more than three and a half hours.

But what if the house is derelict? What if the will had been written decades ago and the tenant was long gone?

If that were true, then why give you the will now?

Sure, but no one had even told me that Aunt Hyldreth was dead.

Your mum?

Didn't ask her.

She sighed. She should have spoken to her mother about the will, instead, sure that she would have been horrified at the thought of her daughter accepting an arranged marriage and talking her out of it, she'd lied about her trip. As far as her mum knew, Cathy was taking a break from life and visiting friends up north. It was a lie, or at least not the truth, but she did need a break, and the tenant was a kind of friend, and he was up north.

'Friend' really is pushing it, Cathy.

Well, he could become a friend. Perhaps it was fate. Perhaps he was even her soulmate!

Or the biggest mistake of your life. What kind of man needs an old lady's help in finding a wife?

What kind of woman accepts an arranged marriage by letter? Mail order bride!

Ugh!

Losing herself to turbulent thoughts she took another sip of coffee. Everything was such a struggle and things didn't seem quite so clear now. Her resolve to kickstart a new life by dumping the old one was perhaps a little hasty. Was it too late to turn around and go back home?

Yes! You've burned all the bridges, Cathy. It's back to living with your mum if you do.

Not a chance!

After another sip of coffee and her attention was caught by movement on the pavement on the other side of the window. A crow, with a single beady eye trained on her, stood watching. It did nothing that normal crows do, like peck at the ground, or hop around and flap its wings, this one just looked at her then cocked its head. It looked familiar, like the one that had pecked her hand as she lay comatose on the doorstep in a drunken stupor.

"Go away!" she said, flapping a hand towards the bird.

"You finished with that, love?" A woman leaned across the table, cloth in hand, and removed the cardboard beaker now drained of coffee.

"Oh, sure, yes," she said, leaning back a little as the woman began to wipe the table down.

The bird continued to stare and then, to her surprise, the cleaning woman sat down opposite her at the table. She looked at her with green eyes smudged with kohl, her dark hair, plaited to the side, a little dishevelled. She took Cathy's hand and drew an invisible circle on the palm with her finger.

Cathy flinched at the light scratch her long nail traced across her palm.

"You are on a journey," she said.

"Of course I'm on a journey, up the M62," she said, pulling her hand back from the woman. "And, if you don't mind, I'm taking a few minutes to sit in peace and quiet."

"Enjoy your peace and quiet," she replied but didn't move.

Too polite to ask her to leave, Cathy focused on her mobile phone, scrolling through the article that examined whether the Beast of the Wither Woods was a myth or a legend and examining the numerous sightings of this half-man, half-wolf creature over the centuries. There were woodcuts from the seventeenth century alongside an eighteenth-century drawing created by an artist who had apparently reconstructed its likeness from a child who had claimed to have seen the beast. There were several reports from the last century too. The woman remained seated as Cathy scanned the article, and when she looked up, the stranger caught her eyes. Cathy grew uncomfortable. It was unusual for a cleaner to sit down during their shift, never mind sit and glare at a customer. Had she done something wrong? Spilt coffee on her newly washed floor?

"Can I help you?" Cathy asked.

"No," the woman replied.

Unnerved by the stranger, Cathy rose to leave but as she stood, the woman clamped a hand around her wrist. She pulled against the grip, but the woman's fingers remained curled around the base of Cathy's hand. She stared at Cathy with eyes narrowed.

"You have much to learn, witch!" she whispered.

"Who are you? And I'm not a witch," Cathy said, casting a glance around the area. Stories of persecution against witches that her mother had told, centuries old tales and ones of her own experience, made Cathy wary of telling anyone that she had the knowledge of witchcraft.

The woman scoffed. "That doesn't matter. What matters is that you realise you are stirring trouble."

"Me? How am I stirring trouble?"

"Was it not you that called upon the aether to cast the spell of disfigurement?"

"I don't know what you're talking about," Cathy lied.

"Was it an illusion then? Did you cast a spell on the observers that they may see what wasn't there?"

Cathy paused. The coven had cast a spell to cause pustules and seeping sores but one that was time limited.

The woman sighed. "You dabble with magic that you barely understand. A novice practicing without true knowledge."

"Who are you?" Cathy asked again, irked at the woman's disapproval.

"Listen to me with care, daughter of Pendle, do not use your powers for spite. Every call to the aether places you in debt. Guard your words well, do not throw them away or use them for harm. Therein lies the pathway to the stake and I see flames in your future if you do not alter your ways."

"They don't burn witches anymore," Cathy said in defiance.

The woman shook her head and her grip tightened. "There are those that do. They hide and they sleep, but wake them, and the fires will light once more."

"Stupid woman," Cathy hissed. "Get off me, before I report you!"

The woman made no effort to release her arm. "Heed this, daughter of Pendle, beware the Curse!"

Cathy pulled her hand and this time the woman let go.

"You're crazy!" she said.

The woman's eyes narrowed but remained locked to Cathy's and a smirk lifted the corner of her mouth. "Maybe I am, but you need to listen to the words of the crazy woman. The aether will demand payment!"

The chair scraped beneath her as Cathy pulled away from the table.

"Only a sacrifice will save you."

Cathy fled the café and returned to her car where she took several minutes to calm herself, the woman's warning repeating.

The aether will demand payment.
Only a sacrifice will save you!

"And how the very hell did she know about Martin?" she said as she pushed the key into the ignition. She sat back as realisation struck. "That's it!" she said triumphant. "One of the girls set this up, probably Lexi, she was the one who really didn't want me to go. It's her way of trying to convince me not to go. Beware of the curse," she laughed. "What a joke."

The thought was satisfying until she remembered that it had been Lexi who had suggested revenge against Martin by giving him the pox. She had even wanted it to last for weeks and leave scars. It had been Cathy who had tamed the suggestion by making it just a twenty-four-hour thing that would disappear just as quickly as it had appeared. "So who could have done it"? Her thoughts turned to the other girls who hadn't wanted her to go and settled on Judy who had advised against using the powerful hex and said something about bad karma. She hadn't listened because she really wanted to hurt someone for what had happened and given that she couldn't bring herself to hurt Dan or the now pregnant Alice, her vitriol had fallen upon Martin.

"Yes, and I don't regret it," she said, remembering the way he had scratched at the rapidly spreading and enlarging pustules, and how the office workers had looked simultaneously disgusted and scandalised.

But was it really a disfiguring spell?
Would he be horribly scarred?
Did she care?
'The aether will demand payment'.

She jolted as a crow jumped onto the car, staring at her with a beady, reproachful eye through the windshield. It shook its head as though in disapproval then flapped its wings and launched from the bonnet as she started the engine. Being in debt to the aether was not something she had ever considered or been taught. Since her teenage years, her mother had become increasingly reclusive and loathe to share her knowledge. Much of Cathy's craft had been self-taught and garnered from the multitude of books published on the subject. Most were nonsense, and she knew the spells they contained didn't work, but there was the odd one that did. She re-joined the road with the woman's warning on repeat and a sense of inadequacy tainted with guilt washing over her.

Chapter Eight

Already weary, her body still suffering the effects of the week-long Prosecco binge, Cathy had a long drive ahead. She chose a favourite playlist and sat back with a weary sigh. Miles of motorway stretched ahead and although she couldn't let her awareness of the other drivers drop, it would be an easy drive until she grew close to one of the cities. Memories of Witherwood Hall rose as she passed yet another truck doing sixty, not all of them pleasant.

Witherwood Hall, from her child's memory, was an enormous house miles from anywhere set deep within a hillside forest. Her family had always been given rooms on the top floor and the view from the windows had confirmed their isolation. Trees stretched for miles in all directions and beyond them, to the horizon, were fields. There were villages and hamlets nestled within the woodlands, but they weren't part of that vista.

Aunt Hyldreth, who Cathy hadn't seen since she was a teen, had been a mysterious figure, barely seen during the day, although always head of the table at dinner which was served at five-thirty pm and announced by a large and circular gong each evening. Watery soup filled with chunks of meat and cabbage seemed to be a favourite and any complaints from Cathy were quickly hushed by her mother.

'It's disrespectful to complain about the food we're served' she'd reprimanded after a particularly tense evening meal. Aunt Hyldreth wasn't an unkind woman; she just wasn't very sociable. Despite the welcoming smiles and halting efforts at making conversation around the table, she seemed distant, and would always apologise for being absent during the day due to 'being busy'. Quite what she had been busy with had remained a mystery, but her mother never questioned it, nor seemed upset by the lack of company. Cathy spent many of her days at the Hall exploring the woods, house, and outbuildings. They were fascinating, but only really became fun when her cousin Fion arrived, and they explored the place together.

Several areas were off-limits: a row of outbuildings with blacked out windows, and an entire wing of the house. There were also a number of doors throughout the house that were locked but neither girl had the courage to ask what was behind them. One particular door, the one that led to the wing that was out of bounds, rose in her mind, surprising Cathy. "I had forgotten about that!" A passing car beeped, and she pulled back into lane, her concentration distracted by the memory. Back in lane, the memories surged.

She was at the Hall, exploring the house after rain had begun to fall, and they'd returned from playing in the woodlands. Fion had looked at her, green eyes glittering with excitement. 'Let's go to *the room*!'

The 'room' was an entire wing of the house rising over three floors plus an attic. Both girls had been drawn to the forbidden part of the house, squeezing through the hedgerow that blocked access to the outside of the wing, to peer through the windows along the ground floor. At the base of the walls were several blacked out and narrow cellar windows.

On one occasion, Cathy had been caught by Aunt Hyldreth looking through the keyhole and she'd grabbed Cathy's shoulder with hard fingers and pulled her to stand, the magic in her eyes flickering. "That room is out of bounds," is all that she had said, but her meaning and the anger bubbling beneath her calm and cold exterior was clear; Cathy was forbidden to even think of going inside.

'The room?' she'd questioned, marvelling at Fion's bravery.

'Yes! The room,' she'd whispered back and pulled a huge and ornate iron key from her pocket.

'Is that the key?' Cathy asked in wonderment. 'Where did you find it?'

Fion glanced along the corridor and pulled her closer to the wall. 'In Aunt Hyldreth's room,' she whispered.

Shock had rippled through her.

Do you remember what we found? Fion's voice rose from Cathy's memory.

"I do!"

Another car beeped its horn as it narrowly missed her wing mirror. Cathy moved into the slow lane between lorries.

She had forgotten the room and what happened after they had unlocked the door.

That summer had been the last Cathy had spent at Witherwood. The last summer she had seen Fion alive.

Memories overwhelmed her.

'What happened to Fion?' she remembered asking her mother.

'She's in the Ever After, Cathy.'

'But how do you know? They never found her body.'

'The Curse took her.'

How had she forgotten? The room. Fion. The holiday from hell!

Stuck between two lorries, Cathy gripped the steering wheel, dazed by her memories.

'She's gone, Cathy,' her mother lamented as Cathy stood on the Hall's steps tugging against her hand. 'She's gone to the Ever After. Come away.'

With her mind flooded with memories, her concentration lost to the past, she pulled into the nearest layby.

Fion had been right, the ornate key did unlock the door, and beyond the doorway were whole suites of rooms over several stories. Stepping over the threshold, she'd felt its energy. Fion had turned to her, and they'd exchanged glances of mutual wonderment. She'd hesitated to step fully inside the room, but Fion had pulled her through. Glass-like and brilliantly lit fragments eddied on the warm rays of sun that shone through the tall windows; the very air seemed to sparkle.

'It's so beautiful!' Fion had gasped, twirling in the brilliance.

The room was magical, like a lost world.

They had spent hours exploring. Moving from room to room, opening drawers and wardrobes filled with clothes from another era, silk dresses with vast skirts and embroidered bodices. The walls held sconces for candles and there were candles in ornate candlesticks on almost every surface. If she had been more observant, she would have realised it was surprisingly free of dust and cobwebs.

Fion had wanted to explore all of the floors, including the cellar and attic, but to Cathy's relief the door beneath the stairs that led to the cellar was locked and so too was the door to the third floor. 'I'm coming back!' Fion had declared as they stood in front of the cellar door.

'I don't want to,' Cathy had blurted.

'Why are there locked rooms within a locked wing?' Fion had asked.

'I don't know,' Cathy had replied, grown uneasy at the thought of descending into the cellar.

Unlocking the door had been exciting and adrenaline had coursed through her teenage veins, but standing in front of the cellar door, she felt a cold energy waft like a draft from behind it and a chill had washed over her. 'Don't you feel it?' she'd asked. Fion had shaken her head. 'There's something down there,' Cathy said, the chill making her hairs stand on end and she'd turned and fled back into the room where the sun warmed motes danced. Fion had laughed and called her 'chicken!' and then tugged Cathy's sleeve and pulled her towards the second floor. 'Let's try on some of the dresses,' she'd suggested with a glitter in her eyes. The thought was exciting but, for Cathy, the fun had slipped away, and her excitement was edged with fear. Nevertheless, she followed Fion to the upper floors but the noise of rustling, of someone or something moving in one of the rooms had spooked them both and they'd fled down the stairs, only stopping to lock the door with the massive key.

'I bet this is where Aunt Hyldreth comes every day," Fion had said as she pulled the key from the lock. "I bet it was her behind the door upstairs!'

Cathy sat with her memories, remembering the excitement on Fion's face as, breathless, she'd declared she would return and discover just what was in those locked rooms.

"Oh, Fion. Where did you go?"

To the Ever After, Cathy. Come away, she's dead.

Sitting in stunned silence, Cathy nursed the revelations of her forgotten childhood, then restarted the engine and continued her journey to Witherwood Hall.

Chapter Nine

Cathy had forgotten just how isolated Witherwood Hall was. Her childhood memories, before she'd remembered about Fion, had it sat in idyllic woodlands, a place of mystery and intrigue, but once she'd taken the junction off the motorway, the roads narrowed as she grew closer until she was driving through a lane overhung by trees with only the occasional passing place to swerve into if a car came her way. The lane meandered and then began to climb as she reached the hillside where the Hall was situated. With no directions to follow, she slowed, and searched the roadside for any sign of the entrance.

The first clue came in the form of a huge standing stone, several feet wide and at least eight feet tall. It sat off the road and was flanked either side by the drystone wall that held back the bank of earth where the road had been cut through the hillside. Lichen coloured the stone yellow and green, whilst ferns grew at its side, hanging over the wall and growing from crevices. In a flash of memory, she remembered passing the stone, her mother breathing a sigh of relief and declaring, 'We're almost there'.

She slowed to a stop beside the stone. Banded along its perimeter were carved runes whilst the centre was taken up by fantastical carved beasts. Her knowledge of runes was limited, but she recognised what could be a wolf-like creature in the carving. She took a photograph and typed a message to Lexi, 'Standing stone outside Witherwood. Any idea what it says?' then changed her mind; she wanted to keep the discovery to herself, at least for now.

With the message deleted, she returned to the car, and drove until she found the familiar entrance. Flanked by stone pillars, the entrance led to a narrow lane large enough to drive down. At its end sat a pair of ornate ironwork gates and beyond them the Hall.

Surrounded by trees, the house seemed hugged by the woodlands and looked more dilapidated than she remembered but not derelict. Relieved to find the house still standing, she drove through the gateway and parked to one side.

The house had a wildness about it; the hedges weren't clipped into subservience by any man's hand and ivy grew up its walls. Despite the apprehension that had clung to her since passing between the entrance stones, she stepped into an energy that was warm and vibrant as she opened the car door. The air shimmered as though a million specks of gold eddied in the warm air of the sun's rays.

Reached by a series of curved and wide steps flanked by trees that overhung the pathway, the front door was made of wide oak planks and furnished with ornate metal hinges that curled across the wood like tendrils. It sat within an ivy-covered stone archway and roots wormed over the edge of the steps. The emerald-green ferns at the base of the trees added to the otherworldly atmosphere and she was thrust back into her childhood, searching for fairies among their majestic and uncurling fronds. An image of Fion appeared on the doorstep. She twirled in the sparkling air, laughing and holding up her hands to catch it, her golden hair glowing as it caught the sun. "Fion!" Cathy whispered as she watched the girl. For a moment the apparition seemed to notice her then she called, 'Catch it, Cathy!' before fading from sight as Cathy held out a hand to the particles. They flowed over her fingers as though on a current. "Fion," Cathy whispered and took a step towards where the girl had stood.

In that moment she was overwhelmed by an intense sensation of belonging. This was her house and she belonged to it, just as it belonged to her. Drawn with an irresistible urge, she knocked on the massive door, and waited.

Surprised when no one answered, she knocked again a little louder. Minutes passed as she knocked and waited but the house remained silent, the only sound the rustle of leaves and the twitter of birds in the trees around her.

Disappointed, she moved back down the steps and searched the windows for signs of movement. The rooms were dark with no sign of light inside, but in an upper room one window was partly open and the curtains moved, blown by the breeze. With no sign of any of the Hall's inhabitants coming to answer her knock, she decided to try at the back.

On one side of the house, a stone wall blocked the way and despite there being a heavy wooden door, she chose the other side where a wide and gated entrance looked as though it could lead to outbuildings and a less intimate part of the house. Although she felt as though she belonged here, she couldn't bring herself to just walk in unannounced to its inner sanctum.

As predicted, there were several single storey outbuildings including a barn-like structure that housed a vintage tractor and a ride-on lawn mower. A track continued past the barn towards a copse of trees and beyond that to an area of pasture. Cathy caught a distinct farmyard whiff and the bleating of a goat or a sheep. The smell triggered more memories; she and Fion leaning over a wooden gate and peering into a sty where a mother pig lay on straw, her piglets suckling.

A high wall surrounded the gardens at the back of the house, and she followed it until she came across a door. Like the front door it sat within an archway and was made of wide oak planks. It had a circular handle of barley twist iron. A large bell hung to the side. She hesitated to ring it, but it would be rude to just walk in.

She reached for the bell then hesitated, lowering her hand to hover over the ring of twisted iron. This was her last chance to turn back; if she returned to the car no one would know she had even been here.

"Hello!"

Startled, she turned to a man towering above her. Dark grey eyes edged with topaz smiled back as she regained her composure.

"Did I startle you? I'm sorry."

She caught her breath, heart hammering, her body releasing the pent-up anxiety that had deepened throughout her journey, but the feeling of breathlessness was the gasp of desire that had flashed through her as he spoke. Like the tenant of her imagination, he was at least a foot taller than her, broad-shouldered and slim, with dark hair peppered grey at the temples. Clean shaven with a strong jawline and high cheekbones, he was casually dressed in jeans and a cambric shirt.

Befuddled by the mix of emotions, she gathered her senses.

"Hi," she managed as his eyes focused on hers. Like the air around the entrance, his seemed to sparkle. He waited with a quizzical frown.

"If you ring the bell, they'll answer," he said, gesturing to the bell on the wall. "Here, I'll do it for you." He reached across her, his body uncomfortably close. Cathy's breath caught in her chest as he leant across and rang the bell. "There," he said as the bell clinked and pulled back.

Cathy took a breath. "Reminds me of school ... playtime ... you know, when they called you in at the end of dinner ..." she rambled, emotions whirling.

The man smiled down. Her eyes caught in his.

"Coming!" a woman's voice called from the other side of the door.

"There you are," he said as the noise of padding feet grew louder. With a clunk of iron the latch lifted, and the door opened. As a woman's face peered at her through a widening gap, Cathy turned to thank the man, but there was no sign of him.

"Oh!" she said in surprise then scanned the area.

"Can I help you, miss?"

"There was a man ..."

"I didn't see no man," the woman replied. "Are you lost?" she asked scanning the area behind Cathy.

"Oh, no, I'm not lost. I'm Cathy ... I think you're expecting me."

The woman stared at her with incomprehension.

"Cathy Earnshaw ... the new Housekeeper. Hyldreth Earnshaw's niece."

"Of course! Oh, Mistress forgive me, please. You threw me talking about a man when there was none to be seen. Come in," she beckoned. "Come in."

Chapter Ten

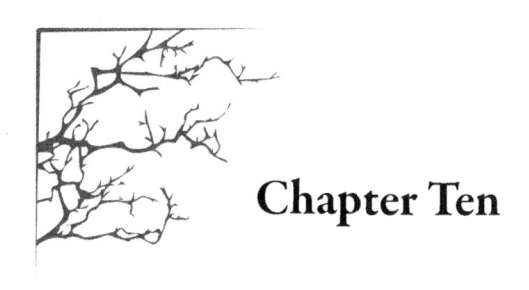

A wave of intense energy wafted over Cathy as she stepped through the garden wall's stone arch and the door closed with a heavy thud and clank of iron. The woman offered a bob curtsey then turned with a swish of her skirt and walked towards the house, beckoning Cathy to follow. She recognised the place from her childhood memories at once, memories that were sewn with magical discoveries and time spent with Fion. She had played under this very arch with her cousin.

Where did she go?
To the Ever After Cathy, come away.

Suddenly hesitant, her memories stirring deep emotions and knowledge she had long hidden, she grew overwhelmed by her senses. Without doubt, Witherwood Hall was as magical as it was terrifying. With a sharp intake of breath, and shrugging off the sensation, Cathy followed the woman, the need for ownership of the Hall suppressing any fear.

A low mist hung over vegetable beds linked by metal arches covered in vibrant green leaves where rambling vines hung with fruit. There were green beans too and rows of peas, their vines rambling within tepees of bamboo. To the far side was an orchard of fruit trees where apples and plums shone like jewels. Against the walls apricot trees had been trained to spread and were hung with ripening fruit.

Closer to the house and marked from the vegetable garden by fruiting shrubs, was the flower garden where rooms were created by arches covered with a profusion of rambling roses, clematis, and honeysuckle, and shrubs that had been left to overgrow. There was a sense of wilderness only just under control and, like the kitchen garden, the effect was magical.

Cathy followed the elfish woman beneath a tall and sturdy arch carrying a profusion of apricot roses, its timber carved with curling and entwined dragons and snakes, and up the steps to the flagstones at the back of the house where a large and ornate patio table sat to the side of an elegant orangery. A coffee pot sat at its centre, a cup of half-drunk coffee and an ashtray with a half-smoked cigar abandoned. A wisp of smoke rose and twisted before melting into the air.

"This way Mistress Earnshaw," the elven woman said and opened a door for her to step through. "Mr. Argenon will meet you in the orangery," she said gesturing to the large glass structure, its interior obscured by the leaves of numerous tropical plants.

Stepping inside the house, the light was suddenly gone, and she was faced with a room she remembered well. A large marble fireplace sat on the opposite wall, a huge mirror above it flanked by silver sconces each holding a candle. A chandelier hung in the middle of the room, hanging from a ceiling rose moulded with the same creatures that had been carved on the rose arch—dragons, snakes, boars, and wolves entwined in an everlasting chase.

In front of the fire was a large velvet sofa strewn with warm blankets and a sheepskin, whilst either side were two leather armchairs, each well-worn. The fire had been swept clean and laid with screws of newspaper and kindling ready to be lit later in the evening and Cathy wondered if she would meet the man who smoked the cigar then. Was he the tenant, the man she was to marry? Her heart tripped a harder beat, but she swallowed down the bubbling anxiety and followed the woman into the orangery. Light filled the space, a contrast to the shadowy room they had just left.

Like the garden, the orangery was a profusion of flowers and foliage and, like the garden, the energy in the room was vibrant. She could almost feel it shimmer. Her mother had the talent to see auras and told Cathy that she had the talent too, she just had to zone into it, but despite sometimes sensing the changes in energy, she had never really believed her. Since driving through the gates with their carved and monolithic standing stones, she had become hyper-aware of the changing energies around her. Here it was fractious, excited. Several cages in white wirework hung from poles that crossed from one side of the orangery's roof to another but rather than birds they held more plants, their leaves growing out through the wires.

Several balloon-back wicker chairs sat around a small filigree metalwork table and the woman asked her to sit.

"Mr. Argenon will be with you soon," she said with a shy smile. Sparkles of iridescent green flickered in her eyes and Cathy wondered if she were actually an elf.

"Thank you ... I'm sorry, but I don't remember your name."

"It's Ellette, Mistress."

"That's a beautiful name," Cathy replied.

The woman's smile broadened. "Why thank you. It's an ancient name, of my people."

Of your people? Elves? "It's lovely, Ellette."

"You must be tired after your long journey, Mistress-"

"Call me Cathy," she offered her a smile.

The elvish woman shook her head. "Nay, Mistress. We all have our place here. May I bring you tea?"

A little taken aback, but unsure how to respond, Cathy nodded and agreed to tea. Ellette gave another bob curtsey and left the room with the promise that 'Mr. Argenon' would be here to greet her very soon.

Mr. Argenon. Was he the tenant?

Chapter Eleven

"Argenon!" Heath called as he slapped his gloves down on the table. "Argenon!"

Argenon appeared through the door that led to the main part of the house. He seemed flustered which was unusual for Heath's faithful servant, particularly for a man who had lived through so many centuries and seen so much.

"Forgive me, Lord. I was attending to business."

"Business?"

"Mistress Earnshaw has arrived."

Heath raised a nonchalant brow though his heart tripped a beat. "She's here then."

"Yes, Lord. Ellette has seated her in the orangery."

"You'd best to it, then. If she's waiting."

"No, no. I'll attend to you first."

Heath nodded. Argenon had become distracted of late, constantly talking about Mistress Earnshaw and how good she would be for the house, how things would change, how their future would be so much happier. It was all drivel. Nothing would change for him. Nothing would lift the dread curse despite Argenon's hopes, unless … unless it did work this time and he hardly dared believe that it would. The uneasy patience he had forced himself to accept began to shatter.

"Good!" he snapped, regretting the harshness of his tone but continuing without apology. "The west wing ... we seem to have an increase of activity there."

Argenon's face grew dour. "Indeed, my Lord."

"Then it is fortunate that Mistress Earnshaw has arrived."

"Oh, but she-"

"Will have to be initiated with urgency, unless we are to call in the Hunter."

Argenon shook his head. "He's otherwise engaged, Lord. He won't be available until after the Winter's Night."

"But that's months away. Action must be taken now!"

"I will assess the situation, Lord, and take the appropriate action."

Soothed, Heath slumped down into his chair.

"Mistress Earnshaw-"

"What of her?" Heath snapped.

"She awaits in the orangery ..."

"What of it?"

"Well, it would be ungentlemanly if you were not to greet her."

"Then I shall just have to be ungentlemanly, Argenon!" he huffed.

"But, Lord-"

"What does she look like? Is she a beauty?"

"It was late when I knocked at her door, but they say that she resembles her aunt, in her younger days, of course, and she was known as a great beauty."

"Yes, yes," Heath replied, a sad note in his voice as he remembered Hyldreth.

"And they do say she carries the gift, as did Mistress Earnshaw, which is why she is such a good choice." Argenon's voice brightened. "She is the one, I feel sure."

Heath batted his hand towards Argenon, but the sense of excitement was contagious. "They have all been 'the one' according to you!" Heath took a deep breath and sighed to ease the tension across his chest. "How did she strike you ... when you delivered the letter?"

Mercurio hopped from the shadows, his indigo feathers gleaming in the light. "She was drunk! Drunk as a skunk!"

"Psht!" reprimanded Argenon. "The lady had had a difficult week-"

"She is a drunkard?" asked Heath, his hopes already dampening.

"No!"

"But she was drunk when she answered the door?"

"Well, yes, she was, but Mistress Hyldreth only ever spoke highly of her."

Heath mulled this over. Over the years he had come to hold a lot of respect for the crone. "Then we will have to trust in Mistress Hyldreth's judgement. Go to the woman. I shall meet her later."

As the door closed behind Argenon, Heath rose from the chair and strode to the window. The room faced out onto the back of the house taking in the vast gardens and woodlands beyond. The moon hung in the sky, a silver orb against the blue. "Waning gibbous," he muttered. Only days left until the full moon. He rubbed at his bicep, a primal ache bubbling deep within his core. The only time he felt at peace, without the grinding ache of disruption within his soul, was when the moon was blotted from the sky. It was a cycle he had endured for centuries, and one Cathy Earnshaw could bring to an end. Hope burned with an intense flame as he looked out over the gardens, but he quickly extinguished it. Failure would be painful and getting his hopes up would only make the crash down to grim reality so much harder to bear.

He peered down to the orangery where Argenon was greeting the new Mistress of Witherwood Hall. The pang of guilt he felt for not greeting the woman was fleeting, and quickly replaced by an uneasy excitement; he wanted to see his new bride, but would she want him?

Unable to get a clear view of the woman seated in the orangery, Heath turned to Mercurio. "What was she like?" Heath asked the bird perching on the chair beside him.

"Drunk, broken."

Heath huffed. "Another broken soul to add to Hyldreth's collection then," he said with a touch of bitterness.

"Pretty."

"Oh? Describe her."

"Dishevelled hair and breath like a hog had taken a-"

"Enough!"

"A bride worthy of you sire," the bird quipped.

"Fie on you, Mercurio! Would that you had died rather than been cursed alongside me."

"Would that I had, sire, would that I had."

Heath growled.

The bird hopped to the windowsill. "Marry the strumpet and let us be done with this life! I am deeply aggrieved and no mistake. Living an eternity with feathers and a beak is beyond my endurance."

Heath shook his head. "Do not worry, old friend. I will make her mine and she shall bear my child," he said with determination.

"Make it so, this time, sire and, for the love of Odin, try to be nice!"

Heath glared at the bird momentarily then turned back to the orangery. "I shall. The Curse shall not triumph again."

With a final scowl towards the orangery, Heath turned and left the room.

Chapter Twelve

Cathy took a sip of tea from the pretty bone china cup and became aware of something fluttering on the other side of the room. The fronds of several ferns bobbed and shivered. She took another sip whilst watching the fronds closely. There was something in the plant and her heart beat a little faster at the thought that it might be mice. As movement was accompanied by more flittering, footsteps alerted Cathy to a man's approach, and she sat a little straighter in the chair, her heart beating just a little harder, the invisible mice forgotten. The bone china cup trembled in its saucer as she set them on the pretty table at her side and took a breath. This was it—the moment she would meet her future husband—Argenon.

As the footsteps grew closer, she imagined him as the man who had helped her ring the bell—tall with broad shoulders, clean shaven with high cheekbones and a square jawline. A little older than herself, but that was fine, she liked her men older—they were so much more self-assured and confident than younger men and the laughter lines meant they'd enjoyed life.

Watching the door as the footsteps approached, she began to stand then sat back down, or rather perched on the edge of her seat, then shifted a little to the side in a pose that she hoped would be at once demur and confident. She flicked her hair away from her shoulder and managed to force a smile to her face—unaware until that moment just how keen she was to make a good impression.

The man appeared at the doorway and Cathy's smile dropped, the light and rapid heartbeat became a dull and heavy thud. A weight seemed to drop in her stomach. The man was old! Ancient. He walked towards her with confidence, a sprightly step, and shoulders squared, without the stoop of age, but he was old. Unlike many older men, his hair was thick, but there was not a single strand of colour. It was perfectly white, just like the huge mutton chop sideburns that began at his temples and ended at his jaw. Slender to the point of being thin, he wore a dark navy suit with a crisp white shirt and tie of maroon silk.

"Good morning, Mistress Earnshaw," he said as he stood before her.

"Cathy," she said, holding out her hand. She dropped it when he shifted his eyes beyond her momentarily. As she dropped her hand he smiled and said, "We all have our place here, Mistress Earnshaw. Let me introduce myself. My name is Argenon-"

"You're the guy who brought the Will!" Cathy blurted in a sudden moment of recognition suffused with relief; he was not the tenant!

A flicker of surprise at her outburst was quickly hidden and his smile broadened. "That is correct. I was indeed given the responsibility of delivering Mistress Earnshaw's Will."

"Aunt Hyldreth?"

"Yes, that is correct."

"So ... so you're not the tenant?" She held his gaze, desperate for confirmation.

"Indeed, I am not, Mistress," he replied with a slight nod of his head. "That honour lies with my Lord, Heath-"

"Your lord?"

"Lord Heath of the Wither Woods is the tenant of Witherwood Hall. He will be joining us shortly. But first, may I ask that you are comfortable? Were the refreshments adequate?"

Cathy grew certain that the attractive man who had run the bell was Lord Heath. "I look forward to meeting him," she replied. "And yes, the refreshments were very much appreciated."

"Excellent. And may I ask of your journey here? You found us without trouble?"

Cathy smiled at the memory of her panic when she couldn't find the location on the map. "I wouldn't say without trouble, the house doesn't appear on any map I could find, but I managed to follow the directions to Witherwood and somehow managed to find the house. I think I remembered the route from being a child."

"Ah, yes, the house has a way of calling its own back home."

The comment resonated with Cathy, she had sensed that she was being drawn to the house as she'd driven through the twisting roads, as though guided by intuition. And then there was the powerful energy she'd sensed on passing through the standing stones. Stepping out of the car into the glittering air there had been the overwhelming sense of belonging, not just of belonging, but of ownership. She wanted the house just as much as it wanted her. "It's certainly a magical place," she smiled.

"Magical is just the exact word, Mistress Earnshaw. Witherwood Hall and the land it sits on are very special. You feel its energy, don't you," he stated.

"I do. I can't explain it, but as soon as I drove through the standing stones, I felt it."

"Mistress Earnshaw assured me that you had the gift, I am beginning to suspect she was correct. Now," he continued before Cathy could reply, "Ellette has arranged a suite for you. Tatwin will collect your luggage and take it to your rooms."

"My suitcase is in the car, I can get it-"

"Tatwin will fetch it," he reassured her. "It is a duty he will gladly fulfil for his new mistress."

"There's just a bag and a suitcase."

"I will instruct him to collect them from your car and bring them to your rooms," he smiled, "where, if you would follow me, I shall take you."

As Cathy stood to follow Argenon from the orangery, the flittering that had alarmed her as she sipped her tea returned. This time she turned to the noise among the shivering fronds of the potted fern and gasped. Peering out from among nodding leaves was a tiny face surrounded by a mass of copper-coloured hair. It reminded her of a dandelion seedhead, one reflecting the light from a brilliantly orange setting sun.

"There's something in the ferns!" she stated.

Argenon turned to her. "Pardon?"

"The ferns," she said, jabbing a finger at the potted fern, its fronds still shivering.

Argenon's lips pursed a little as he followed her finger, his eyes narrowing.

"I saw a face. It had an enormous mass of copper hair."

Argenon took a deep breath then tutted. "I must ask your forgiveness, Mistress, but since your aunt passed, we've had an infestation, but it's nothing to worry about. If you'll follow me-"

"Infestation! It didn't look like a mouse."

Argenon chuckled. "Forgive me. We're struggling with an infestation of fairies."

"Fairies!" she exclaimed. "I can't believe it! I mean, I do, but I spent hours searching for them with my cousin, Fion. There were fairy rings in the meadow. We were sure there were fairies here, but we never found any."

Argenon's brow creased but it quickly smoothed. "They're harmless—to an extent. Left to their own devices, they can become troublesome, but now that you are here equilibrium will return to the Hall and they will grow quiet once more."

"Are they the inhabitants I am to control?" she asked referring to the Will's Codicil.

"They are some of them," Argenon replied.

With a final look among the leaves and wondering what other 'inhabitants' she was to 'control', Cathy followed Argenon out of the orangery and through the house to the entrance hall. Light from the side panels beside the door and windows on the staircase filled the dark space. An elaborately carved mahogany staircase wound up to the next floor and an enormous cast iron chandelier ringed with antlers and squat candles hung at the centre of the room.

A side table held several glass cases displaying taxidermy. One held a fox fixed for eternity snuffling at the ground, another held a kestrel ready to leave its perch. Above them a stag stared out across the hallway, but it was the table beside them that caught Cathy's attention. Both held the most hideously stuffed creatures she had ever seen. In one a quartet of wigged mice dressed in satin breeches with matching waistcoats played fiddles and flutes. Their faces squashed, and eyes askew, they looked to be in varying degrees of pain as they played the instruments. The other held a mangey black cat so badly stuffed it was barely recognisable. One eye looked at the ceiling, whilst the other stared at the fiddling mice with a forever glare of hunger. Intrigued, Cathy stopped to inspect the hideous display.

"They were a gift to your aunt from one of her oldest friends," Argenon explained.

"They're ... different."

"I'm afraid that your aunt was rather taken with them despite their ... unusual appearance and she insisted it would be a slight on her friend if she didn't display them."

"She had some interesting friends."

"Oh, yes, she did. Your aunt was a wonderful woman. Her passing has been a drain on us all."

Cathy only nodded, unsure of what to say. During her visits her aunt had been a fleeting figure, a little austere, though not unkind, but with the formal air of a Victorian school mistress that Cathy had been in awe of.

Leaving the hideous taxidermy behind, Cathy followed Argenon up the winding staircase. He walked with a brisk step and Cathy quickened her pace to keep up. As they passed through a doorway that led into another corridor the sensation of being watched made the hair on the back of her neck prickle. She turned to look back along the landing but there was nothing but an empty space and the noise of something sliding, like a sash window being pulled up or down.

Chapter Thirteen

Heath made his way back through the passageway to his suite of rooms, brushing the cobwebs from his hair and shoulders as he stepped through the door. It shut behind him, disappearing into the dark panelling.

The woman had been attractive with a slender body and dark and glossy hair worn in a messy style piled in curls on her head. Argenon had been correct, she had the look of a very young Hyldreth. The same jawline and overly large green eyes ringed with dark lashes. Sweetheart lips and a flush to her cheeks, but she was old, in her late thirties! He clenched his fists as he walked through the room and leant up against the now cold fireplace.

A half-drunk glass of whisky placed there after last night's overindulgence remained on the mantle and he swallowed it in one large gulp, relishing the burning sensation as he swallowed—for one second it blotted the roiling turmoil in his soul.

He slammed the glass down then pulled the bell beside the fire. It rang in the butler's pantry and would be heard by one of the creatures that cared for the house. He rang it again, pulling on the cord several times in an irritated manner not caring if it grew annoying, glad that it was annoying, as long as it served his purpose—to bring Argenon to his rooms.

He refilled the glass then stalked to the window that overlooked the gardens and swallowed the fiery liquid. After pacing the room for several minutes with no sign of Argenon, he decided to take a walk in the woods to ease his tension.

Mistress Earnshaw was to be his salvation. It was her role to set him free of the Curse. But if she was a shrivelled maid, a barren wasteland, then what use was she to him? No use, absolutely none! He swallowed the remainder of the whisky, talked himself out of pouring another glass, then looked out to the woodlands. His grip on the glass tightened and it shattered, dropping to the floor. Blood dripped onto the glass and carpet.

He huffed as he noticed the sound of footsteps in the corridor outside. "Argenon! How long must you make me wait?" he growled as the door opened.

Argenon responded with a frown that was quickly smoothed. "You saw her then?"

"Indeed, I did. What are you trying to do to me? For certain she is an old maid!"

"But-"

"Old and dried up. What use is the womb of a woman that age!"

"Lord, I do not think-"

"I need a younger woman, this one is no use to me."

"Lord, she is young enough, many women-"

"Many women! Many women what, Argenon?"

"Many women are mothers for the first time in later life. And the runes predicted-"

"Fie on it! Fie!"

Argenon swallowed. "Lord, we must trust in Mistress Hyldreth's judgement. She felt sure-"

Heath batted a hand towards Argenon, disappointment twisting his guts. Despite his best efforts, his hopes had been raised and, in his mind, he had already imagined the wedding ceremony complete with the claiming of his conjugal rights—the apprehension in her eyes, a little resistance and fear, and then her acceptance and passion and then the fulfilment of his needs. He had imagined the fruit of their passion growing in her belly: the seed taking form, her belly swelling as the months passed, and then the fruit of his loins emerging—a firstborn child that would break the curse and save him from this life of torture.

"She is very pretty, Lord. A wife worthy of you."

"Is that a joke?" Heath scowled, catching sight of his face in the mirror. The hideous wide and extended jaw and overly long canines had disappeared, the skin was no longer covered in hair, and his brow was smooth bar a few lines. His hair, dark and glossy was no longer coarse. Long sideburns, no longer melded into his neck and cheeks, were peppered with grey. Staring back at him was the face unchanged through the centuries, the face of the man he used to be before the curse took hold and destroyed his life—the only evidence of the monster he would become that evening hanging in the despair within his eyes.

"Of course not, Lord. I only meant that she is a beautiful woman who would make a beautiful bride, one that you could be proud of."

"Proud! Psht."

Argenon took a breath.

"What is it? You have something to say."

The man who had been at his side decades before the curse was cast upon them took another breath. "There is news I must impart though I fear your reaction."

"You think I am so much of a monster I cannot listen to bad news without lashing out in a rage?" Heath replied with bitterness.

"No, Lord," Argenon replied.

"Then out with it!"

"The lady ... when she arrived, was not greeted at the front door."

"And?"

"And she made her way to the back of the house where she was assisted in gaining entry by a man."

Heath frowned. "Go on."

"I am afraid, Lord, that Linton-"

Heath hit his hand against the mantle. "Do not speak that name!"

"I apologise, but I thought it was important that you know."

"So he knows."

"Suspects, perhaps. He could not know."

Heath stared at his reflection in the mirror. There were several hours before twilight, precious hours before the curse took hold once more and transformed him into a hideous beast that no woman could love. A monster that no woman would take to her bed unless forced. The mention of his enemy brought with it a reignition of Heath's resolve. "Is she expecting me?"

"Aye, Lord. I have promised that we shall all three sit together and read the Will. She is curious to meet you and understand her duties as Housekeeper."

"And when is this to take place?"

"This afternoon."

"And you say she has agreed to the terms of the Will?"

"She is here, so I presume that is so."

"And when can the marriage take place?"

"When all is settled. And she has given her consent."

"After the reading?"

"Nay, Lord, not that quick. We must not hurry the lady for fear of frightening her off. You must woo her a little."

Heath huffed again. "What good is wooing? We are purchasing her consent by offering her the house, all its lands, and Hyldreth's monies."

"A dowry, my Lord, as is right. The lady had no father to offer it for her, Mistress Hyldreth offered her wealth as the girl's dowry."

"Pah! Hardly a girl."

"A figure of speech. But she is fair and if Linton has shown signs of interest, then you can be sure he finds her attractive."

Heath remembered the emotion of desire he'd experienced as he'd watched Cathy walk along the landing. "She is attractive," he agreed. "She has good hips, a narrow waist."

"Childbearing hips, my Lord, and breasts-"

Heath cast a glare at Argenon.

"Breasts that will suckle a child, Lord."

A knot formed in Heath's belly. "You know that will not be necessary."

Sadness passed over Argenon's face. "No, it will not," he agreed.

Heath walked back across to the window. "I will take a walk in the woodlands before meeting my bride. What time is it arranged for?"

"Four o'clock, in the drawing room."

"I will be there," Heath replied.

Chapter Fourteen

Cathy lay back on the bed, tracing the patterns of the intricately woven fabric of the canopy atop the fourposter bed with her eyes. Entering the suite of rooms had been like taking a step back in time. More than that. It was as though the world she had stepped out from had been the fiction.

A smile curved onto her lips as joy skipped within her. Her rooms were beautiful. Apart from the bedroom, there was a small sitting room, and a bathroom, and the three rooms were larger than the footprint of her entire house back home. Home? No, even after such a short time, the house she had left did not feel like home; this suite of rooms, this entire house, felt like home. She had never experienced a sensation of belonging as strongly as she did here. Memories of past holidays spent at the house flitted in her mind, rising from deep within her, sensations, smells, noises, all wafted across her memory. Some strange, some unsettling, but many joyous, and filled with fun.

The curtains at the side of her bed matched the canopy—a heavy brocade in a Jacobean pattern of green hillocks and running deer. The fabric looked hand embroidered but was without sign of age. The bedroom was large with tall sash windows that filled the space with light and were hung with complementary and equally heavy, embroidered curtains. The sitting room was of a similar size and, like the bedroom, had a large fireplace. In both rooms the fires were made up ready for lighting although would not be needed for another month or two. Warmed by the sun streaming through the windows, sparkling motes danced in the air.

Unlike the orangery and the room they had passed through on the way to the hallway, her rooms were clear of ornaments and the bookshelf beside the fire was empty. Argenon had informed her that the room had been cleared of paraphernalia in order to house her own 'nicknacks'. She'd replied that she had travelled light and that most of her belongings were in storage. He'd nodded then and said she would be within her rights, once the terms of the will had been fulfilled, to take what she wanted from the house to decorate her rooms—given that they would all belong to her.

After putting the few possessions she had brought on the shelves, a framed photograph of Lexi with her children, another of her mother taken during a holiday with Cathy's prized polaroid camera, and a leatherbound notebook with its collection of spells, she made her way to the sofa. Leaning back into its cushions, she surveyed the ceiling, her thoughts returning to the polaroid of her mother. At the very edge had been a fraction of a figure, just a sliver of an arm, hand, and foot. Someone dressed in jeans. "Fion!" she whispered and returned to the shelf, taking the polaroid in hand. "It is you," she said as she scrutinized the photo. The memories returned. The photograph had been taken here, in the garden, only days before Fion had disappeared. Her mother was smiling, Fion's image was blurred by motion as she had walked towards Cathy. 'Come on, Cathy,' she had whispered as the camera had whirred and the photograph began to roll out from its base. "Let's go to the forbidden room! I've got the key."

"Where did you go, Fion?"

She's gone to the Ever After, Cathy. Come away.

Despite the warmth of the room, a chill dropped over Cathy. Fion had disappeared without trace and her body never found. It was a tragedy that Cathy had obliterated from her memory until today. Now, the pain of losing her beloved cousin felt raw. There had been no funeral that she could remember, but a solemn darkness had descended over her remaining days at the Hall, and they had never returned. She had no memory of her mother speaking of Fion again, not even in remembrance.

In her memory there was no recollection of police searching the estate, or there even being a hunt through the house or woodlands by the staff or her aunt or her mother. It was as though the girl had disappeared and no one cared.

"Why were you forgotten, Fion? Why?"

Unnerved by her returning memories, Cathy decided to take a walk in the gardens. As she walked beneath the rose covered arches, taking in the heady scent of the blooms, and mulling over the last days of that fateful summer, movement at an upper window caught her eye. She looked up to see a man staring down at her. He stood massive in the window, broad shouldered with a full and dark beard, and long hair, but it had been his eyes that made her heart tap harder—they were dark and hard.

"The tenant," she whispered, realising with disappointment that it was not the attractive man who had rung the bell at the back gate.

The figure was quickly replaced by Argenon, distinctive with his mass of white hair and huge lambchop sideburns. After noticing her presence, he too disappeared from sight. Both men had seemed displeased to see her. She turned back to the garden, breathing in its perfumed air to ease her tension and followed a walkway overhung with trees. It led her down a path that was vaguely familiar and ended in a gate that separated the garden from the woodlands. As she reached for the iron handle, she was overwhelmed by a memory so intense and vivid that it transported her back in time to when she stood at the gate with Fion.

The woodlands were dark, moonlight casting a silvery light upon the leaves, and Fion tugged at her sleeve. 'The Beast of Witherwood,' she whispered in dramatic tones. 'He prowls the woodlands at night. Let's find him!'

Heart pounding, the wood's dark spaces barely lit by the moon's light, Cathy had remained still.

'It's a full moon! They say he comes out at the full moon.'

'Let's go back to the house,' Cathy had suggested pulling her sleeve from Fion's grip.

'No! I want to find the beast,' she had declared.

'There's no such thing. It's just a myth.'

'Or a legend, Cathy. What if it's real?'

Cathy had shaken her head, not sharing her cousin's sense of excitement, or courage. Fion had refused to return to the house and disappeared into the dark spaces between the trees with a tinkling laugh, excitement bubbling.

Not wanting to abandon her cousin, but too afraid to follow, Cathy had stood at the gate and waited, torch in hand, growing more anxious with each passing moment, relieved when Fion emerged, eyes glittering. 'I saw it, Cathy!'

'You did not!' Cathy had retorted.

'I did! It was huge and had fangs and enormous eyes.' She'd laughed then roared and clawed her hands making Cathy jump. Cathy had screamed and Fion had crowed with laughter and then they had both run back to the house.

The vision faded, and Cathy returned to the present.

With the woodlands lit by dappled sunlight, she stepped over the threshold and was drawn through the trees until she grew tired and stopped to rest beneath the boughs of a massive oak. Leaning against its trunk she gave herself over to thoughts of the house and Fion. Her cousin had disappeared inside the house which meant someone had to know what happened. Determined to discover the truth about Fion's disappearance, she decided to begin questioning the staff, and find the key to the forbidden wing.

As she pushed away from the tree, impatient to return to the house and search for the key, she noticed several long gouges in its trunk. Long and deep, they resembled claw marks where talons had scraped through to the living tree beneath. That they were old wounds was obvious from the weathered flesh and bark that had thickened along their edges. Cathy traced the gouges with her fingers, barely able to cover them even with her hand splayed to its limit. As she drew her fingers down the scars, she felt their energy and withdrew her hand as though scolded; they oozed rage and dark despair.

"The Beast of Witherwood," she whispered, taking a step back to distance herself from the toxic energy.

Her foot knocked against a hard object and metal clinked. She crouched, brushing away rotting leaves to reveal a massive hoop of iron secured into the tree like a huge staple. Attached to it was a chain. She pulled and it snaked from beneath the leaves to reveal thick links, the remnants of a once longer chain. The chain and staple were rusted and looked unused for some time. Had the creature that had scored the trunk been chained here? A chill ran over her. Or had the creature attacked whatever had been chained here?

She scanned the woodlands, suddenly wary, a ripple of fear running through her. Like the house, the woodlands had a dark history. As she turned back to the tree, she noticed another large staple hammered higher up on the tree. It held a single link from a chain. There were also four deep holes that she took as evidence of where two more staples had been hammered into the trunk, enough to hold a man by his arms and legs. Standing with her back to the tree, she imagined herself shackled at ankles and wrists.

'I saw it, Cathy! And it was huge!' Fion whispered in her memory.

Beside her twigs snapped underfoot. "We meet again."

Startled, Cathy spun to the voice. Towering above her, eyes glinting with magic and a gleam she recognised as desire, was the man who had rung the bell.

Chapter Fifteen

"Odin's ravens!" Cathy blurted.

The man raised a surprised brow then laughed whilst holding her gaze. "I'm sorry! I didn't mean to startle you," he said.

A crow cawed in the treetops.

With a glance to the canopy, the man narrowed his eyes, then returned his gaze to Cathy. "I had hoped to see you again," he said with a smile, the amber glinting in his eyes.

"Oh?" *Lame, Cathy!*

"Yes. You seemed so flustered this morning and leaving you at Witherwood," he glanced with meaning at the chains. "I was concerned."

"Oh?" she replied, once again berating herself for the lack of intelligent response as she was caught in his gaze. "Well, I'm fine," she said, managing to return his smile. "Witherwood was my aunt's house," she said. "I've inherited, well at least I'm the housekeeper and-" *Shut up, Cathy! Don't tell him you've accepted the house in return for an arranged marriage; he'll think you're a nutter.* "I'm here to take care of the house," she finished.

"Ah! I see," he said with a glance in the direction of the Hall. "So, you are Hyldreth's niece?"

"You know my aunt? Knew her?"

"We have been neighbours for many years," he replied. "I won't lie and say that we knew each other well, but I have always been here should she require any help."

"That was kind of you. I didn't know her too well either. I mean, she was my aunt, and we used to come on holidays here until ... but I haven't been here since I was a teenager."

"It's a beautiful place. Full of magic," he said.

"It is!" agreed Cathy with enthusiasm. "It has this amazing energy that just ... just seems to wrap itself around me."

He threw her a quizzical frown then nodded. "Do you know that it is built upon an old pagan site?"

Cathy shook her head. "No. Obviously, I know that it's old but I'm not familiar with its history."

"It's ancient," he said. "The house was built close to a sacred spring known for its power to heal. Its magical energies run deep. Many volvas would drink from its waters. It heightened their powers to see what lay ahead."

Cathy remembered the concentration of sparkling fog to the side of the house. "I think I know where you mean."

"You do?" he asked, a flicker of excitement passing through his eyes. "How?"

His response caused her to pause; he seemed greedy for the answer. "I ... I think I saw the sides of a well. It was overgrown but I think that's maybe where it is."

The excitement left his face. "You could be right. There is so much about this land that is special, which is why I love to walk here."

"I remember it from being a child," she replied.

"So," he said. "We haven't been introduced, but I hope that you'll forgive my forwardness." He held out a hand in greeting.

She took his hand, instantly aware of an electrifying current sparking through her fingers. He gripped it whilst holding her gaze. "I'm Edgar Linton," he said as the fizzle of energy passed between them. "And I am truly delighted to make your acquaintance."

His words were peculiarly formal for a man dressed in modern jeans, casual shirt, and walking boots, but the day had been filled with peculiarity, so she took little notice.

"I'm Cathy," she replied.

"Catherine Earnshaw," he said drawing her hand to his lips. "Welcome to Witherwood, long may you reign as Keeper of the Hall."

Cathy laughed at his formality, the sensation of his soft lips on her skin sending shockwaves across her hand.

"Now that we've been introduced, we can relax," he said with a broad smile. "Would you like to take a walk through the woods with me?" he asked gesturing to the deeper forest.

"I'd love to, but I have to get back to the house. Argenon ... I mean, I have a meeting with the staff. It's my first day on the job," she said, "and I don't want to be late for my first meeting."

"I understand," he replied. "Then join me for a drink this evening. There's a lovely pub in the village where they do great food. Their steak and ale pie is amazing."

"Sounds great, Edgar" Cathy agreed. "I'd like that."

"Wonderful! But you can call me Ed."

"Okay, Ed," she smiled.

"Great! We can get to know each other, and you can tell me all about your first day at work. Cry on my shoulder if you need to."

"Thanks," she laughed, "but I don't think it will be that bad."

"Shall I meet you there then? The *Wolf & Lamb*. You can't miss it. The village is tiny and there's only one pub. If in doubt, look for the thatched cottage with the sign hanging at the front. It's painted with a wolf devouring a lamb." His eyes glinted with desire and the shiver that ran through Cathy's body held the thrill of fear at its edges.

"That would be lovely," she managed.

"Eight o'clock?"

She nodded. "I'll be there."

A caw from the trees was followed by a crow springing from the branches as it launched itself to the sky.

As Ed disappeared among the trees, Cathy stepped away from the iron shackles and the oak tree's canopy, hugging the moments of their meeting to herself. There was something about Ed beyond the obvious physical attractions of his broad shoulders, lean body, and strong jaw, that intrigued her. His eyes were captivating, and he exuded a deeply sensual energy. He had eyed her with hunger, even giving his lips the slightest lick as he'd spoken of the wolf devouring the lamb, and she'd felt the tug of desire deep between her legs.

She stared into the trees where Ed had disappeared with longing, excited to be meeting him again later, but with the guilt of deception already washing over her; she had agreed to marry the tenant of Witherwood Hall and produce an heir. Was it wrong of her to go out for a drink with this man if she had agreed to marriage?

Of course!
But nothing formal has been signed.
You lose the house if you don't.
It belongs to me!
If you marry.
I belong here. Ed could live here too.
But he's not the tenant.
Never heard of divorce?

She shook her head, pushing out the subversive voice. It was ridiculous to consider divorce before she had even met her groom.

In the distance a gate clacked shut and she came back to the present. Argenon had called a meeting with the staff at three o'clock to be followed by a tour of the house. After those formalities there was to be high tea with the tenant. She swallowed, her belly doing a queasy flip; would they become betrothed at that meeting if she agreed to the terms of the Will? She felt like a cheat already.

Turning in the direction of the house, she retraced her steps and returned to the garden through the arched gateway. As she made her way through the gardens, she remembered Ed's comment about the sacred spring and followed the wall to the area where she had seen the thicker sparkling fog, sure that was the place. She had lied about seeing the walls of the well, but not about sensing the magic of the spot.

Thickening mist sparkling with iridescent particles led her to an area close to the house. A narrow pathway was hemmed in by hedgerow that had been left to rise high and at its end was an ornate gate decorated with fantastical creatures each following the other, mouths open to grasp their tail. The gate pushed open with surprising ease given its size and weight and she walked beneath the overgrowth of honeysuckle to an open space. Briars ringed the area and at its centre sparkling mist rose in a twisting plume from a small pond. Something flittered in the corner of her eye moving behind a tall flag iris at the edge of the pond and a dragonfly swooped across the water. Bees crawled among the flowers, and a frog jumped from the pond, disappearing into a cluster of reeds. Something chittered close to her ear and she caught sight of a tiny creature with an explosion of copper hair as it swooped into the ivy that threaded through the briars circling the garden.

Unlike the quiet of the forest, the garden was alive with noise. A frog croaked and jumped from the pond to the gentle bank, disappearing beneath the massive leaf of a dock, its skin iridescent green.

Stepping closer to the spring, she crouched, taking a scoop if water in her hand. It sparkled in her palm. Ed had been right, this water was magical.

Don't tell him! The voice whispered from the hedgerow.

Don't tell him. Another voice repeated.

Keeper of the Hall. Keeper of the Spring. A different voice called. *Keeper of all. Beware the Curse!*

Unnerved by the voices that belonged to no visible creatures, but surrounded her, she allowed the sparkling water to trickle through her fingers into the pond and returned to the house.

Chapter Sixteen

Heath returned to his rooms, rage churning, and slammed the door shut. After struggling with the thoughts that tormented him, he had decided to take a walk in the woods in an effort to ease his fractious energy. It had been a mistake, but also reinforced his suspicions that Edgar Linton had already begun to work against him, another battle to be fought in their never-ending war.

Despite his misgivings about the woman's age, he had felt a strong attraction to her as he'd watched her walking through the house from the secret spaces behind the walls. She was shapely with glossy dark hair and an attractive face. Argenon had been correct about her 'child-bearing' hips, and his hopes had soared that she would be the one to set him free but there was something more. He yearned for companionship, someone to talk to and hold close through the night. He huffed. Holding a woman close to his chest through the night was impossible whilst the curse kept its grip around him.

He reached for the empty glass on the table beside his chair and filled it to the brim with whiskey, swallowing the fiery liquid in two massive gulps. Tapping at the window distracted him from pouring another glass but he intended to drink enough to blot out the scenes he had witnessed in the woods.

Striding to the window, he pushed it open and let Mercurio enter. His indigo feathers glistened in the sunlight, becoming black as he took flight and landed on the chair's back. He eyed Heath with beady, accusing eyes.

"Getting drunk won't solve our problem."

Heath batted a hand towards the bird.

"Did you not see?" he asked. "Mistress Earnshaw has betrayed me already."

"How so?"

"How so, bird? She allowed Linton to kiss her hand. Is that the behaviour of a woman betrothed?"

Mercurio shook his head. "I saw nothing in her behaviour that would suggest disloyalty and she is not yet betrothed—a free woman still."

"Then you are blind or bewitched! He kissed her hand. She allowed it," Heath stated.

"She was being polite. He used his magic upon her."

Heath poured another glass of whiskey and took a mouthful.

Mercurio eyed his master with a challenging glance. "She has agreed to dinner," he stated.

"Then I have already lost."

Mercurio cawed. "What has come over you? You cannot give up so easily. If Linton wants a fight, he can have one."

"Another fight I am bound to lose."

"You will not lose this time, sire. I feel it in my bones."

"You too," Heath gave a bitter laugh. "Everyone feels it in their bones. Everyone bar me."

Mercurio gave an annoyed caw. "Thor's hammer, sire. You were once a brave warrior—be that warrior again. I am heartily sick of feathers and beaks."

"As you have already made plain," said Heath. "Try fur and claws and fangs!"

"Self-pity will get you nowhere and at least you get to become your own self during the day. I do not. I demand change. It is beyond endurance."

"Hush, stupid bird."

"Unkind," replied Mercurio. "Remember that I am still here, sire, the man who fought by your side, trapped until you overturn the curse."

Heath gripped the glass, his memories returning to the days of his youth. "I do remember," he said staring down into the glass.

"For Thor's sake man, you are the only one that can reverse the curse and set us free."

"It has held me within its grip for centuries. What makes you think this time will be different?"

Mercurio flapped his wings, springing up from the back of the chair to land on the mantle, staring at Heath from his perch. "She is different, sire. She is of Mistress Earnshaw's bloodline and has the gift of magic as did she. She is the only worthy successor to care for Witherwood. If we have her on our side, Linton's power over us will be broken."

"You hope!"

"I know! I feel it in my bones."

Heath shook his head, the image of Cathy staring up at Linton with a look of wonderment and desire scratched at his core. "And you think he is using his magic on her already?"

"I guarantee it. His magic is what he used to lure your brides before, and I am certain he will try again."

Heath clenched his teeth as the memories of long forgotten brides surfaced, sneaking out of the box he had forced them into. There had been five serious attempts to procure a bride to break the curse and each time Linton had managed to destroy any chance of success, seducing the women away from him, humiliating him, working against him, plotting, and lying about him. Each time the women had believed Linton and turned their back on Heath, horrified when the curse had been revealed to them. They had run into Linton's arms, destroying any chance Heath had of breaking the curse. Could this time really be different?

"You say she has the gift?"

"Yes, Mistress Hyldreth was sure of it. She said she showed the signs of it as a child and Mistress Catherine's mother confirmed that it was so."

"Hyldreth was a powerful and knowledgeable crone," he relented.

"Indeed, sire, and given the magical properties of the house, which Linton has not been able to access, then we have a chance of victory this time."

"Victory! Hah! You make it sound like a battle, Mercurio."

"It is!" he replied with passion. "It is the greatest battle of your life."

"But I am weary of fighting, old friend," Heath sighed.

"Are you about to give up when we have a real chance of breaking the curse?"

Heath remained silent, sighing before taking another mouthful of whiskey. His throat burned.

"Are you about to let that snake steal another of your brides? Are you about to let him make a fool of you and defile your woman?"

A jealous rage began to kindle.

"Are you going to let him take your place in your bed, take your place between her legs.

"Enough!" Heath spat, his grip tightening around the glass.

As turmoil began to burn in his belly, the door opened and Argenon appeared. "Lord, Mistress Earnshaw awaits an introduction in the library."

"Take her to your bed, sire."

"Hold your peace!"

"Don't allow Linton to get there first," Mercurio pushed.

"Damnable bird! You are insufferable, Mercurio."

"But I am right," he cawed as Heath followed Argenon out of the room. "Claim your bride, sire. Set us free!" he squawked.

The journey down the stairs and through the house to the library to meet Mistress Earnshaw was a torture and he was glad of the whiskey running through his veins, but his heart still beat with rapid insistence against his breastbone. Women! They had been the thorn in his side too many times, but Mercurio, for all his insolence, was correct; he needed this woman, and he had to take her to his bed before Linton took her to his. He swallowed down the rising anticipation, squared his shoulders and lifted his chin.

As Argenon swung the library door open, light filtered in through large sash windows illuminating the room and golden dust shimmered in the air, collecting around the woman as though drawn by a magnet. She stood with her back to him turning the pages of an ancient book on the desk. His eyes skimmed the contours of her body as she turned and his heart seemed to stop for a single, painful second. With the shimmering dust collected like a halo around her form, her skin took on a honey-like hue, her dark hair shone in glossy curls, and her green eyes, ringed by black lashes, glittered with iridescent magic. Heath stalled in the doorway, the shot of desire he felt as their eyes met overwhelming his senses. She was beautiful and he wanted to claim her as his own with an intensity that took him by surprise.

Argenon coughed, breaking the spell. Heath stepped into the room and waited as the door was closed and the manservant stepped to his side.

"Lord, I have the great pleasure of presenting Mistress Catherine Earnshaw to you."

"Pleased to meet you," she said, and he noticed the slight flush at the base of her throat.

"I have taken the liberty of ordering tea. Mistress Earnshaw, if you'd like to take a seat ..." Argenon moved to the table set with cups, saucers, and a plate of cakes before the windows. Without speaking Cathy walked to the table and sat. "Lord," Argenon urged as Heath remained standing whilst watching Cathy's every move.

The intense emotion Heath had experienced as he'd entered the room grew stronger as he sat opposite the woman. Although past the first flush of youth, she was still beautiful and the streaks of white that were beginning to run at her temples only made her head of glossy black hair even more striking. The halo of shimmering particles had followed her, and she sat opposite him as though framed by magic. Correction, she was framed by magic. He had seen the phenomenon before on several occasions when the particles had surrounded Hyldreth, but they had never been as dense as now. If it was an indication of the power of her gift. Mercurio was correct, she was the one who could help, perhaps his last chance to break the curse. *His last chance for love!* He swallowed, mouth suddenly dry, the disparaging remarks he'd made about her age and the barrenness of her womb, regretted.

Chapter Seventeen

Sitting across from the tenant Cathy remained silent, her thoughts scattered. As she'd waited in the library after being introduced to the small group that made up the staff at Witherwood Hall, her thoughts had become lost in the forest and the meeting with Edgar Linton. She remembered every detail of the experience—the sparkle in his eyes, the sensation of his lips on the back of her hand, the thrill it had sent through her body and, despite the guilt that stroked at her for accepting the invitation to the pub, she was excited to see him again.

Everything changed the moment the door to the library opened and the tenant stood within its frame.

Ellette appeared as if from nowhere and poured tea into the fine bone china cups. Steam rose as the cups filled. After replacing the teapot Ellette lifted the tiered stand of cakes. "They were made fresh this morning," she said offering the cakes first to Cathy and then to Heath. "I hope that you like them." Cathy took a tiny square of chocolate cake topped with a whorl of cream and a raspberry and placed it on her plate. Heath did the same. Neither ate.

"Thank you, Ellette," Argenon said, "you can leave now."

Ellette gave a quick bob curtsey and left the room, the lightness of her step barely audible. The door closed with a soft thud and Cathy became aware of Argenon watching them as though they were two particularly fascinating insects. With the room silent, and both men watching her, Cathy grew self-conscious, and took a bite of the cake.

Heath continued to watch her. His eyes locked to her mouth as she chewed.

"Lord, perhaps you would like to enquire as to Mistress Earnshaw's comfort?" Argenon suggested as the awkward silence continued.

The huge man glanced at Argenon, a frown momentarily creasing his brow, then said, "Yes, of course, forgive me. How was your journey? I hope it wasn't too difficult."

Cathy nodded, now regretting her cake-filled mouth.

Argenon coughed.

"And ... and how do you find Witherwood Hall?"

Cathy swallowed the cake. "I love it. It's such a beautiful place."

Heath took a sip of tea, the cup ridiculous in his large hand. He replaced it on the saucer with a heavy clank, spilling some of the liquid.

"And the staff are ... lovely," Cathy said, her mind returning to the peculiar collection of people Argenon had introduced her to. She suspected that they were the 'inhabitants' that the Will referred to and she had become convinced that Ellette and her husband Tatwin weren't human. They were beautiful people, but in an ethereal and quaint fashion. She had wanted to take photographs and send them to Lexi just to get a second opinion but resisted the impulse. "And the neighbours seem nice too," she said.

"Neighbours?" Heath's brow furrowed.

The change in his countenance surprised Cathy. "Yes, your neighbour. I met him when I arrived and then I bumped into him again whilst out for a walk in the woods. He spoke highly of Aunt Hyldreth," she said.

"What does he know of Mistress Hyldreth?" Heath snapped.

"You met a man in the woods?" Argenon deflected as Heath's furrowed brow deepened to a scowl.

"I ... yes, Edgar Linton."

Argenon stiffened. "Ah, yes. Mr. Linton. You are correct that he is one of our neighbours."

Heath's jaw clenched and the sparkle that had sat within his eyes grew hard. "Mistress Earnshaw has agreed to dinner with our neighbour, Argenon," he stated with an edge of bitterness.

Argenon glanced from Heath to Cathy and then to the scene beyond the window. "Ah!" he said then forced a smile. "I'm afraid that may cause us some problems, Mistress Earnshaw. There are a number of issues in the house that require your attention this evening. I think cancelling the arrangement, at least for tonight, would be best."

Cold energy wafted from Heath as the atmosphere in the room became tense, but the guilt she had felt at making the arrangement morphed into outrage. "I try to keep my promises," she replied with defiance, irked at Argenon's efforts to control her.

Heath's eyes narrowed.

"Mistress Earnshaw, let us discuss the contents of your aunt's Will. It is why you have come to Witherwood after all."

"Well ... yes. Fine," she replied, her mind whirring. *How did Heath know about her date? Had he been spying on her?*

"Yes, let's," Heath snapped.

Argenon spoke to him in a language she didn't understand, and he seemed to relax, easing back into his chair though his gaze remained cold. Cathy squirmed under his judgemental gaze, annoyed with herself for believing they had made a connection as he'd walked through the door. Witherwood was a magical place, but its energy was playing havoc with her senses. Heath seemed to be wallowing in a quiet fury as Argenon continued to speak.

"As you know, as per the contents of your Aunt Hyldreth's Will, you have been offered the role of Housekeeper with especial duties towards the inhabitants of the house."

Cathy nodded.

"Do you accept this role?"

She grew quiet, remembering the last painful and turmoil-laden weeks she had endured: the lost fiancé, the lost job, the lost chance of being a mother. Witherwood was her future. "Yes, I do."

Argenon gave a formal nod whilst Heath continued to watch her without comment or reaction. "Good. Then welcome, Keeper of the Hall."

"Housekeeper," she corrected.

"Yes, of course, Housekeeper of Witherwood Hall and its inhabitants." Argenon smiled. "Now, to the Codicil."

Heath stiffened in his seat, shifting his gaze to Argenon and then back to Cathy, hands tightening around the armrests. The butterflies in her stomach began to swarm.

"Your Aunt was most insistent about the Codicil. I spoke to her at great length about the terms. She was most passionate about it and only had your best interests at heart," he said. "She was an insightful woman, Mistress Catherine, a woman of great power."

"A witch, you mean."

Argenon nodded. "Yes, a witch, but one with great powers. She believed that you too have that gift and assured me that you are the perfect candidate to take over responsibility for the Hall, alongside your husband. However, I digress, back to the Codicil. It was her dearest wish to see you, her only relative, continue her important work, and that you be wed to her great friend, Lord Heath of the Wither Woods, who she took to her side as a son."

Heath nodded, a smile barely making it to his lips.

"She adopted you?" Cathy asked, directing her question to Heath. "I never knew."

Heath rolled his eyes. "No, of course she did not adopt me," he replied with an edge to his voice.

"What my Lord is trying to say is that during his time here, he grew indispensable to Mistress Hyldreth, and that the relationship they had was more akin to mother and son than landlady and tenant."

"She was like a mother to me," Heath said in an unconvincing tone.

"And it became her dearest wish that her closest relative and her dearest friend wed and produce an heir."

Cathy glanced at Heath, her cheeks now stinging. His eyes held a flicker of contempt.

"In short, you shall inherit the house if you agree to marriage and give him the child."

This was it, the moment she signed her life away. The room grew silent as the men waited.

This is your last chance, Cathy, the last chance to have a baby. He's good looking too. The child will be strong and handsome and inherit the Hall.

"Do you agree to the marriage and the gift of a child?"

She swallowed.

You don't have to like him to be married. Just get pregnant, have the child, and the house will be yours.

It belongs to me!

Only if you give him a child.

This is your last chance, Cathy!

With both men watching every nuance of reaction, she replied. "Yes, I agree."

Argenon sighed and Heath's stiffly held posture relaxed a fraction.

"Then I declare your betrothal."

From the desk Argenon pulled out a sheaf of parchment and unrolled it. Written in the same insular script as the Will was a formal declaration of their intention to marry. Heath was the first to sign.

Chapter Eighteen

Back in her room Cathy flung herself down on the bed, heart pounding. The meeting in the library had been surreal, a whirl of confusion and emotion. When Heath had appeared she had experienced desire so profound that it had overwhelmed her senses and she felt sure that Heath had reciprocated. The energy that surged from him as their eyes locked was unmistakable. One side effect of coming to this magical place was that her ability to sense the energy of others had become much clearer. However, the meeting had quickly become awkward and Heath's energy decidedly hostile.

She was engaged to a man who appeared to hate her, at least he had held her in contempt.

You agreed the go out with another man. You betrayed him before you had even met.

How did he know?

He spied on you!

He doesn't trust me!

Why should he?

"Stupid! You are so bloody stupid, Catherine Earnshaw." There had been the smallest flicker of pain in Heath's eyes as he'd told Argenon that she had arranged to go out with Ed that night. "But how did he know?" Her brow furrowed.

EXPECTING MAGIC

There was no way he could have known unless he had been spying on her, but they were out in the woods and the only evidence of life when she'd been talking to Ed had been the crow cawing in the treetops.

"The crow! It was that bloody rude crow!"

It made sense now, albeit in a crazy, paranoid way. If she told anyone but Lexi that she thought a crow was spying on her and tittle tattling to her fiancé, then they'd want her locking up.

"But it was real, the crow was real, and there was no one else in the woods, so it had to be him." She mulled it over. Talking to the crow at home, she had been unsure whether it was an hallucination, everything that had happened since she'd been jilted had taken her life into a downward spiral of crazy, but she was a witch, and talking crows were a reality that she had to embrace, even celebrate, for it proved that there was a world beyond what all the normies could see. She wasn't crazy or cuckoo or stupid for believing in a magical world as she'd been accused of more times than she cared to remember, and neither was her mother.

Cathy hadn't realised there was something different about her mother until she started school. Her friends' mothers didn't pore over a massive book filled with archaic writing, symbols, and drawings, pulling out recipes for everything from soothing ointments for rashes, to elixirs for a broken heart, or potions that would help a wife keep her husband from straying. Cathy smiled at the memory. Her mother had grown quite a reputation for helping couples keep their marriages alive and on one occasion she'd overheard her talking with a friend and promising to help her put a stop to her husband's affair with the office 'bike'. The term had confused Cathy who couldn't understand what the husband could be doing with a bike or why there should be one that belonged to the office. The friend had brought items belonging to the 'bike' who turned out to be a woman called Stephanie. There was an earring the friend had found in her husband's car, a mug Stephanie had used when she'd visited whilst the friend was out of town, and a pair of knickers found in the pocket of her husband's work trousers—the item that had finally confirmed her worst suspicions.

From a step on the stairs, Cathy had listened to the women talking in the kitchen as they'd giggled about their plot for revenge over a second large glass of wine. Her mother had begun, reciting ancient words as the house had filled with the scent of burning mugwort. The energy in the house had changed as she'd chanted the words, and although Cathy couldn't understand them, she knew their meaning—a call to the aether for intervention. Several weeks later, the friend had reported success: her husband couldn't keep his hands off her and Stephanie 'the bike' Wilson no longer worked at the office. That her friends' mothers weren't the same confused Cathy, but she quickly learned to keep her mother's strangeness a secret.

Her thoughts returned to the crow. If it had told tales to Heath, was it his familiar? Or did it belong to Argenon? Both men exuded an energy she had never picked up from a male before. Did they have the ability to call to the aether too?

Half an hour passed as Cathy relived every second of the meeting until finally, with the sun lowering, she realised that only fifteen minutes remained before she was meant to meet Ed at the *Wolf and Lamb* in the village. As she rose from the bed, filled with a queasy unease, she was distracted by chittering and then movement in the periphery of her vision, and she yelped as something swooped down from the top of the curtain and across the room to the fire.

"What in the world!" she exclaimed as the tiny figure landed and perched on the mantlepiece. Its hair gleamed in the light, burnt orange with dark copper at its ends, framing its face like a dandelion's seedhead. She took a step forward. The creature chittered and then another swooped from the chandelier and landed beside it. It too squatted on the mantle. Like the first creature this one had a mass of dandelion seed-like hair, but instead of a vibrant copper, this one's was flaxen. Both creatures watched Cathy as she stared at them in disbelief. "Are you really fairies?" she asked, taking a step closer. The orange haired creature stood and was quickly followed by the other, both chittering and growing skittish as she continued to stare at them with interest. Wings that had folded behind their backs extended and began to buzz, glassy and iridescent, like jewelled dragonfly wings.

"Yes, you are!" she whispered. "You are real."

They were exquisite, tiny, and doll-like, with large emerald-green eyes framed by dark lashes, their lips blush pink. She gave a soft laugh and held out a finger. "You really are real," she repeated. The orange haired one chittered in annoyance, bared a mouth full of dagger-like teeth, rose, then darted forward, speeding past her like an Exocet missile. The second followed, only just missing her cheek and both darted to the ceiling, disappearing among the shadows.

After waiting several minutes for them to reappear, she made her way to the bathroom to get ready for her meeting with Ed. With no way of contacting him to cancel, she felt obliged to turn up; she may be betrothed to Heath - her belly did a queasy flip - but that didn't mean she could treat Ed badly. After a short deliberation she decided to have a single drink with Ed, make her excuses, then return home.

Dressed in skinny jeans, strappy sandals, and silk blouse in a green that Lexi said complimented her eyes, she made her way to the door. One of the creatures chittered and as she reached for the doorknob it swooped in front of her. Hovering, it chittered as she reached once more for the doorknob, then swooped to the ceiling before diving back down.

"What is it? Do you want to go out?" she asked as it hovered above the handle. She tried to reach for the knob and once more the creature swooped, bit down into the base of her thumb, then shot to the ceiling. "Ow!" Cathy yelped as pain like a bee sting shot through her hand. She took a step back in disbelief; the creature was trying to stop her leaving the room. "Right!" said Cathy. "I'm leaving this room, whether you want me to or not." Wings buzzed. "I'm going to open the door now." She reached a tentative hand to the handle and when the creature didn't swoop down to attack her, opened the door and stepped through, pulling it shut behind her. "Can this day get any weirder?" she asked as she took the first step down the stairs.

During the short tour of the house earlier, Argenon had shown her the kitchen, the pantry, and the servant's room where the unusual collection of staff often gathered, and she made her way there unsure of who to tell she was going out. The corridors to the wing that housed the servants' quarters had grown dim with the falling sun. Oil lamps lined the walls but hadn't yet been lit and she retraced her earlier steps, making her way down the flight of stairs to the kitchen, pleased to find Ellette busy drying pots.

She bob curtseyed after recovering from Cathy's hurried entry. "Ellette, I'm going into the village," she said. "I won't be long."

A frown flitted across the petite woman's face. "At night, Mistress?"

"Yes" she replied, surprised at the flicker of disapproval on her face. "So, if Mr. Argenon asks for me, could you tell him that I've gone out, I'd appreciate that."

"Certainly, Mistress," she said bowl in one hand, cloth in the other.

For a moment she appeared to want to say something but then turned back to the sink and Cathy made her way to the entrance hall. She was late, and Ed would be waiting.

Chapter Nineteen

Cathy felt the first pull of the house as she stepped out of the front door and stood at the bottom of the steps, suffused with thoughts of turning round and going back inside. But it was when she reached the standing stones at the top of the drive that it became intense. The car's engine thrummed as she sat behind the wheel, indicating right, car in gear, and waited between the stones. The house seemed to be calling her. 'Come back, Cathy. Come home.' Only it wasn't the house. The voice that seemed to call from her heart was Heath's.

"It's just a drink at the pub," she mumbled. "I'll be back as soon as its polite to leave."

'Come back, Cathy!'

Taking a breath to ease the tension across her chest, she pulled out onto the road. "Just one drink and then I'm coming back," she whispered, a sense of loss already pervading her senses. As she drove away the intensity of the feeling faded until finally it receded and gave way to thoughts of Ed.

The village was several miles down the road and the main road into the village ran through its centre where the pub with its large sign hanging from the wall, complete with wolf devouring a bloodied lamb, was impossible to miss. She parked up then made her way inside.

Quaint beneath a thatched roof, the pub was built of stone and retained much of its original features including dark beams on the ceilings complete with wooden posts to hold them up and a large fireplace big enough to sit within. Despite being high summer a low fire burned in the hearth, taking the coolness from the air. She scanned the room, surprised not to see Ed, made her way to the bar, and asked for a glass of wine.

The barmaid smiled and reached for a bottle just as a figure drew by her side. "I'd almost given up on you!"

She turned to see Ed smiling down at her, the sparkle in his eyes instantly mesmerising. He towered above her, his chest opposite her face. The early sensation of desire returned, and she broke his gaze with difficulty. "It's been a busy day," she replied.

"I can imagine. Need a shoulder to cry on?"

She managed a laugh. *Yes!* "Not quite. It's been ... different."

He took the glass of wine and paid the barmaid. "Come on, let's sit by the fire. You can tell me all about it."

They made their way to the table beside the fire and Cathy sat, glad of the warmth and the kindness in Ed's eyes. In the past she'd always had Dan to talk to, or Lexi, if he hadn't been around, but the day had been so strange she needed someone to talk to in the flesh. There was no way she could tell him the truth but having someone to share some parts of her first day with was a relief.

He took a sip of beer whilst she took a sip of wine. Full-bodied and red, it filled her mouth with a gentle and soothing warmth. Ed watched her above the rim of his glass then smiled. "So, tell me all about it. How did it go?"

Amazing. Crazy. The weirdest day of my entire life. "Good," she smiled whilst her brain scrambled for words that wouldn't betray just how crazy it had been. "The house is amazing, and the staff are great. I'm going to love working there."

"And you're the housekeeper?"

"Yep," she nodded. "Keeper of the Hall, is my official title."

"Keeper of the Hall," he replied whilst raising a brow. "Sounds archaic."

She laughed. "I guess, but in keeping with the house."

"It is ancient ... did you discover the magic well?" he laughed. "The locals claim it is a fountain of youth, the source of the Hall's power," he joked.

"Oh, that one!" she threw him a smile. "Why yes, and I captured some of the magic in a jar and brought you some." She feigned reaching for her bag, surprised at his gasp and the look of excitement that flickered in his eyes. "Only kidding," she said curious at his reaction. "I haven't seen a well." She took another sip of wine as Ed leaned back in his chair. Once again at ease, he exuded charm like a rich perfume, and they sat for several moments in silence.

"What would you like to eat?" he asked.

"Oh!" she said remembering her decision to have a single drink and return to the Hall. "I can't stay for dinner! Sorry."

"That is a shame," he said with disappointment. "I was looking forward to spending some time with you."

"I am sorry, truly," she said. "It's just ... I have some business to attend to this evening."

"I see," he said with a slight frown.

Cathy cringed at the look of disappointment on his face, unsure how she could have let him down more gently. She certainly couldn't tell him the truth that she had agreed to marry a man she had only met this afternoon. He would think her a lunatic, or worse, desperate. "I'd like us to be friends," she said in an effort to smooth the conversation.

He caught her eyes. "I'd like that," he replied. "Perhaps you could come to dinner another night? I cook a mean stroganoff. It's the mushrooms from my garden that make the difference."

Relieved that he no longer seemed offended, she laughed. "It sounds wonderful, and yes, I'd like that."

"Are you sure you have to leave so soon?"

She nodded. "I promised to stay for one drink."

"Promised? Who did you promise?"

"I ... myself. I promised myself."

"Are you sure?"

She laughed despite a flitting sense of unease, he didn't appear to believe her. "Yep!" she said lightly. "I'm sure. I'd love to stay longer but with it being my first day I want an early night so I'm bright and breezy in the morning."

"Well, if you're sure." He leant forward. "Cathy, you're not being coerced, are you?"

"Coerced? Whatever gave you that idea?" she asked with a bemused laugh.

"I don't know. Just a feeling."

She shook her head, confused.

Ed swallowed the last of his beer and Cathy drank the final mouthful of wine.

"Will you take a walk with me, before you go?" he asked. "The village is quite extraordinary, almost untouched by the modern hand. I think you'll love it."

"I already do," she said glancing around at the handcrafted wooden beams and whitewashed lime plaster walls of the ancient pub.

As she stepped out onto the path beneath the wolf devouring the lamb, twilight had begun to darken to night, and she hooked her arm through the crook of his.

"This cottage," he said as they passed the low and whitewashed walls of a thatched cottage with a series of tiny multi-paned windows, "belonged to Old Mother Crofton. She was known throughout the area for her knowledge of healing herbs." Cathy glanced in through a window, quickly looking away as she caught sight of an elderly woman sat at the kitchen table peeling apples. "In the past, they would have called her a witch. Did you know that witches live in the village still?"

"No, although, I did come across an article about the pagan roots of the witches of Witherwood. I haven't had time to read it yet."

"Ah! Well, then you will be delighted to discover that Mother Crofton's family live here to this day. Once you've been here a while, you'll realise how little it changes over the years. Witherwood isn't a village that takes to change well," he said.

"How so?"

"It just doesn't. We don't have the usual movement of people. Family's stay put, handing their houses down to relatives."

She scanned the row of houses on the street. Unlike the towns and villages at home, there wasn't a single 'For Sale' sign in sight.

"It's a tightknit community," he said as they continued to stroll past another quaint cottage, this one decorated with window boxes filled with vibrant geraniums. "Which has its drawbacks."

"Drawbacks?"

"People are nosey!" he said in a stage whisper. "And they know all the gossip. Take us, for example, walking in broad daylight, well, broad twilight," he laughed, "by tomorrow the entire village will be alive with gossip about the new woman Edgar Linton was seducing."

Cathy gave a nervous laugh. "I'd hardly call walking through the village being seduced."

"Ah, but there you see, the facts don't matter. They see me, a well-known bachelor, with a young and lovely stranger, and they'll weave a story around us, particularly if we kiss!" With a quick turn on his heels, he faced Cathy, planting a hard kiss on her lips before she had a chance to refuse. He chuckled as she gasped. "There! There's grist for their mills."

"I ... but ..." Cathy glanced along the street, scanning the windows for twitching curtains, her mind filled with Heath, her cheeks beginning to sting.

"Don't worry," he laughed. "No one saw. I'm only teasing."

Unable to think of anything to say that wouldn't sound petty or trite or suggestive, Cathy suggested they walk back to her car. Her lips tingled with Ed's touch, and the intense desire to feel the strength of his arms around her returned. In that moment she realised she couldn't see him again, not if she was going to marry Heath and inherit Witherwood Hall, and nothing would get in the way of her doing that.

"I've enjoyed tonight," she managed.

"Me too," he said and leant forward as though to kiss her.

She turned her head, avoiding his descending lips.

He held her gaze. "I'm concerned for you, Cathy," he said as he took hold of her hands.

"Concerned? Why?"

"Witherwood Hall. It's a strange place."

"I'm happy there," she replied. "There's nothing to be concerned about."

"I've heard things," he said whilst looking across her shoulder and gripping her hands a little tighter.

"What things?"

"There are stories about the place ... and its tenant."

"What do you know about the tenant?" she asked.

"It's gossip, really, but they say he has a history. I think prison was mentioned. I know that your aunt was a wonderful and generous woman, and she gave a roof to those in need, but sometimes people are in need for a reason that is not always ... how can I say it ... Cathy, there are dangerous people in this world ..."

She had to agree that there was an undercurrent of anger about Heath, but dangerous? Surely her aunt wouldn't have given him a home if he was truly dangerous. Would she?

"The staff don't seem afraid of him," she managed.

His gaze became intense. "Cathy, have you ever wondered how your aunt died?"

Chapter Twenty

The journey back to Witherwood Hall seemed to take only moments as Cathy reeled with the information Ed had shared. He'd suggested that Heath had a dark past that involved going to prison but his comment about her aunt had sent a chill through her bones. How had she died? She realised that she didn't know. Her mother had only said that she had gone to the Ever After and she'd assumed the lady, already ancient when Cathy visited as a teenager, had died of old age. But then why hadn't they known about her death at the time and why hadn't they been invited to the funeral? The questions churned in Cathy's mind as she drove between the standing stones but any sense of dread at returning disappeared as the wave of energy hit her and she was once again drawn to the house. It appeared in all its majestic glory as the car left the narrow woodland driveway. Golden dust sparkled in the twilight taking on a violet iridescence. It was a place of magic, the one place in the world she truly belonged, and nothing would take it from her. Nothing.

This time she entered through the massive front door. Candles lit the entrance hall, pushing back the failing light. From deeper in the house came the clatter of pans and she followed their noise to the kitchen and then the butler's pantry where Argenon sat at the table oiling a leather tunic. On the table were various leather items including several pairs of gloves.

"Good evening, Mistress Catherine," he said with an affable smile. "I thought that tomorrow we could go over your duties. You must be tired after such a taxing day," he said, standing to pull out a chair at the table.

She sat ruminating on how to broach the subject of his master's criminality and involvement in her aunt's death.

"I have the kettle on the stove, if you'd like a cup of tea," he said with a gesture to the woodburning stove. A kettle sat atop, steam beginning to rise.

"Thank you."

As he moved about the kitchen heaping tealeaves into the pot and placing mugs on the counter, she summoned the courage to ask the questions.

"Argenon, you have known Heath a long time—at least that's the impression I get."

"Oh, yes. I've known him man and boy. He came to me as a child to learn our ways."

"Came to you?"

He nodded as he poured water from the boiling kettle. Steam rose in plumes to the ceiling, curling as it hit the beams.

"Yes, for lessons in court etiquette, swordsmanship, falconry, horse riding." He beamed as he placed a jug of milk on the table. "He keeps a falcon still," he said lifting up the large gauntlet from the table. "A peregrine falcon."

"Here?" she asked.

"Yes."

"I haven't seen it."

"Witherwood Hall has extensive grounds, Mistress. It is impossible to see everything in one day. The Hall itself will take you weeks to become familiar with as it has so many rooms and floors and then there are the wings."

Cathy remembered the wing that had been forbidden to her as a child, the one they had entered on the day that Fion disappeared. Thoughts of Heath and her aunt's death receded to the back of her mind.

"Will you show me the wings ... tomorrow?" she asked.

"Certainly. I have drawn up an itinerary for tomorrow. Your Aunt was most particular in the way she ran the Hall and was quite insistent that you should receive full training," he said. "Now, where did I put it?" He scanned the kitchen then patted the front of his apron. "Ah!" he said with a smile and dipped his hand in the pocket pulling out a fold of thick paper. "Here it is," he said and flattened it out on the table. "Your aunts 'To do' list," he chuckled and then retrieved a pair of glasses from the counter. After a quick glance at the paper he refolded it and returned it to his pocket. "Exactly," he said and began to pour the tea.

When he placed a cup in front of her and offered her the milk without further explanation, she asked, "Exactly what, Argenon?"

"Eh?" he said as he poured milk into his mug.

"The 'To Do' list, what's on it?"

"Ah, yes, sorry, it quite distracted me. There is so much that I have to tell you that I struggle to know where to start."

"Oh," she replied. "Well, I've met the staff, and had a tour, but I'm still unsure of my duties."

"Ah, yes, well, obviously as Housekeeper the house must be maintained both inside and out, and the estate, its gardens and outbuildings, must also be kept in good and fruitful order, but your main duty will be to care for the inhabitants of the Hall." Before she could question him about what exactly this 'care' entailed he continued. "It is best to leave this all until tomorrow. I have a full day planned for you. We will be touring the entire estate and then the Hall itself."

"Perhaps I could shadow the staff?" she suggested.

"Shadow the staff?" he asked with an uncomprehending frown.

"Yes, accompany them as they go about their duties, so that I can understand exactly what it is they do."

"Ah! Yes, a good idea. Shadow the staff—what a strange way of terming it."

"I think it's a general term used when new staff come on board. At work it was often how new employees were inducted."

"Inducted ... yes, precisely, then we shall induct you with shadowing of the staff," he replied.

She smiled behind her cup. It was the first sense she had that Argenon was not all knowing.

With the tea drunk, thoughts returned to Heath and her aunt. "Argenon, how did my aunt die?"

He looked at her with surprise. "Why she passed to the Ever After, Mistress."

"Passed?" *Or was pushed?*

"It was her time."

"We weren't told that she was ill, or that she had passed."

"She was adamant that she pass with the minimum fuss."

"Without a funeral? Without her family?"

"We had a ceremony."

"Why wasn't I invited?"

"She did not ask us to invite you."

"Was she angry with my mother for not visiting?"

"Oh, no, that was entirely understandable."

"So you know why we didn't visit?" she asked.

"I ... well, your aunt didn't talk about it often, and I know it saddened her that your mother stayed away, but after the ... incident ... then she understood why she didn't come. I think leaving the Hall to you was her way of making amends."

Cathy grew excited; Argenon knew about Fion. "Incident?"

He threw her a surprised frown suddenly wary. "Yes ... incident."

"Which was?"

"I'm sorry, Mistress, I thought that you were aware of the ... incident."

"I'd just like to know if we're talking of the same incident."

Argenon held her gaze. "Your young cousin. I believe she disappeared and was never found."

So he did know. "Were you here then?"

"Me?"

"Yes, you, and Heath, were you living here then?"

"We were here before and after but absent at the time of the incident."

Convenient. "Could I ask where?"

"Oh, in another part of the country," he said and picked up the teapot and placed it on the side. "If you'll excuse me, Mistress, it is late, and I rise early."

With that signal to end the conversation Cathy agreed to meet him at eight o'clock in the morning and begin her first real day as Housekeeper of Witherwood Hall.

Cathy returned to her suite exhausted, the emotional toll of the day finally registering, and sank between the covers of her bed with a pounding headache and burning eyes. Despite her tiredness, each hour of the day took its turn to present itself to her memory, and she turned in bed, unable to find comfort or a safe place from her thoughts until the early hours of the morning. When she did fall asleep it was filled with dreams of being enveloped in golden dust and pulled feet first down into the pagan waters as Ed and Heath leered at her from above whilst the crow sat on the tenant's shoulder squawking 'down she goes' repeatedly.

AS CATHY FELL INTO sleep, Heath pulled against his chains, growling at the bird as it hopped just close enough to be out of reach.

"Woo her, sire. Make her think that you love her and do it tomorrow. Linton is drawing her to him, charming her with his lying smile."

Heath growled, snapping at the bird. "Don't mention that monster's name."

Mercurio squawked as Heath lunged forward and was then jerked back by the chains.

"She seemed reticent to accept his advances. You have a chance to win her."

Chapter Twenty-One

The following morning, Cathy woke to the sound of birdsong and a grey light filtering through heavy curtains. Despite the earliness of the hour, she knew that sleep would escape her, and rose from the bed then made her way to the window, drawn to look down on the garden.

The grey sky was already brightening to blue, and obelisks and arches rose from the low and rolling mist that hung over the garden, seeming to float. To her right, tucked away behind its protective hedges a haze of golden particles rose from the sacred waters.

Movement towards the back of the garden caught her attention as a group of people emerged from the walkway that led to the forest. Dressed in drab trousers and full-length skirts, a couple walked across the garden with numerous children, each one carrying a glass jar, a wire wound around its lip to make a handle, just like the ones she and Fion would use to dip into the stream when they tried to catch sticklebacks. She recognised the woman as Ellette and her husband Tatwin, the others were children, carbon copies of their mother and father. Fascinated she watched their progress across the lawns and between the flowerbeds as they made their way to the house. She counted the children as they skipped, the jars seesawing in their hands. She counted eleven children altogether, six boys and five girls, each with flaxen hair the same hue as their mother and father's. Like the adults, the children wore similar outfits, the girls with knitted shawls belted at the waist. Each wore a bonnet from which their plaited hair hung in golden ropes across their shoulders. The boys wore trousers just a little too short and waistcoats in the same roughly woven fabric as that of their father. And, like their father, their ears pointed through flaxen hair.

"A family of elves," Cathy whispered, captivated by the quaint family. Were these the 'inhabitants' she was to 'control'? If so, the instruction did not sit well with her.

The children skipped ahead but instead of entering the house they made their way to the sacred water and its sparkling mist, disappearing beneath the foliage that hid its entrance.

Minutes passed and Cathy was about to turn from the window when they reappeared. Bright and golden light sparkled in the jars, and they danced in the grey light of early morning like fireflies at twilight.

Intrigued, Cathy watched the scene with renewed interest, certain that the jars hadn't been filled for creating light against a darkening sky, it being morning. When all eleven children had reappeared Ellette and Tatwin followed, but whilst the children skipped off into the garden leaving a trail of golden particles in their wake, the adults turned to the house.

The children headed straight for the door in the garden wall where Cathy had first entered the house and made their way through. With the garden once again empty, she let the curtains drop back and made her way to the bathroom to shower and then to the breakfast room where Argenon had explained she would be expected each morning to break her fast before meeting the staff and giving them directions for the day. What 'directions' she was to give remained unclear.

With the mystery of the magical mist-filled jars being carried out of the garden by the elvish children turning in her mind, Cathy dressed then made her way downstairs. The breakfast room was empty and held a slight chill and, after sitting for several minutes unattended, she grew unsure if she was supposed to wait for her breakfast to be served or make it herself and then eat it in the room. Uncertain of etiquette, she made her way to the kitchen. Inside the log burning stove had been lit and unlike the breakfast room was already warming. A kettle sat on the stove, steam beginning to rise from its spout, and Tatwin sat at the table with a plate of porridge liberally sprinkled with sugar and ringed with milk. He greeted her with a look of surprise holding a spoonful of porridge to his mouth then nodded and glanced to Ellette. She stood with her back to them both, busy at the sink, her flaxen hair shining in the yellow lamplight.

"Morning, Mistress." He replaced his spoon on the plate whilst simultaneously rising and offering her a small bow.

"Please don't stop eating because of me," Cathy said, uncomfortable at their deference but charmed by their old-fashioned ways.

"Sorry, Mistress, we didn't expect you down so soon. 'Tis early yet."

Cathy glanced at her watch; it was barely five o'clock. "I had no idea it was so early!" she said.

"Did you not sleep well?" Ellette asked. "Were you not pleased with the bed? I chose the best linens."

"Oh! Yes, I slept very well," Cathy replied. "It was very comfortable, thank you. I was waiting in the breakfast room-"

"I'm sorry, Mistress, I haven't had time to light a fire in the breakfast room."

"I hadn't realised it was so early. Ellette, please don't worry. I can eat in here. It's lovely and warm and-" She stopped as she noticed the looks passed between the pair. "Or I can eat in the breakfast room, in a little while, when the fire is lit?"

"I'll light it now, Mistress," Tatwin said.

"Thank you, Tatwin, but please, eat your breakfast first. I'll take a walk around the gardens." Reluctant to leave the warmth of the kitchen and taking the opportunity to ask the couple about themselves, Cathy remained. "Have you been married long?" she asked.

"Aye, been married many a long year now," Tatwin replied. "And we are blessed with much fruit."

"Fruit? Oh, you mean your children. I saw them in the garden this morning. So beautiful!"

"Thank you, Mistress." A blush of pink stained Ellette's cheeks, making her look even younger and it seem even more impossible that the elven-like woman could have so many children.

"I counted eleven in the garden."

"Aye, and that's them as were sprinkling this morning."

"Sprinkling?" she asked.

"Aye," Tatwin replied. "Sprinkling." He picked up his spoon and scooped up more porridge, eating it without further explanation.

Cathy waited for him to finish eating and then explain, but he only scooped up more porridge.

"Can I ask what you mean by 'sprinkling'?" she asked.

Ellette turned from the counter and prodded at his shoulder. "Tell her then."

Surprised at the forceful prod, he replaced his spoon. "Forgive me, Mistress, I didn't mean to ignore you. It's been a while since we had anyone new around here that doesn't know our ways."

"They filled glass jars at the spring."

"Aye. That's for the Sprinkling."

"Ah, I see. And where do they sprinkle the water?"

"All around," he replied circling his head with the empty spoon.

"Tsk!" Ellette said. "They take it round Witherwood Hall, round the walls where the toadstools grow."

"Ah! I see," Cathy said. "And why would they do that?"

Tatwin shook his head and helped himself to more porridge.

"It's for protection, Mistress. Sprinkling the waters around Witherwood stops the Unwanted from entering."

"Aye, no one wants the Unwanted here. They cause too much mischief," Tatwin said.

"We have to keep the protection fresh, Mistress, to keep it strong, that way they don't get in."

"Who are they?"

"The Unwanted," Tatwin replied, then left the room declaring that he would light a fire in the breakfast room.

His plate was quickly removed and replaced with a steaming cup of tea in a bone china cup with matching saucer. "I bid you sit, Mistress. Ease your feet whilst you wait. The days are long at Witherwood. Mistress Hyldreth would always sit and have a cup of tea with me before her duties," Ellette smiled and sat on the opposite side of the table with her own cup of tea.

Chapter Twenty-Two

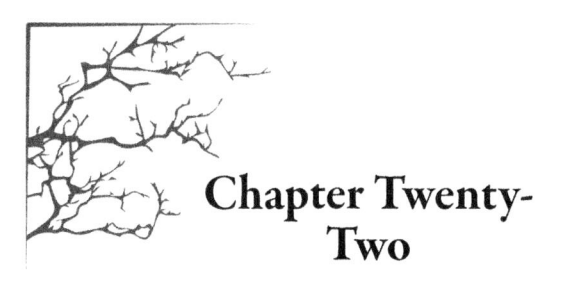

Whilst Cathy sipped tea with Ellette asking questions about her family and the children, Heath began his daily walk around the estate. This morning the job which took priority was inspection of the Sprinkling and he traced the steps Tatwin's children had made checking that each portion of the ring was secure. Golden particles glittered where the magical water had splashed. It gave off its energy with force, as though one magnet were repelling another. For him, it was easy to step either side of the line, but for anyone unwanted, particularly those named in the repelling spell cast by Hyldreth all those decades ago, such as Edgar Linton, it would be impossible to cross.

Leaving through the front door he made his way to the side of the house where the side wall became the brick garden wall and then a hedge of hawthorn and hornbeam interspersed with self-set trees migrated from the forest. Silver birch and poplars grew tall, casting their shadows across the open field to his right. The sprinkle of golden particles continued into the forest following the thicker bushes until they passed the back of the walled garden and around to the other side of the house. Heath would prefer it if the entire estate had been cast with the protective shield, but Hyldreth had argued that it would take too much magic, too much of her strength, to keep it intact if it extended beyond the house and walled garden.

The Tatwin children had done a good job this morning leaving no gaps in the perimeter. Satisfied that the protective circle was intact and strengthened, he made his way to the barns where the chickens were kept overnight. He had a busy day ahead. One of the ewes had been found lame yesterday and with tupping season less than ten weeks away, the condition of the flock was upmost in his mind. Several had looked a little lean last week and needed reweighing to check on progress since he'd adjusted their food. The rams too needed their yearly pre-tup checks, the 5T's of testicles, teeth, toes, tone, and treatment, taught to him by a local farmer who had long since passed.

As he approached the stables to check in on his stallion and its harem of purebred mares, one of Ellette's brood ran past with a basket on her way to collect the eggs. She was followed by two of her sisters, and one brother. The boy slowed to walk beside him, matching Heath's huge strides with his own.

"How do," he said with his typical greeting. "'Tis a beautiful morning."

"Indeed, it is," Heath replied.

"And were you pleased with the Sprinkling this morning, Master Heath? I was particular careful."

"You did a good job, son of Tatwin" Heath replied, slowing a little to help the small creature keep apace.

The creature beamed. "Thank you," he said. "And how do you find the new Mistress?"

"She is fair," Heath replied giving the child a sideways glance remembering the first awkward moments they had shared, the intense need to own her, and crushing disappointment that she had already deceived him by flirting with Linton.

"Fader says she is a comely wench."

Heath snorted. "Then you father had best keep his eyes on your mother."

"Aye," the child replied. "Modor says she is a beauty. Just like Mistress Hyldreth in her youth."

"There is a passing resemblance," Heath agreed.

"Fader says you shall be a courting her and that you will bring forth fruit, like Modor and Fader."

"Your father has much to say, young Tatwinson."

"Shall you be awedding her then, before you tup?"

"Cheeky rapscallion!" Heath laughed. "Be off with you before I clip your ear."

The boy's eyes glinted a bright and emerald green, the points of his ears poking above his flaxen hair. "'Tis what they be saying. That you be awedded to her before Freysblöt."

"We shall see," Heath replied.

"And will the curse lift? If you tup her and she births your fruit."

Heath cuffed the boy at the back of the head with a light tap, too amused by his cheek to be angry despite the flush rising to his cheeks. "Be off with you, son of Tatwin before I set you to cleaning the pigsty."

"Not again!"

"Aye, again, for your cheek. Now, be off!"

With a mirthful glance, the boy darted to catch up with his sisters and disappeared into the barn.

At the stables, Heath checked the stallion over and inspected the bedding for each of the mares then saddled his working horse, a large Fresian with a glossy black coat, that he used to make his way around the estate on his daily inspection of the fields, flocks, and herds. The horse was a magnificent creature, a true noble among its breed, and he preferred it to the stallion, which was kept for breeding, the sale of his thoroughbreds bringing him much needed income. The one problem with living such a long life, Heath mused yet again, was maintaining one's wealth. Over the centuries he had gone from being master of his own lands, complete with tenant farmers, to living as a tenant, protected by an elderly crone from the man who hunted him through the years, delighting at each rung Heath had fallen further down the ladder until he now had nothing left but his horses and his curse.

He patted the stallion. "Come Sweyn, we have work to do."

The flaxen-haired boy reappeared, so alike were the fruit of Tatwin and Ellette that he could only tell it was the same boy by the distinctive diamond shaped fleck of dark green in one of his eyes. He took the stallion's reins and led him to the mounting block, a large stone, worn to a dip along one side through long use.

"I warn thee not to mention Mistress Catherine to me, young Tatwin."

The boy nodded his agreement with a barely suppressed smile but then his face grew serious. "The woods were alive last night."

Heath continued to mount the horse and once in the saddle focused on the boy. "Alive?"

"Aye. And the herd was fractious this morn. One be sitting by its calf. It be too weak to move."

"Why didn't you tell me this before?" Heath growled and pulled at the rein, steering the horse towards the gate. "Open it boy, before I regret not cuffing you harder."

Recognising the surge of anger, the boy ran to the far side of the yard without another word and unlatched the gate, swinging it open for Heath to ride through.

"Let's to it, Sweyn," Heath said with a squeeze of the animal's flanks as he urged it into a trot and then a canter.

The fields where the herd grazed was almost half a mile from the house, but the horse made its way easily along the track, keeping the pace.

With the son of Tatwin jogging by his side with ease, Heath arrived at the field where he had driven the herd only days before. Thinking back to his last visit, he scoured his mind for evidence of illness but there had been nothing that would have alerted him to any problems. The field was shrouded in low-lying mist and several of the cows stood as though floating, their heads nodding above the mist. This particular herd was kept at around nine beasts, with a single bull to service the females kept several fields away. There were two young calves making a total of twelve beasts. Heath counted only six cows.

After dismounting, he climbed over the gate, jumping over with a thud then strode across the field searching for the missing cows within the thinning mist. He found another two cows sitting beneath the mist, both lethargic.

Squatting beside one, it eyed him with dull eyes then laid its head down. Its calf sat resting against its belly. Apart from the lethargy and dull eyes, the cow's udder was empty, and the calf bleated mournfully, nudging at the teat, and suckling without success.

"Tis what you fear?" asked the boy.

"It's hard to say. I haven't seen sickness among them for a long time. A long, long time."

"Tother is on the ridge," Tatwinson said, pointing up the hill to where the land jutted out. Above it sat another area of woodland. A falcon wheeled in a circle, riding the currents then returned to its branches.

Heath followed the boy's pointing finger, hand against his brow as he peered up the hill. Towards the top, a cow lay prostrate as though dead. The calf beside its mother gave a mournful bleat. Another cow answered.

"Is it dying?" the boy asked glancing at the mother, as it began to gasp for breath.

"Yes, I think we are too late to save her," Heath said with anger bubbling.

Leaving the dying cow and its calf, Heath made his way to the cow beneath the ridge. It lay lifeless, flies already swarming around its eyes and tail. Its belly was concave and the udder that should have been filled with milk ready for its calf was empty. Further along the ridge a smaller reddish-brown mound lay unmoving. Heath groaned. Both mother and her calf were dead, both emaciated as though every ounce of moisture had been drained from their bodies.

"They're dead," stated the boy. "Is it what we fear?"

"Aye, lad. I've not seen it for many years, but it is what we fear, I would stake my horse on it."

"Can I have your horse if you're wrong?"

Heath turned to the boy with a frown. He shrugged.

"You said you would stake your horse on it!"

"Impudent boy," he said without any anger. "Your tongue will bring you much trouble if you do not learn to tame it."

"That is what Modor says," he grinned then returned his gaze to the dead beast.

An inspection of the calf proved it to be in a similar state to its mother—emaciated and drained of moisture. He returned his attention to the herd below, instructed Tatwinson to inform his father that the sick cow must be rehydrated and taken to the barn until she had regained her strength and the calf taken with her and bottle fed.

"But what of the others?" Tatwin asked as Heath left the field and began to mount his horse. "If it is what we fear-"

"It is."

"Then the others will be next."

"We call in the Hunter," Heath replied with a gentle tug at the rein and a squeeze of Sweyn's flanks. The signs had been there, the increased activity in the West Wing, but he hadn't acted upon them and now the herd was being destroyed. If it was only the herd that had been attacked, then there was time to put it right.

Chapter Twenty-Three

As Cathy finished a breakfast of scrambled eggs and bacon, both, Ellette proudly informed her, from their own chickens and pigs, a door slammed, and Heath's demanding voice could be heard shouting for Argenon. Too curious to ignore the sense of urgency in his voice, she made her way to the kitchen, but the men stepped outside as she entered.

"Is there a problem?"

Ellette seemed unperturbed by the shouting. "Something to do with the herd on top hill," she replied whilst reaching for a cloth and wringing it out. "One of the cows isn't well." She began to wipe the already clean table. "Master Heath is most particular about the health of the animals. He checks them over every morning."

"Argenon had mentioned showing me around the estate today."

"Aye, there's much to see. It stretches far, almost to the village."

"And Master Heath ... he looks after the animals?"

"Aye, he's the estate manager. Has been since ever I can remember. Mistress Hyldreth was much thankful for his expertise. He keeps the sheep and pigs in top condition, and they're sought after throughout the country for their meat."

"You sell the meat?"

Ellette laughed. "Why of course, they made Mistress Hyldreth a good income, enough to keep the house running. And Master Heath's knowledge of animal husbandry is what has saved us all from ruin."

"Ah, I see," Cathy replied, beginning to understand Aunt Hyldreth's admiration for the arrogant man.

"And then he has his horses, which he breeds, but they belong to him alone."

"Horses!" she said with surprise. "I love riding although I haven't been on horseback for such a long time."

Ellette smiled. "There's another thing that you have in common." Her eyes widened. "I'm sorry Mistress, that was too personal." A flush rose to her cheeks and she turned back to the sink.

"Don't worry, Ellette. I don't mind."

Ellette rubbed at the dishes in the sink.

"So, Argenon has gone with Heath to see the sick sheep?"

"Oh! No, Mistress. To the herd on top hill—the herd we keep for ... we keep a herd of cows for milking."

"If we had some solar panels and a wind turbine then we could be completely self-sufficient," Cathy laughed, admiration for Heath, the staff, and her Aunt Hyldreth growing. Witherwood Hall was a functioning and productive farm as well as being a place of secrets and magic.

"Solar panels?" Ellette asked with a confused frown. "What is solar panels?"

Taken aback, Cathy stared at the elvish woman for a moment then explained that they caught the sun's energy and transformed it into electricity to power lights and other electrical appliances.

"Oh, my! That is surely magic, but we have no need of that here, the spring gives us all that we need."

"So, we are off-grid?" Cathy questioned with a glance to the electric light that was brightening the room.

Ellette responded with another look of confusion.

"Ellette, where do the lights get their power from?"

"The sacred spring, Mistress," she said with a smile then returned to washing the breakfast plates.

Cathy glanced at the lamp hanging from the large hook on the ceiling as it illuminated the room with a soft and sparkling golden glow.

With Argenon gone from the house, and unsure of what she should do next, Cathy decided to find the key and explore the rooms behind the locked door. Fion had said she had found it on a hook in Aunt Hyldreth's day room, the room now allocated as her sitting room.

As she stepped inside the room another memory arose though not as intense as the vision in the woods. She was a child again, peering round the door. Aunt Hyldreth had been sitting at the table, reading from a book, glasses perched on the end of her nose, a bright aura skimming her form. The aura ebbed as their eyes met, fading to a light pink, and the flow of words stopped. The room had smelled of burning mugwort, and smoke from a wand burning on the windowsill twisted to the ceiling, the energy radiating from her aunt shimmering as it collided with the particles.

With the memory fading, she walked into the room, closing the door with a soft thud. Cathy's immediate impression of the room was one of comfort. A dark green velvet sofa overlaid by a large sheep's fleece and strewn with several cushions bright with blown roses and peonies sat before a fireplace. A mantlepiece of marble in a chalky white stone was carved with gentle curves whilst above it were several differently sized oil-paintings, all depicting flowers. Along the back wall sat an enormous Welsh dresser loaded with ledgers, books, stoppered jars, and glass bottles in various colours and sizes. Before it was a round table and chairs, an oil lamp at its centre. Light flooded in from two sash windows that looked out to the gardens at the side of the house, again adding colour and beauty to the room.

She scanned the room for the hook that held the large iron key to the forbidden wing and found it beside the door, but the key was missing. Disappointed, she turned her attention to the Welsh dresser and its drawers and then the old sideboard behind the sofa. An iron key sat in one of the locks. It turned with a little effort and the door swung open to reveal three leatherbound books.

"Your grimoires," Cathy whispered, running a finger across the edge of the largest book then removed it and placed all three on the table before checking inside the cupboard for the key. It wasn't in the sideboard and, disappointed, Cathy sat at the table, to examine the books.

The largest was bound in dark brown leather and tooled with runes around its front edges with a design of entwined wolves, snakes, and boars at its centre. With the book opened before her, Cathy lost herself within its pages, the hours passing as she pored over its pages. Made from parchment, each quire sewn with waxed string, new booklets had been added over time. Unlike modern books that were glued together or permanently sewn into place, the grimoire was a moveable feast, the quires, with a little effort at unknotting their laces, could be removed, and reordered, the book easily added to, and there was space within its binding for more to be added. The quire at the front was only partially filled, which Cathy took to mean that it was the newest to be added. She turned to the back where the pages were thicker and pitted with holes. Closer inspection revealed the remains of follicles that meant the 'paper' was not paper, but parchment, animal skin. Any skin could be used but sheep skin was common and for really expensive books calf skin known as vellum was used, Lexi had told her. The skins would be soaked in a lime solution to remove the hair and flesh and then stretched on a frame so that it could be bleached and scraped to make it an even thickness. Once dry, the skins were cut into sheets then folded to form pages. Given the self-sufficient nature of the Hall, Cathy wondered if her aunt had made the parchment herself.

"You will love this, Lexi," Cathy said, taking several photographs of the books before sending them to her friend with a message of, 'You must come up soon and check these out!'

She turned to the end of the large manuscript. Without a table of contents it was a book only traversed by a knowledgeable owner. The parchment of the final quire was of a thicker and rougher quality than the earlier quires and the ink brown rather than black, confirming to Cathy, that the final quires were the oldest. The final quire differed from the rest too in that it contained mostly drawings that were labelled with runes. Much of the book was given over to botanical drawings and lists of medicinal plants and different combinations and recipes and charms to be said whilst preparing or administering, much like a medieval herbal. But the final quires were entirely given over to drawings of supernatural and mythical creatures. In one, she recognised the features of a spritely woman, similar to Ellette with her large eyes, flaxen hair, and pointed ears. Next to it were a series of runes that she couldn't decipher.

Fascinated, Cathy continued to read through the grimoire finding several more quires with drawings of trolls, fairies, imps with creatures labelled *draugar, dweorg, dokkalfar, Ljosalfar, fossegrimen*, and *huldra*. Each depiction of a creature was accompanied by drawings of various implements, and charms which Cathy presumed gave information on how to deal with them. Among the pages she found several spells she was familiar with, but the majority were new to her and carried warning labels such as, 'Warnynge thys be a spell filled with power' or 'greyt care must be taken,' and 'a great debt to the æther thys spelle desyres'. On another page, written along the side were several lines carrying the title, 'To repaye a debt to the aether offerre a sacrifyce.' She read them to herself, remembering the words of the cleaning woman at the services, 'do not use your powers for spite. Every call to the aether places you in debt. Guard your words well, do not throw them away or use them for harm. Therein lies the pathway to the stake and I see flames in your future if you do not alter your ways'. "Silly woman," she said, but re-read the charm.

"Oh, Aunt Hyldreth, I wish I had visited you," she sighed as she realised the richness and depth of her aunt's collection. With many of the charms, hexes, and spells written in either runes or a language she did not understand, there was much in the grimoires that Cathy had no access to. The medium sized book also contained numerous charms though, Cathy noticed with satisfaction, there were a number of pages that she could read. The third book was the smallest and contained the least number of pages.

Unlike the other books, the black leather of this book remained undecorated and inside, on the frontispiece carried a single word, 'Déaþscufa'. As she leafed through the pages, she came across several drawings of hideous-looking beasts and creatures. She realised that the book was divided into sections, with each section beginning with the drawing of a beast, and a title above it. This was followed by botanical drawings and then charms, each relevant to the beast depicted. The first showed a wolf-like creature, an amateurish depiction of what could be a half-man half wolf hybrid and on the following page was a botanical drawing labelled 'wolfsbane'. The pages that followed offered various repelling charms.

On another page was a fearsome looking creature with fangs. Beside it were a number of drawings including a sickle, a pointed stick, and a hammer. At the top a title was written in large runes but above that, in a later, cursive hand, was written, 'blódgeótan déaþscufa'. On the following page was another botanical drawing, this one labelled 'garlyc flowere'.

Again, there were charms that used the flower in repelling the creature. "Déaþscufa," she read, taking another look at the drawn figure, noting the fangs at its mouth. She laughed. "It's a vampire!" The following pages depicted the same figure showing it with a stake thrust into its heart. Another showed it within a drawn rectangle with the label, 'to keep the shadowe walker in the grave'. The creature was drawn with a curved object over its neck and an object placed in its mouth carrying the labels 'syckle sharpened beneethe the moon' and 'large stowne'. Beside them were charms, instructions of how to prepare the sickle and the stone. "It's an instruction booklet on how to kill vampires and werewolves," she said.

"Ah! You are here." Argenon said from the doorway.

Cathy jumped, startled at the sudden intrusion.

"You've found your aunt's books, I see" he said taking several strides into the room.

"I was just reading them," she said feeling like a small child caught with stolen cake.

"Mistress Hyldreth bequeathed the books to you, Mistress Catherine. They are yours to do with as you wish although ... I assume they must be treated and used with great care," he said.

"Yes! Yes, of course. They're fascinating, but there's so much in them I can't read because I don't understand the language."

"Is that so?" he asked and walked across to the table, leaning over the book to peer at the page depicting the vampire with the stake through its heart.

"Ah, yes, the shadow walker. It seems clear to me."

"This page is, I mean the language is quite old-fashioned but it's the earlier pages in the large book that I can't read. They're written in Old English, I think, and some of them in runes."

"And you can't read runes?" he asked with a hint of surprise.

"Oh, well, I have cast runes, and see what is foretold, at least I'm practicing but there are whole pages of charms and spells and I have no idea what they mean."

"Show me," he said.

Cathy turned to the oldest quires with their depictions of mythical and supernatural beasts. "Ah, yes," Argenon said and proceeded to read from the book.

Cathy sat back in the chair. "You can read them," she said, impressed.

Argenon nodded. "I can, although it has been some time since I've read such ancient words."

"What about this?" she said turning the pages to what she believed was the earliest form of English.

He read the text to himself. "Ah, yes. This is a charm against dwarves," he said, then read the first line.

"That is amazing!"

"Thank you. I was taught the language as a child."

"There are so many charms in this book. So much I can't read," she said unable to hide her disappointment.

"And hexes," he said pointing to the opposite page. "This one is to curse a dilly man who does not clean the privy with care."

Cathy laughed. "I'm not sure I'll need that one," she said.

Argenon smiled. "I wouldn't be so sure of that, Mistress Catherine. We are not connected to the main sewers at Witherwood Hall, and part of your job, as Housekeeper, is to ensure the smooth running of the house."

"You can't be serious," she said, expecting him to laugh and agree that he was joking.

"Indeed, a functioning privy is essential," he said in earnest. "If the cesspit becomes blocked ..." He shuddered.

Cathy had expected there to be some element of cleaning to be involved in her role as Housekeeper, but cleaning sewage pipes and cesspits had not entered her thoughts. Images of her wandering around the house like lady of the manor evaporated as she imagined herself pulling on rubber gloves and wellington boots to inspect the cesspit and ensure the 'dilly man' had done a good enough job. "Oh," she said and returned to the book, reading the hex despite not understanding the words. A hand clamped down upon her shoulder. "Take care, Mistress, a call upon the aether carries with it a burden of debt."

"I- ... Yes, of course," she said.

"Will you teach me how to read them?"

"Me?"

"Is there anyone else?"

"Master Heath is proficient in several languages," he replied. "You can speak to him about it. Which reminds me of why I am here. Master Heath requires your company, Mistress. If you would accompany mc, I will take you to him."

"Why does he require my company?"

"He has asked that you accompany him this afternoon. I took the liberty of suggesting that you shadow him whilst he carries out his duties," he smiled. "It is a good opportunity of becoming familiar ... with each other."

"What should I wear?"

"As you are, but perhaps boots rather than your shoes," he said with a glance at Cathy's strappy sandals. "The farm can be a little muddy at times."

Cathy wrinkled her nose.

Argenon gave a small chuckle. "Don't worry, you won't be inspecting the cesspit, at least not today."

After changing her shoes for a pair of walking boots, Cathy followed Argenon from the house, through the garden, and out of the gate to an area of outbuildings and stables.

Heath stood at a stable door, patting the neck of an enormous black horse. He barely smiled as she approached, and she avoided meeting his gaze.

"Good afternoon, Mistress Earnshaw," he said with a slight and formal nod of his head in greeting.

"Good afternoon," she replied, forcing a smile.

"I took the liberty of saddling Gefyon for you. She's of a calm temperament and pliable."

A young boy with flaxen hair, one of the many children she had seen with their jars of sparkling water that morning walked around the corner, reins in hand. The horse, a stocky chestnut mare, snorted as it walked forward. The large black horse nickered, nodding its head as though speaking to the smaller horse. The chestnut mare clopped to a stop.

"You do ride, I take it?" Heath said.

"Yes, I do," Cathy replied. "Although I haven't been on horseback for years, since I was a teenager to be honest."

Heath sighed. "Decades then," he muttered and returned to his own stallion, and opened the stable door.

"Yes," Cathy said, biting back her annoyance.

"Never fear, Mistress," soothed Argenon with a faintly disapproving glance at Heath. "It will all come back to you as soon as you are in the saddle."

"Argenon, you have duties to attend to, I believe," Heath said.

"Indeed, Lord."

"Then to it, man!"

Without argument, Argenon gave a small bow then left.

Chapter Twenty-Four

After finding the herd in a poor state, Heath had instructed Argenon to contact the Hunter and urge him to attend, and then listened to the man's plea that he spend time with Cathy and allow her to 'shadow' him during the day. 'It will help ease her into the duties she must carry out,' he had said. 'Hyldreth was quite determined that she take over from her, and if the Hunter refuses, then she will have to take up those duties without an apprenticeship.' Heath had agreed but, already tense, seeing Cathy again was a jolt to his senses. As she'd walked across the yard, he experienced a wave of turbulent emotions. This was the woman who could save him, but the woman had already been disloyal by going on a date with Linton. As she walked across the yard, he imagined her undressing for him on their wedding night, allowing her nightdress to drop to the floor to reveal the alabaster curves in all their glory. His heart tapped a hard beat and he turned to the horse, patting its neck a little more enthusiastically than was usual, forcing himself to think of the day ahead to dampen down his growing need to take the woman to his bed.

Argenon walked away after throwing him a meaningful glare, and Cathy stepped beside him. The need to slip his arm around her waist and pull her tight against him grew overwhelming. Taken aback by his need, he clamped his jaw tight.

Stay in control, fool! The woman is to be used for producing an heir, nothing more.

What if she's your last chance for love?

She is a means to an end. Nothing more.

She could be everything!

Ignoring the thoughts worming in his mind, he held Cathy's gaze, hardening himself against the emotions rolling over him. Argenon had insisted that he show the woman around the estate. 'See it as a way of getting to know her, my Lord,' he'd said and, despite Heath's objections, had finally convinced, nay bullied, him into spending the day with her.

'She needs to be wooed, my Lord, whether she has signed a contract or not. Remember, a happy woman is more likely to conceive. And the Hall *needs* her.'

'Pah!' he'd scoffed, 'what nonsense you speak, Argenon. A woman does not need to be happy to be impregnated with *my* seed.'

Nevertheless, Argenon had been adamant, and Heath had relented; being 'nice' to the woman wouldn't do any harm, as long as he kept his own emotions at bay. He had loved no woman since Agata had been so cruelly taken from him. Yes, he had taken his pleasure with them, but love, no, and this one would be no different. He would fill her with his seed, take great enjoyment from the act, but keep his heart locked in its box where it could do no further harm.

"So, we shall take a tour of the estate," he said. "Son of Tatwin, hand Mistress Earnshaw the reins."

The young creature's face broke into a broad grin.

"Thank you," she said as the boy handed her the reins.

"Have you forgotten how to mount a horse?" he asked as she remained beside the mare.

She answered with widening eyes that held a flicker of fear. "No. It's just been a while, that's all."

"Fine," Heath said with forced resignation and cupped his hands below the stirrups. "Put your foot in my hands," he instructed.

"I ... Well, I'm sure I could use the stirrup," she replied defensively.

"Good." He straightened up. "Then to it!" he said a little more forcefully than he intended, the effort of remaining calm with her so close becoming a struggle. The curse had done far more than disfigure him each night, it had superpowered his senses, and her scent, and the sensual energy that wafted from her, was intoxicating. His body responded with a primal urge. He clenched his jaw a little tighter. At night, when he transformed, the primal instincts of the beast were ascendent, but controllable, until the moon grew close to being full, and then they became a torment. Tonight the moon was waning gibbous, and he felt his control slipping. He faced it with a weary, frustrated sigh.

"Thanks! I will," she snipped.

He bit back the urge to apologise.

Her foot slipped from the stirrup as she placed it through the metal loop and she fell back against the horse, making it snort with surprise. "Sorry!" she said.

"Here, let me help," he said, grown irritable with chafing emotions. His heart beat hard as his future wife, the woman with the power to break the curse, slipped her foot into his cupped hands. As she grabbed the saddle, he pushed, lifting her up. "Swing your leg over," he said with a grunt as he held her aloft, her thighs close to his face. With an awkward tilt, she swung her leg over. "Are you sure you've ridden before?" he asked, allowing the edge of annoyance to slip into his tone.

"Yes, I have," she replied. "It's just been a long time."

"Too long," he said with a huff.

She cast him a defiant glance. "I'm more than capable of riding a horse," she said. "I just need to get comfortable in the saddle again."

"Make it soon. Gefyon is of good temperament, but even a well-bred mare such as she, doesn't have the patience of a saint."

Be nice!

"Well, I-"

He slapped the horse's flank, and it moved forward. "Walk her on. Head for the gate."

Gefyon walked forward with a slow gait then came to a standstill. Heath chuckled. Despite her protestations, the woman was rustier than she realised, or was exaggerating her experience. "Squeeze her flanks," he suggested as he took Sweyn's reins from the boy and mounted the stallion. As Cathy squeezed the mare's flanks and the horse began to move towards the gate, he drew parallel. *Be nice! Woo her. A child comes quicker from a woman who feels loved.* He swallowed. "You're doing well," he said recognising the patronising tone.

"Thanks!" she replied.

He tried again. "It will come back, once you're more comfortable in the saddle."

"It will," she said whilst focusing ahead.

As they steered the horses through the gate, Heath moved ahead. "Follow my lead."

She steered the horse to the right and followed behind without comment, her body stiff in the saddle. He sensed her fractious energy and was at once displeased with himself for causing her resistance against him, but thankful for it too. Once their wedding night was over, and the union consummated, he would be able to relax, until then, allowing her to see his true self, the man that battled with the monster he had been cursed to become, had to be kept from her.

With Cathy behind they made their way to the fields where the pigs were kept during the summer months. "We farm the pigs for slaughter," he explained. "Some we keep for ourselves, and the others we supply to local butchers."

"And when you say that we keep them for ourselves, how do you ... how are they slaughtered?"

"We do it here," he replied.

"Oh!" she said wrinkling her nose. "So, you don't get a professional in? I thought there were laws about that."

"We are professionals," he replied. "Tatwin and his brother Alfwith have been helping to raise pigs here for decades."

"And the ones we keep ... do you butcher them here too?"

"Of course."

"Do Tatwin and his brother butcher them?"

"Nay, the butchering is left to the ladies of the house."

"Allette?"

He laughed. "And you."

"Me!"

He nodded. "Yes, you, but don't worry, Ellette is a master butcher and will give you training. Did you know that your Aunt Hyldreth made the best pork pies I have ever tasted."

She nodded. "I remember them. They were delicious. And the bacon we had in the mornings was just the best," she enthused, remembering the aroma of breakfast that would waft through the house each morning.

"Indeed, and it all starts here, with good animal husbandry."

She looked out over the herd. "They do look to be in good condition."

"They are. This last year's litters were some of the best. We had seven sows each giving birth to a healthy litter. Only one runt, and that was brought on to survive."

She gave him a sideways glance, the irritation gone. "So, these are our pigs; they feed us and make us money. And, as Housekeeper, I'm expected to help prepare them for the table," she stated.

He beamed, relieved that she seemed to be taking the news in her stride. "Exactly."

"Cesspits and slaughter," she said with a shake of her head. "It's not quite what I imagined a housekeeper would do. What's next?" she asked, scanning the fields.

"Next we visit the sheep."

"Please don't tell me I'm expected to help shear them," she said, this time managing a smile.

He laughed, his tension easing a little. "No, but spinning their wool-"

"Now I know that's not true!" she said, searching his eyes.

He shrugged his shoulders. "Isn't it?"

"You're joking, surely?" she asked with a quizzical frown.

He relented. "Okay, yes, I am joking about the spinning. Tatwin and his family help to wash and prepare the fleeces."

"And you sell them too?"

"Indeed. The house needs maintaining, and magic will only help so far. It can't make roof tiles, or bricks, or mortar, or all the fixtures and fittings that need repairing. It is an old house with ancient roots. Hyldreth made it her life's work to keep it from rotting, I will not let her down."

A gleam appeared in her eyes as she spoke. "Do you think that's why she wanted us to marry, so that we could both help look after the house?" she asked.

"... I think so ... yes. I would think that was on her mind as she devised the Codicil."

"And the heir ... will inherit the house and continue the work," she stated looking back to the fields.

"Let us continue," Heath said. "I want to show you the sheep. Tupping season is close and they must be in good condition beforehand."

"Tupping season? What's tupping?"

"It is when ... it is when the ram is allowed to join the ewes."

"Oh, I see."

"We shall have lambs in spring if they tup in November," he explained and tugged at Sweyn's reins, steering him to follow the track up to the fields where the flock of Lincoln Longwool sheep grazed.

Chapter Twenty-Five

As Cathy followed Heath along the track that led to the flock of sheep, he spoke with knowledge about the creatures, and she began to warm to him after their initial disastrous few minutes. That he cared deeply for the animals reared at the Hall was obvious. That he cared for her was not. In fact, her presence seemed to irritate him. Twice he had flinched as she asked a question, curt in one reply, dismissive in the other. Her hopes of growing close to the man she was to marry faded with each step up the hill and her thoughts turned to Ed and his offer of dinner and the suggestion that Heath had at one time been in prison. There was definitely something edgy about the man.

As they dismounted beside the fence to observe the sheep. Bristling energy waved from Heath and Cathy began to wonder if he was hiding behind his brusque exterior. Was he as nervous as she? Afterall, it was an arranged marriage for them both. As she stood beside him, she grew acutely aware of his strength. Broad shouldered and tall, he stood at least a foot above her five-foot four height. Dan had been tall, but this man was a monolith of muscle. She stole glances as he talked about the sheep, noticing his large hands, the tanned skin weathered by the sun, the veins on the back of his hands standing proud. He was far from the foppish, brattish, Lord of the manor; here was a man who worked for his living, rising at dawn to tend to the animals on the farm. As he continued to talk, it became clear that Heath was the catalyst behind the Hall's flourishing farm, working daily with the animals and business side of the operation too.

"And I'd like to branch out into cheese production." He glanced her way, their eyes catching for the first time since leaving the stables. His glittered, matching the excitement in his voice. "I have plans, Cathy! And when we wed ... Well, having you by my side will be the help I need to make it happen."

Her heart jumped as he mentioned their arrangement. She glanced back to the house. "Witherwood is my future," she said. "I'd be glad to help."

"There are many duties you will be asked to fulfil, Cathy. Do you have a strong stomach."

She paused. "I think I can butcher pigs if it helps the business."

He turned to her, giving her his full attention. "And you are happy to marry me, then?"

Unable to answer him truthfully by saying yes, she swallowed. He noticed the hesitation and stiffened. "We barely know one another," she said in a moment of honesty. "I'd like to get to know you better. Could we have dinner tonight?"

"Is this not enough?" he asked casting a hand as though throwing seeds.

No! "Actually, no. I know that I've agreed to marry you-"

"You have."

"But I'd like to get to know my future husband a little better before the ceremony. If we could have dinner-"

He frowned and looked out across the fields. "What would you like to know?"

"Well ..." she stalled struggling to know where to start. There was so much she wanted to know but standing in a field asking questions without humour or tenderness was not how she wanted to get to know her future husband. She and Dan had spent hours talking in their early days, usually entwined in bed in the aftermath of making love. "I ... Have you been married before?"

He gave a dismissive snort. "No."

"Really?"

"Are you accusing me of lying?"

"No! I just meant that I'm surprised. You ... you're a good-looking man ... I just thought that given your age you would have already been married."

"You are not exactly young yourself!" he returned with another frown.

"I ... no, but-"

"But you *have* been married before."

"Me? No."

"You were a common law wife," he said with a curl of his lips.

Taken aback by the derision in his voice, Cathy recoiled from his gaze. "I was engaged to be married."

"But he broke off the engagement. Why?"

It was a question Cathy had struggled with over the past weeks. Pain ripped through her once more as the images of Dan and Alice walking along Cathy's idyllic honeymoon beach burned in her memory. "It was my fault," she said catching his gaze. "I put our relationship on hold whilst I focused on my career."

"But why now? Why did he leave you after so many years of waiting?"

"He met someone else and got her pregnant," she snapped, the pain grown overwhelming. "They're having a child together. There was no way I could compete with that."

"And you blame yourself?" he asked in a softer tone.

"Yes, I do. I was stupid. He wanted a child. I kept putting him off. There was always another promotion to grasp, another rung of the ladder to climb."

His eyes trapped hers. "So, you want a child now?"

"Oh, yes!" she said, surprised at the all-consuming need that overwhelmed her. "More than anything." She looked away, seared by the look of contempt in his eyes. "I don't blame Dan, not now, but Alice was my friend."

"They both betrayed you, Cathy," he said.

The tumultuous flow of his energy was unnerving; one minute he seemed to pity her, even understand her, but the next despise her.

"I guess. It was my fault though. I should have realised how much I was hurting him, but I was too wrapped up in myself and my career."

"Do you think that you have learned your lesson? That you can put your husband first?"

Once again, he sought her gaze. "I ... well, it's not exactly-"

"I want a wife, Cathy," he said. "An honourable wife who will be loyal and pleasing."

She frowned. "You want someone who will do as they're told?" she asked, riling at his attitude. "Pregnant and barefoot in the kitchen?"

He frowned. "Your feet would become cold on the tiles, and we have Ellette to cook and clean."

Eyes widening, expecting him to laugh, and for them to share the joke, she waited in vain. He was serious!

"So, no, I do not want you barefoot and in the kitchen, but yes, I hope that we can produce a child. Those are the terms of our contract."

Contract! Was that all their marriage was to him?

"I have my concerns," he said in a softer tone, "... given your age-"

"Concerns! Given my age!" she snapped.

He seemed startled at her reaction. "Why, yes, you are old-"

"Old! I'm ... I'm only forty-three."

"Forty-three! I had thought younger." His frown deepened. "Are you sure that you are fertile?"

"What? Of course I am fertile!"

"How do you know? Have you had a child out of wedlock?"

"Have you sired bastards?" she returned.

He flinched at her words, then narrowed his eyes. "Not that I know of, but I have had many lovers as have you, I think."

Cathy pursed her lips, suddenly angry. She hated him. "How dare you!"

"How dare you!" he replied. "I have sired no bastards, as you so crassly put it, but you have not answered me. Have you been delivered of a child out of wedlock?"

"No!" she spat. "This is too bloody much. What did you want? A virgin mail order bride?"

His eyes grew wide and dark, and Cathy sensed the rage behind his darkening scowl.

"A virgin would be preferable, Mistress Earnshaw," he said, "but these are degenerate times and when the devil drives, needs must."

"Then perhaps you should order one!" Turning from him, she mounted the horse. "And no, I have never had a child and nor will I if it is you that I must marry!"

"Cathy!" he called as she began to ride away.

She turned. "What?"

"Don't go into the woods after twilight."

She frowned, turned back to face the Hall, and squeezed the horse's flanks. "Onwards!" she instructed. "Get me away from that arrogant pig of a man now!" she muttered.

Chapter Twenty-Six

"The wedding date has been set," Argenon said as Heath strode back into his rooms.

Heath huffed in return.

"Lord, are you displeased?"

"She accused me of siring bastards!"

Argenon frowned. "Well, it's not an impossibility."

"Fie on it, man! The woman is a termagant. And did you know that she is forty-three years old?"

"She does not look so old, Lord."

"Well she is and what is the chance of a woman that old being able to conceive?"

"You shall have to give her a test run," said Mercurio hopping down from the windowsill and onto the back of Heath's chair.

Heath swivelled to the bird. "A test run? Foolish bird."

"A try out then."

Heath scoffed. "You are talking nonsense. No child of mine shall bear the name of bastard."

Argenon took a deep breath and sighed. "Let us concentrate on what is important. A child must be born in order for the curse to be lifted."

"She said she didn't want to marry me."

Mercurio squawked. "What have you done! She is our last hope."

Heath growled. "I have done nothing."

"Forgive me, Lord, but I thought we had agreed to treat the lady well-"

"Hah! For a start she is no lady. A lady would not live with a man for a decade as his common law wife. And she did not even bear a child during that time. She is barren. Find me another bride."

"Lord, your tenancy here is dependent upon you marrying the heir to the estate. Mistress Hyldreth was most insistent upon that. If you do not marry Mistress Catherine, then you forfeit the tenancy."

"And then we will be without a roof over our heads—again!" squawked Mercurio.

"What does it matter to a bird?" Heath said with a contemptuous glance. "You can live in the forest quite happily."

The bird snorted. "If I were a bird! Verily, sire, I am sick of living in this form. You are the only one who can save us all. Marry the woman."

"She has refused me."

"She signed the contract," returned Argenon. "She forfeits the house if she reneges on her sworn oath. She signed the paper. It is binding."

Heath sat in his chair. Argenon filled his glass with whiskey. "Drink. It will ease your discomfort," he said with a glance through the window. "It is the moon that is making you dissatisfied."

"You mean disagreeable."

"Yes!" squawked Mercurio. "And selfish."

Heath flapped a dismissive hand at the bird. It squawked and launched itself to the windowsill, staring with sullen irritation at the garden below.

"If I may ask, what was it that caused her such offence that she refused to marry you?"

"I asked about her fiancé and why he left."

"And?"

"And when she told me her age, I questioned whether she would be fertile."

"Stupid man!" Mercurio muttered.

Heath growled. The bird hopped from the sill and flapped across to the furthest window.

"And she took it badly?" Argenon gave a martyred sigh.

Heath shook his head. "Yes," he said, beginning to realise he had handled the situation badly.

"Lord, I understand your frustration, and do not blame you, but-"

"Win her back!" demanded Mercurio.

"It's too late," said Heath.

"Let us focus on what is important," Argenon repeated. "She is contracted to marry you and produce a child. She will go through with the ceremony, I feel certain, but in the meantime, as Mercurio said, you should win her affection."

"Hah!"

"You can be charming when you want to be, Lord. You are not without attractions for a woman."

"Oh?"

"Yes. You are of strong body and mind. Your visage is not displeasing, and you have good breeding."

"Until night falls."

"Which is exactly why you must try your best to be patient and tolerant. Put aside your prejudice and take her as your bride."

Heath nodded. "I was perhaps a little harsh."

"And do not forget, Linton will be making his best efforts to stop the union, as he always does."

"Don't let him win this time, sire," Mercurio said. "Don't let him take another of your brides."

Heath's jaw clenched as he remembered the brides Linton had stolen away from him. Mercurio was right, he was allowing emotion to take control and distract him from what was important, consummating the marriage and impregnating his bride.

"Go to her, Lord. There are still several hours before twilight. Take a turn around the garden. Apologise."

"Hah!"

"Flatter her. Tell her how beautiful she is, what lovely eyes, and glossy hair. They all love that," Mercurio advised.

"Do you think I don't know how to woo a woman, bird?"

"I know that you don't," Mercurio returned. "You have told this one that she is a shrivelled spinster with a barren womb."

"I did not."

"Not in those words, but that is how it translates."

Heath sighed. "She is comely," he said. "And ageing well, I suppose," he said remembering his surprise at her age. "I just did not think that she was so old. Forty-three is old to be having a first child-"

"Hark who's talking!" Mercurio interrupted. "He hasn't had a first child and he's centuries old."

Heath threw the bird a glance. "There have been many women."

"So perhaps you are the one who is firing blanks."

Heath glared at the bird. "I ... of course I am not."

"Then why have you not sired any bastards," he snorted.

"Impudent bird! Leave my rooms before I pluck out your feathers," Heath growled, the truth of Mercurio's words sinking in. What if it were true and he was the one who was infertile? Never! It was impossible. He cast a glance to his lap, then swallowed the remainder of the whiskey. If it were true – he could hardly tolerate the idea – then he would give himself over to the curse completely and descend into the vicious madness that consumed him. He would become the beast of the Wither Woods Linton had cursed him to be and cast off what remained of Heath completely.

"Lord," said Argenon, "the Hunter is unavailable."

Heath groaned. "The herd cannot sustain the attacks. And you know what follows once they have been drained."

Argenon nodded his understanding. "Which is why Mistress Catherine must be made aware of her other ... duties."

Heath nodded whilst taking a deep breath. "I shall leave that to you, Argenon," he replied. "I shall do my part and 'woo' her, as you say."

With another slug of whiskey in his system, Heath made his way downstairs to find Cathy, suffering the nagging caw of Mercurio in his ears.

At the sitting room door, he knocked, and was taken aback when it swung open. Cathy stood before him with a look of surprise that quickly became a frown. Her eyes were red and a little puffy. She had been crying.

"Yes?" she said without inviting him in.

Standing so close to her, seeing the pain in her face, he wanted to slip his arm across her back and hold her tight to his chest.

Last chance for love, Heath.

No!

"Can I come in?" he asked.

"Sure," she said without enthusiasm and stepped aside.

The room retained the scent of Hyldreth although Cathy's energy was beginning to overpower it.

"This was your aunt's room," he said, noticing Hyldreth's books on the table.

"Argenon said I could use it," she said with a defensive tone.

"Yes, of course, I didn't mean that you shouldn't use it."

"Good," she said and stood with her arms folded in front of the unlit fire. "What can I do for you?"

Pain wafted from her.

"I ..." He took a breath. This wasn't going to be easy. What if his clumsy attentions had ruined everything? "I came to apologise. I was rude ... earlier."

Cathy batted a dismissive hand towards him.

"I'd like to make it up to you. We can go for a walk in the garden ... if you'd like?"

She remained silent, arms still crossed.

"You were right. We should get to know one another."

"That didn't go so well the last time!"

"I'd like to try again," he replied. "I was too ... hasty in my ... in thinking ..."

"That I'm too old to get pregnant? A whore because I lived with a man I loved for a decade before he dumped me for a younger woman he'd knocked up?"

"No! Not a whore. Of course not."

"But old?"

"You're younger than me." He managed a smile.

"I am," she said, and a slight curl grew on her lips.

"So, will you walk with me ... in the garden?"

The smile broadened and he relaxed, then offered her his arm.

The early evening was warm, and although the sun hovered close to the horizon, there was still time to take a walk around the garden before twilight would make it impossible.

Heath picked a rose from a shrub and presented it to her. "Be careful of the thorns," he said as she took it from his hand and held it to her nose.

"Thank you," she said. "It smells wonderful."

He plucked another, this time keeping it for himself. "Hyldreth planted many roses and honeysuckles," Heath explained. "She particularly wanted the garden to smell of joy in the summer, those were her words."

"I think it's a perfect word to describe the garden," Cathy replied.

"Come this way," he said and led her to the far side of the garden where the sacred water lay. The golden particles released from its depths thickened as a light mist, gathering around Cathy as she walked, although she seemed to be oblivious to it. As they passed beneath the overgrown archway that separated the waters from the garden, he felt the pulse of its magical energy.

Cathy followed him down the narrow walkway and they both stood beside the water's edge. "The waters here are sacred, filled with ancient magic," he said as the sparkling air shimmered. "They say that if you make an offering your wish will come true." He threw the rose into the spring. It landed with a soft splash, and he recited an ancient charm as it fell then closed his eyes, asking in silent fervour, for success in defeating Linton.

"What did you wish for?" Cathy asked.

"That you would become my bride," he said. "Your turn."

"Okay, but I'm not going to tell you what I'm wishing for."

She threw in the flower, reciting the same charm. Particles rose and whorled as she recited. "There done it," she said.

A happy bride conceives more readily.

He took her hand, and lifted it to his lips, kissing the back of her hand. She gave a girlish laugh.

"The date for our wedding is set."

"Oh? It is?"

"So Argenon informs me. We are to be wed the day before Freysblöt. Does that please you?"

Her face had paled, and he waited as his heart pounded a little harder.

She gave self-conscious smile. "Yes," she replied. "I'd like that."

He sighed with satisfaction. Argenon had been right, being nice did wonders.

Chapter Twenty-Seven

Cathy returned to her room, emotions on fire. This morning she had grown irritated by Heath, even hating him when he pointed out that she was old and may have little chance of becoming pregnant. Then she grew mortified as she realised he thought badly of her for living with Dan out of wedlock. She'd ranted in Aunt Hyldreth's room, calling him 'a bloody pig' and a 'stupid out-of-date oaf' whilst searching for a spell to cast against him—just something to make him itch for a while or blurt nonsense and feel the mortification she felt, until the gypsy's voice returned to her mind. '... do not use your powers for spite. Every call to the aether places you in debt.'

She had closed Hyldreth's largest grimoire with a gentle thud. If the old woman warned that being vindictive would rebound on her, and she was right, even if calling on the aether didn't put her in some sort of moral debt, it was a toxic thing to do. She always felt a little grubby after casting any kind of harmful spell against someone, even if they had deserved it like Martin Shaw. She giggled, remembering the look on his face as she'd suggested it was a sexually transmitted disease; he had stood in shock, frantically trying to remember past lovers who could have infected him. How much debt had that petty revenge cost her?

Picking up one of the smaller books, she sat on the large velvet sofa and tried to relax, but thoughts of Heath intruded on her efforts to study. He was such a contradiction and her feelings towards him didn't just ebb and flow, they crashed against rocks!

And then there was Ed!

Cathy let out a groan as she remembered the attraction she'd felt towards Edgar Linton. It was instant and exciting, but when she compared it to the primal emotions that Heath aroused within her, it paled to a damp squib. The thought of being with Heath aroused her most primal needs to be loved and made love to. And the promise of filling her with life, a child they would share and raise together, was overwhelmingly erotic.

But he's a pig!

Was a pig. Look how different he was at the spring.

I thought he despised me.

Probably just scared, like you are, Cathy. The marriage is an arrangement for him too.

Aunt Hyldreth played matchmaker.

Yes.

But what if she got it wrong?

Time will tell. Tick tock, Cathy. Your biological clock is reaching midnight.

She huffed. Heath was her last chance for a child, she felt that truth deep within her bones. "Then I must marry him, whether he thinks I'm too old or not, or a slapper for shacking up with Dan for a decade!" After several more minutes of being unable to concentrate on reading the grimoire, she returned to her room, to call Lexi and ask her to be her maid of honour.

Back in her room, mobile in hand, she headed for the bed, and noticed a small jewellery box on her pillow and by its side a note.

She opened the box first, perturbed that someone had been in her room, but made a small gasp of amazement as it opened to a wide gold bracelet decorated with fantastical creatures entwined in an eternal hunt.

Cathy slipped it onto her wrist and held it to the light. It gleamed as it caught the golden particles that hung in the warm air, and she was captivated by the shimmering creatures.

She opened the letter, breaking the wax seal. Inside was a single slip of folded paper with a message written in an old-fashioned hand. She read it aloud as a whisper:

'Mistress Earnshaw, Cathy,

Please accept my gift as a seal of our betrothal.

Heath'

No kisses, no 'love Heath', no 'I love you to the moon and back', just accept the jewellery to seal the contract. She remembered the sensation of excitement she'd felt standing beside him at the spring as they'd made their wishes, her desire to stand even closer, the tenderness she'd seen in his eyes even if it had quickly been hidden.

"We can love each other, if we try." She said as she admired the bracelet, holding it to the light. "I accept, Heath," she whispered, remembering the silent wish she had made with intense desire; *Please let him love me.*

Tired after another emotion-filled day, Cathy undressed, and climbed into bed, falling asleep thinking of the bracelet and the note.

Several hours later, Cathy woke to a pitch-black room and the thud of something falling to the bedroom floor. Instantly awake, she sat up, eyes blind in the dark. Air was displaced close to her face as something wafted past and she yelped, pulling the bedcovers up to her chin as the hairs on the back of her neck stood on end.

Reaching for the mobile on the pillow at her side. The noise of buzzing close to her ear was followed by the zipper of her bag being undone. Someone, or something, was in her room. Another thud was followed by chittering.

Fairies! Argenon had said they were mischievous and Ellette had mentioned they were becoming troublesome. After listening to the noises, heart hammering against her breastbone, she turned the mobile's light on and shone it towards the dressing table.

Chittering squeals erupted and a bottle of perfume clinked against her moisturiser then rolled off the table and onto the floor. Several creatures swooped in the light then disappeared into the shadows. Swinging the light around the room showed an empty space and Cathy left the security of the heavy blankets and turned on the light. Her large holdall had been unzipped and several items of clothes pulled out, but it was the dressing table where the most damage had been done. Her makeup bag had been emptied and her eyeshadow palette and lipstick opened. The lipstick lay broken on the carpet, its tip blunted by the fall and the eye shadow had gouges in it, the palette surrounded by tiny shiny footprints in 'caramel noisette' and 'velvet cocoa'. "You naughty little things!" Cathy scolded to the now hidden creatures. "Those were expensive." She retrieved her clothes and replaced them in the holdall, fixing the lock in place, then began to replace the make up in the bag, leaving cleaning the shiny mess of powdered eyeshadow until morning. Picking the lipstick up from the floor she was relieved to see it had left only a tiny mark on the carpet. After clearing the dressing table of any lotions and makeup, she placed them in her suitcase, securing it with the lock, then scanned the room for the creatures.

"I know you're up there," she said, only a little uneasy at the thought of their presence within her room, "so leave my stuff alone. Okay?" Her question was met with silence. "I'm going to bed now, but if you touch my stuff again, I'll tell Argenon about you." Chittering from the corner of the room followed. Unsure whether the creature was agreeing or answering her back, she returned to bed deliberating whether to pull the curtains around the four-poster bed. She decided against it, preferring to see into the room.

Despite the disturbance, sleep took her down to its depths with ease. Her dreams were turbulent and in one she heard tapping at the window. Rising from bed, she made her way to the window and pulled back the curtains.

Hovering outside was a girl, her skin as pale as the moon.

"Fion," she said.

The girl raised her hand and tapped at the window. Tap! Tap! Tap!

From behind her there came the angry buzz of swooping fairies. She felt a tug on her hair, but the pain in her scalp barely registered and she took a step closer to the window.

Tap! Tap! Tap! Fion grinned to reveal bone-white teeth, sharpened to points, the canines overly long.

"Open the window, Cathy. Let me in." she sang. Her voice was soothing, an enticing melody.

Fairies sped around her, their wings beating furiously, the buzzing a high-pitched whine. They chittered angrily. Some screeching. Others tugging at the curtains, pulling them closed.

Long fingernails tapped at the glass. Fion rose, twisted her head to look behind her then disappeared.

Cathy staggered back, the spell broken, and the curtains dropped, concealing the window.

She woke with a shiver, standing beside the dressing table, confused. The dream had been intense, and the division between waking and sleeping blurred.

From the distance came the low mooing of a cow. It was followed by a plaintive howl. And then she heard a woman scream.

Pushing the curtains back, Cathy looked out across the garden, noticing the woman almost immediately. She was running towards the house, obviously in fear.

A flitting and dark form passed her window. Startled, Cathy caught her breath. The fairy chittered, dropping down in front of her face, baring its teeth. When she tried to take a step closer to get a better view outside, another fairy swooped down and both flew in front of her, making it impossible to see outside.

After pulling on a jacket to cover her nightdress, Cathy ran out of the room and downstairs, making her way to the kitchen. She planned on grabbing a knife before going outside.

As she reached the bottom of the stairs, Argenon stepped out of the shadows. Startled, she stopped with a jerk. "There's a woman in the garden! I saw her running across the lawn."

Argenon frowned although didn't seem surprised. "It's dark outside. Perhaps you are mistaken," he said.

"No! I saw her, and I heard her scream. And there was a wolf. I heard it howl."

"Foxes," he replied.

"But it howled"

He shook his head. "It's nothing to concern yourself about, Mistress. Just foxes."

"But the woman-"

"Just a lost motorist. I have given her directions."

"But you just said ... she was running. She seemed scared. And something tapped at my window!"

"You didn't open it, did you?" he asked with a flash of concern.

"No, the fairies wouldn't let me."

He tutted. "Dear me, things are becoming problematic."

"Argenon, what is going on?"

Chapter Twenty-Eight

Cathy made as though to push past Argenon, and he grabbed her arm. "It's late, Mistress."

She pulled her arm from his grip.

"We can talk about it in the morning."

"Talk about what in the morning?"

His countenance became grim. "There are some particular duties that I need to inform you about."

"But the woman ... there's something going on, and I want to know what it is. She wasn't a lost motorist. That's a lie!"

"Very well, but it is highly probable that she had lost her way, although where she became lost, I do not know."

"This makes no sense, Argenon. The woman needs our help."

He shook his head. "Nay, Mistress. She is beyond our help ... now."

"But ... the police-"

"No!" he barked. Cathy flinched at the anger in his voice. He sighed and managed an apologetic smile. "Forgive me. It is late and I am tired. Come," he said gesturing for her to follow, "let us go to the kitchen and have a cup of tea. I will explain everything to you then."

Cathy waited with trepidation as Argenon busied himself boiling water and placed tealeaves in the pot. She considered finding a sharp knife from one of the drawers and holding it as insurance against attack. There was something very wrong at the Hall, and she felt the threat of danger like an oppressively heavy blanket.

"There's something wrong, here, isn't there," she said as he poured tea into a mug and passed it to her.

"I wouldn't say 'wrong', but there is something that needs attending to. I'm afraid we have issues with some of our less appealing inhabitants."

"There are other 'inhabitants'? I thought it must be the fairies the Will alluded to."

He nodded. "Yes and no."

She remembered the chains stapled to the oak in the forest, and Edgar Linton's suggestion that Heath had a dark and dangerous past. "Does this inhabitant have anything to do with the disappearance of my cousin?"

Argenon nodded.

Sickness swirled in Cathy's belly. "Heath killed her!" Cathy gasped. "I knew it. Ed tried to warn me about him."

"What? No! Lord Heath had nothing to do with her disappearance."

"Then who?" Cathy pressed, scrutinizing his face, unsure if she could believe him.

"Your aunt … your aunt was a very kind woman, some would say it was a weakness."

"Go on."

"She … I really don't know quite how to say this without it sounding outlandish."

"Just spit it out," said Cathy with a touch of impatience.

"She was wont to take in waifs and strays—she had such a good heart-"

"Was Heath one of her 'waifs and strays'?"

"To an extent, yes, although it is a complex story."

"But he hasn't got anything to do with the woman running across the garden, or my cousin?"

Argenon shook his head. "As I told you, Mistress, Heath was not present at the time of her disappearance. In fact, he was not even in the country. And tonight ... he is away from the Hall."

"Then who *was* present?"

Argenon took a deep breath. "You have already seen who they are, in your aunts' grimoire."

Cathy scanned her memory. "But it was filled with charms and hexes and pictures of mythical creatures."

"Of other realms, not mythical," Argenon corrected.

"Are you trying to tell me that my aunt ran a B&B for trolls, pixies, and werewolves."

Argenon took a quick breath. "Not, trolls, no."

"Then what?"

"Vampires."

Stunned, Cathy stared at the man, waiting for a smile to break across his face, but he looked at her with deadly earnest. "You're serious," she said.

"I am."

"Which is why there was a whole section in the book about them," she said remembering the numerous drawings of vampires and charms and hexes to deal with them.

Argenon nodded.

A chill ran down Cathy's spine. "And they killed Fion?"

"I'm afraid it is far worse than that, Mistress. Fion became one of them."

"I don't believe it! It's just too ... too ridiculous. There's no such thing as vampires!" she said, unwilling to believe that Fion was not in the Ever After.

"I understand your revulsion and unwillingness to believe. It is an outlandish reality—when you first discover the truth."

Cathy took another sip of tea. Lifting the cup to her lips and swallowing the liquid, was reassuringly normal.

"I had a dream, or at least I thought it was a dream ... she was at my window. Tapping at my window, asking to be let in."

Argenon shuddered. "I take it that you did not let her in."

"No! I woke up. I thought I was sleepwalking. The fairies were going nuts, swooping, and diving in front of me."

"They have their uses, our little friends," Argenon said.

"So ... it *was* her at the window," Cathy said, the chill sinking into her bones.

"Yes, I'm afraid it was." He took a sip of his own tea. "Now ... how to continue?" he murmured. "There is no easy way to introduce this ... you are going to have to sort them out."

"What?"

"The woman ... the herd ... vampires tapping at the window ... it's all evidence that the colony is getting out of control."

The hairs on Cathy's scalp rose. "There's a colony?" she asked with a touch of horror. "Are you telling me that there is a ... colony of vampires around here?" Her eyes widened in disbelief, and her bowels grew watery.

"Yes," Argenon said and smiled as though relieved. "Yes, there is, and it is your job to keep it under control. So," he reached for a large leather bag sat on the kitchen counter, "you will need this." He landed the bag on the table with a thud then prized the top open. The leather creaked. From inside he drew out a mallet and a polished wooden stake sharpened to a point. He placed them in front of Cathy.

"What are these?" she asked despite knowing the answer.

"Your tools."

She picked up the stake. It was surprisingly heavy in her hand and evenly weighted, its surface smooth.

"It's a stake," he said, "for driving into their undead hearts."

He delved in the bag, bringing out a crescent of metal. "And this is to place across their throats until we can dispose of them, just a precaution, but your aunt always insisted on a 'belt and braces' approach—for security."

"I thought that they disintegrated once you drove the stake through the heart?"

"That's just in the films, and only the new ones where they have fancy special effects. No, vampires only shrivel to nothing when they are exposed to the midday sun, and it is a horrible death—very painful. This," he said, taking the stake from her hand, "is far more ... what is that modern word? Humane! That's it, humane. We expose them to the sun after their souls have been freed."

"This is crazy," Cathy said, still struggling to process the revelation. "And anyway, I don't think killing vampires is part of the agreement."

"Oh, yes, it is. It distinctly says it in her Will, 'care and control of the inhabitants'. Your Aunt Hyldreth often took matters into her own hands when the Hunter was busy. Just think of it as culling the herd as we used to do in the old days before winter or if a poor summer had produced too little to overwinter them. It's got to be done."

"Why didn't you tell me about them when you were explaining about the Will?"

"We didn't want to scare you off. Having an infestation of fairies to deal with is one thing, but vampires ..."

"Can't we just ask them to leave?"

He shook his head. "This outbreak needs nipping in the bud," he said, "before we have a plague on our hands! They have already started laying waste to the herd we keep for their sustenance. Once they finish with them, then I'm afraid they will seek food elsewhere. Their numbers need depleting and the troublemakers ousted."

"Can't someone else do it? What about Heath?"

Argenon shook his head. "I'm afraid not, Mistress Catherine. It's you or no one and I'm afraid that if we wait for the Hunter to become available, we shall be overrun. They're drawn to the house you see, and we live as uncomfortable neighbours. They are bound by rules, as are we all, but when their numbers begin to grow it is a sign that one of them has gone rogue and is actively recruiting to grow their numbers or has simply buckled under the stress of adhering to the rules."

"And what are the rules?"

"They don't eat humans."

"I see."

"You don't want a vampire plague on your hands, do you?"

She shook her head. "No! Of course not," she said with a shudder.

"It would be apocalyptic, you see. Imagine mice."

"Mice?"

"Yes. Mice. In Australia. Now, every few years, when the conditions are right, they breed like rabbits, or mice," he chuckled to himself. "Anyway, it results in a plague of mice. Millions of them devouring the farmers' stores and destroying their crops. The same happens with vampires. It is part of your duties, as Keeper of the Hall, to help keep them under control. It is pest control, Mistress Cathy, and your Aunt took it very seriously."

He held out the stake and mallet once more and this time she took them.

Life had taken an odd turning in the past few weeks, but this was bizarre. Marrying a stranger wasn't the craziest thing she could have imagined doing in her life, but become a vampire slayer? She didn't even realise they were real.

"Are you sure they're vampires?"

"Oh, yes." He delved into the bag and pulled out an old newspaper, unfolding its yellowed leaves for her to see. "Here," he said, stabbing at the page, "a local story. Granted it is from a few years ago but illustrates the point. "Seven cows found drained of blood. That's from when we last had an outbreak. Your aunt was on the job immediately; stamped it out right away." He nodded in the direction of the mallet and stake. "We learned the hard way that our guests quickly turn to the human population once they've drained the animal supply. And back in 1942 that is exactly what happened. They descended like a pack of rats on a convoy of soldiers heading out to the front and killed the lot of them. We had to step in quickly and cover that one up—it took quite some effort on your aunt's behalf, and her magic was never quite the same after that. Drained her you see, making the local populace, and then the entire country, believe that they had been bombed by the enemy, and then there were those that had turned. We had to hunt them down too."

"So the herd on the top hill, the one that Heath is upset about-"

"Drained!" Argenon said dramatically. "Drained of blood and life. They live on the blood from the herd. Did you know that there are tribes of humans that do that too?"

She shook her head.

"In Africa, there's a tribe of cattle herders that live off their blood as they move the herd finding food and water."

"Are the vampires African?" she asked, confused.

"No dear," he gave her a quizzical frown. "I'm just trying to make the comparison. Vampires prefer human blood, but they can subsist on that of cows. It is a term of our agreement that they only feed on cows. We offer them sanctuary and maintain a herd for them to feed on, but they must adhere to the terms of the agreement."

"And they've broken it?"

Argenon nodded. "The cows being drained is one indication that their numbers are growing beyond what can be sustained, and the woman in the garden," he shook his head, "most unfortunate, is another. Which is why you must do what you must do."

"But I've never done it before."

"Of course you haven't!" he said with a laugh. "But it really isn't that difficult and don't think for a second that it is gruesome. One tap with the mallet and poof they are gone."

"They disappear?"

"No, but they are no longer in this realm!"

"They go to the Ever After."

"Or thereabouts. So, you see, it really isn't that bad."

"Well, I guess if it's not ... messy, then I could give it a go."

"Oh, you must do more than give it a go, dear. You must succeed."

"No pressure then!"

He threw her another quizzical frown then rose whilst checking his watch. "It's late and we both need our sleep. Your aunt always took on this particular challenge during the morning, so we shall set to work after daybreak. Agreed?"

"Agreed," she said, although her head swam as it tried to process the information.

How had she gone from inheriting a house and signing up for an arranged marriage to becoming a vampire slayer?

"As soon as there's a single whiff of them growing in number, we have to act," he said to reinforce his point.

"Yes, I see. So, where are they, these vampires?" she asked, imagining a desecrated stone church complete with belfry set somewhere on the estate.

"That's the spirit! They live in the cellar."

She glanced at the floor. "Here?"

"No, no, dear. Don't fret. They're not in this part of the house, and they can't enter unless you invite them in. They're in the west wing."

Chapter Twenty-Nine

Sleep eluded Cathy and she faced the rising sun with trepidation. Today Argenon was going to school her in the art of vampire slaying, with a practical test at the end of the session!

Noise from outside caught her attention and she rose from bed and walked to the window. Outside, the day was already bright, and the golden haze hung as a low mist across the gardens. Several of Ellette's children ran from the pathway that led to the forest and made their way to the house and in the distance a horse and rider galloped up the track to the higher fields.

She watched the rider's progress for several moments before realising it was Heath. He was making his way to the upper fields where the cow herd - the vampire's larder - was kept. The field was bounded by hedgerow on two sides and the forest on the others. She could make out several dark shapes in the grass but only two cows were standing. She remembered Argenon's warning with a shiver, 'They have already started laying waste to the herd we keep for their sustenance. Once they finish with them, then I'm afraid they will seek food elsewhere'. She realised exactly what he meant by them seeking food elsewhere—they would turn to the closest village and then spread out to the towns. The woman Cathy had seen being chased across the garden last night had been an unwilling victim, a lucky find for the vampires, who would now be resting in the cellar until this evening when she too would begin to hunt and increase their numbers. That their numbers could increase exponentially and take on plague-like proportions within the coming weeks was something Argenon had insisted was no fear-mongering fantasy. It could really happen, and the Hall would become inundated whilst the surrounding area was decimated of living souls.

The rider dismounted and climbed the gate, making his way to the dark objects in the grass. That they were cows drained of blood Cathy felt sure.

"Only two left," she said.

The sight of Heath inspecting the ailing, perhaps dead, cows, spurred her to action and she washed and dressed in practical clothes she hoped would be suitable for the job – she shied away from thinking of it as slaying – and made her way downstairs. Determined to face her responsibilities without fear, she experienced the surge of adrenaline as a thrill of excitement.

Ignoring protocol, she made her way to the kitchen where Ellette was serving bowls of porridge to five of her eleven children.

"Good morning, Mistress!" Ellette said with surprise as Cathy strode into the kitchen. "I'm sorry, but I haven't laid the table in the breakfast room yet."

"It won't be necessary this morning, Ellette," she replied with a smile. "I shall have some of your delicious porridge and eat it here."

"With the children?"

"Yes," she replied. "With the children. It's a little lonely eating on my own," she admitted.

Five pairs of eyes watched her as she pulled up a chair and sat down. Ellette filled a bowl with creamy porridge and set it before her.

"Thanks," she replied before taking a spoonful from the steaming bowl.

"Argenon mentioned that you would need a full belly this morning," she said hovering beside her with the pan. "You'll be working in the cellar?"

The mention of the cellar made Cathy's stomach somersault with a watery flip. "Later in the morning," she replied.

"And will he teach you how to strike them through the heart?" one of the children asked. Each child at the table waited with wide-eyed expectation.

"Do they bleed?" asked another.

"Fader says that you must pull them out into the sunshine. He said to hope for a sunny day." All five children glanced to the window.

"'Tis a sunny day." The smallest of the flaxen-haired girls said and threw a pitying smile at Cathy.

"Now, now, children," Ellette chided. "Don't be putting Mistress Catherine off. Her work is sorely needed. We're headed for difficult times if she fails."

"Oh, I'm sure she will be the best slayer we have had."

"She can't be better than Mistress Hyldreth," one of the boys said.

"Nay, not better, but the best anyhow."

As they continued to chatter among themselves, Argenon arrived in the kitchen.

Dressed in dark trousers and a leather tunic, shirtsleeves rolled up, and with his profusion of white hair hidden beneath a flat cap, he looked ready for work. He carried the leather bag in one hand and a second leather tunic in the other.

"Good morning, Mistress," he said with a broad smile. "It is good to see you looking so well this morning."

"She's excited about the slaying," one of the children said.

"Elspeth!" chided Ellette. "I'm sure she's not excited about it."

"She is," the child insisted. "I can tell from her aura. It sparkles and shines."

Ellette shook her head with a warning glance at the child. "Forgive her, Mistress. She thinks she is better than she is."

Cathy laughed, intrigued that the child could see auras. "I think she may be right. I spent the entire night awake worrying about this morning, but when I looked out over the field and saw Master Heath making his way to a field full of dead cows, I realised the gravity of my responsibility and I no longer felt fear."

"See!" the child threw back at her mother.

"Elspeth, you were correct, but you mustn't cheek your mother," scolded Argenon.

The child dropped her eyes. "Sorry, Modor," she said.

"That's right," said Argenon. "Now! Let us to it, Mistress. I have already removed the covers to the cellar windows to allow light to flood the space."

"Can we watch?" asked the smallest boy.

"Tsk!" chided Ellette.

"Can we?"

"Nay, young Tatwin. This is not a job for young eyes."

The boy rolled his eyes and returned to his porridge.

"Here," Argenon said, handing the leather vest to Cathy. "Put this on."

The leather vest was shaped like a waistcoat but was fastened with metal hooks rather than buttons and its front was reinforced with several layers of leather and the collar rose to cover her neck, ending just beneath her jaw. She stroked it with a thrill of fear, realising it was there as a protective measure.

"It is just a precaution. As are these." He handed her a length of braided leather thongs intertwined with long leaves, stems, and tiny white flowers. It stank of garlic.

"Here, Mistress, let me put it on for you."

Ellette took the braided leather and placed it around Cathy's neck. The odour of garlic grew overwhelming. "It's strong!" she said wafting her hand.

"Just a precaution. Nothing to worry about."

"You keep saying that," Cathy replied, "but I'm not sure I believe you."

With her vest and garlic necklace fitted, Argenon led the way through the house to the west wing.

Chapter Thirty

"I thought that we were going to practice ... before we went in," said Cathy as they stood outside the door.

"The best practice is doing," replied Argenon.

"But ... you've got to tell me what to do!" she exclaimed.

"Well, it's simple," he replied as he placed the large iron key in the door's lock. "You just get the stake and hammer it in."

"This is too much!" she said.

"You keep saying that, Mistress, but yet here you are. You are far more courageous than you give yourself credit for. So far you have been introduced to a talking bird, agreed to an arranged marriage, taken upon the responsibility of running an extensive house and managing its staff, and learning new languages so that you can become the powerful witch your Aunt Hyldreth knows you to be."

"Yes, but vampire slaying!"

"Is just another responsibility for you to assume. It is not unlike the butchering you will supervise once the pigs and sheep have been slaughtered. I would have thought that was much more distasteful."

"Well ... it's a new skill I guess, but the animals are dead."

"As are the vampires or rather they are the undead. The only difference is that you're not going to butcher them and then prepare them for market."

Cathy grimaced. "That is a revolting thought."

"Indeed, Mistress." He managed a smile. "Shall we?" he asked and twisted the key in the lock.

The room looked just as it did in Cathy's memory, an elegant space with a crystal chandelier glinting in the sun, and golden particles shimmering in the warmth from the large sash windows. On the opposite side of the room a huge mirror in an ornate goldleaf frame hung above a black marble fireplace. Either side of the fire were matching armoires in black lacquer painted with oriental birds. A wide velvet sofa in dark green velvet sat before the fireplace. There was no sign of dilapidation or surfaces left to become dusty.

"They use this room," she said looking round. "It's where they live."

Argenon gave the room a cursory look. "It is. I believe they use the rooms each night, after fulfilling their dietary requirements."

"We came here when I was a teenager. It wasn't dusty. I should have realised it was being used, but I didn't."

"Ah," Argenon murmured as though unsure how to respond, then said, "Before we go down into the cellar, there are several things I need to tell you."

"Thank goodness!" Cathy said with a sigh of relief.

"Now, the first is that our normally resident vampires, the ones that are permitted to live here, will be in the caskets. You do not need to concern yourself about them. The vampires we must exterminate this morning are the ones you will find ... unboxed." He chuckled, his shoulders heaving.

"If they're 'unboxed' then where will they be?"

"In the shadows. The darkest corners."

"And is there light down there?"

"Only that which comes from the sun through the windows. But do not worry. Vampires are dead to the world during daylight hours. They are as vulnerable as new born babes—utterly defenceless and harmless to us."

"Are you sure?"

"Absolutely. It is only after twilight darkens to night that they are able to rise."

Cathy shuddered. "So they ... come out and use the rooms?" she said gesturing to the comfortable sitting room.

"They do. Obviously, I have never joined them for an evening, so I do not know anything about their culture, but generally the colony remains within the west wing, only venturing out to play in the forest and feed from the herd."

"But you said that they've expanded in number which means that one of the residents has broken the rules. How do we stop them breaking the rules again once we've ... dealt with the new members?"

Argenon looked deep in thought. "That is a good point, Mistress ... I don't have an answer at this point."

"Should we destroy the colony? To make sure it doesn't happen again?"

"Oh! No. That would never do. There is an agreement in place. We can't renege on it."

"Can I see that contract, once we've finished here?"

"Certainly."

"Good," Cathy replied, curious to see what exactly had been agreed to between the vampires and her aunt and if there was any way out of it.

"Are we ready, then?" asked Argenon and motioned to the door under the stairs.

Cathy took a deep and calming breath. "As I'll ever be."

Argenon descended the steps first and Cathy was relieved to find the cellar lit by sunlight from two large openings.

She stalled on the final step, taking in the depth and breadth of the room. Held up by six brick pillars the ceiling was low, but high enough for Cathy and Argenon to stand to full height. Between the pillars were several caskets, each one made of thick oak planks.

"Mistress Earnshaw had these made after the contract was agreed."

Cathy approached the closest casket. With its large iron hinges and curling ironwork braces, the top resembled a door. Curious, she placed a hand on the lid. A wave of cold energy fizzed at her fingertips. Argenon walked deeper into the cellar as she began to lift the lid. Heart beating hard, she inched it open, ready to drop it in an instant if there was any sign of movement or noise.

Unsure what to expect - hideous monster or preserved, ethereal beauty - she lifted the lid to expose the vampire within.

Laid in a state of peaceful sleep, lay a bearded, middle-aged man. Surprisingly large and well-built he was nothing like the slender vampires that she had been fascinated by as a teenager. This man could be a builder or a logger. She eased the lid down and allowed it to close with a soft thud.

Argenon stepped to her side, making her gasp and grab his arm.

"Sorry, Mistress," he whispered. "I didn't mean to startle you."

"It's okay," she said, tapping at her chest. She motioned to the box. "He looks so normal. Nothing like I imagined."

Argenon chuckled. "It is unexpected," he agreed. "Although the paleness of their skin and the redness of their eyes does give me a creeping sensation when I encounter it."

"I thought he'd be ... more Dracula-like, I guess."

Another chuckle. "There is a count among them somewhere." He scanned the boxes, "but I suggest we find the illegals and dispatch them forthwith.

"How many are there?"

"I've seen two so far. Both women, which leads me to believe that the culprit is one of the men," he said gesturing to the box, "and Boris here, is a well-known philanderer, at least he was when he was alive. It wouldn't surprise me if it wasn't him that turned them."

She glanced back at the box. "How can we find out who did it?"

"Catch them at it?" he said with a shrug of his shoulders. "Although once we've dealt with the new additions, I think whoever did it will realise we're on to them and desist for some considerable time."

Cathy wasn't convinced but decided to follow Argenon's instructions and seek the illegals.

"This way," Argenon said and beckoned her to follow.

He walked to the deepest recess of the cellar where the light barely pushed at the shadows. From his pocket, he pulled a light, a jar filled with the magical water. It gave off a warm and sparkling light, illuminating the bodies laid within the shadow.

"Do you have a light?"

Cathy shook her head.

"A witch light perhaps?"

Cathy frowned. "A witch light?"

Argenon tutted. "There is so much for you to learn. Nevermind, you have many days ahead in which to study. Now," he said turning his attention to the prone women, "we will dispatch these ladies first."

Both women were young, neither could be more than twenty years old, both dressed in short skirts, their blouses unbuttoned to show the tops of their breasts. "They look like two women who had been out for a drink," she said. "Do you think they're locals?"

Argenon shook his head. "I doubt it. At least not the local village pub. I would hazard a guess at the nearest town. The pickings are easier there—more nightlife."

Just as Argenon had promised, the women made no sign that they were aware of their presence. There was also no sign of life, no breath being inhaled and exhaled, no movement of eyes beneath eyelids as they dreamed. "Are you sure they're not just dead?" Cathy asked as she focused on the women, double-checking for any signs of life and wishing she had a mirror to check for breath.

Argenon took hold of the chin of the woman with shorter hair to reveal her neck. It showed two puncture wounds where incisors had bitten down. "If they were dead, they would be showing signs of rot." These women arrived several days ago." Tatwin witnessed it. They have a homing instinct you see. They home in on their sire, returning to his lair."

"So he could bite them miles away and they would find their way here?"

"Yes, that is correct." He opened the bag and removed a single spike and passed it to Cathy. "Place it over the heart and then use this," he said passing her the mallet. "I'll wait whilst you dispatch the first, then scour the cellar for any others."

Horrified, but driven by the need to protect Witherwood Hall and its inhabitants, Cathy held the sharpened stake above the heart of the woman with the shorter hair.

"That's right. Now, let it rest against the flesh," Argenon instructed.

Obediently, Cathy held the spike vertically then pushed it against the woman's chest. She made no sign of being aware. Cathy took the mallet.

"Now, just whack it down, as hard as you can. This is no time for feminine niceties. Hit it hard and fast!"

Cathy held the mallet high.

"Now!" Argenon demanded.

Cathy brought the mallet down upon the metal head of the spike. As it plunged down into the woman's chest, she opened her eyes, stared into the void beyond Cathy, and hissed, revealing needle-sharp and inch-long fangs.

Cathy squealed and dropped the mallet. Red eyes blazing, the woman swivelled her head to Cathy. In the next moment, Argenon grabbed the mallet, grasped the spike, and hammered it with force. The woman lay rigid, blood-red eyes staring at the ceiling, mouth agape.

Cathy shuffled back. "I thought you said it was easy, one tap and 'pouf!' they were gone."

"Well, if you hadn't lost your nerve, it would have been one tap, but for your first time you did well." He reached for another spike and handed it to Cathy along with the mallet. "Now do this one and I shall look for any others." Cathy took the tools without comment, still in shock at the vampire's reaction.

"But I can't," she complained.

"Oh, you can, Mistress, and you must," Argenon replied then disappeared into the shadows.

"You can and you must," Cathy repeated, then moved across to the other woman.

"Practice makes perfect, Mistress," he called from the other side of the room.

There had been five squatters in the cellar, all young women. Cathy had driven a spike through each of their hearts, saying a prayer of passing for each as she hammered. All the women had reacted as the first, blood-red eyes staring, fangs gnashing, but dispatching them had become easier. It helped that the kills were clean. No blood seeped from their wounds.

"It's clotted you see," Argenon said as he hammered a sickle across a brunette's neck, "what little there is that's left.

As far as I can tell, the sire drains them of blood and because they are dead, it is not replaced."

"Makes sense," Cathy replied standing back to consider her work.

Five bodies were laid in a row on the lawn, each with a sickle placed over their necks, and a stone pushed into their mouths.

"When do they disintegrate then?" Cathy asked.

"When we get a break in the clouds," Argenon replied with a glance to the sky. "See, there's a patch of blue."

"And what if we don't get a break in the clouds? What if the sun stays hidden?"

Argenon took a deep breath. "Then we bury them, until we can be sure of a sunny day."

"This job is not getting any easier," Cathy sighed.

She crouched beside the body of the brunette. "This was someone's daughter," she said with a note of sadness.

Argenon stepped to her side. "Yes," he agreed.

"She was so young, and pretty. She had her whole life ahead of her," she continued. "Argenon," she said, "we must make sure this never happens again."

"Agreed, Mistress."

As she spoke, the clouds blew past the sun, brightening the lawn and falling upon the tethered bodies. Smoke began to rise as a mist. The woman's hand shivered, seeming to move, and Cathy took several steps back. Minutes passed as the smoke thickened and the bodies beneath began to sag and collapse into themselves then disintegrate until there was nothing left but piles of ash.

"Is that it?" Cathy asked as the smoke dissipated.

"That's it, Mistress," Argenon replied. "And you did brilliantly."

"Thank you, Argenon. It was easier *and* more horrifying than I imagined it would be."

"Yes, but you are saving lives. The situation was getting out of control."

Cathy nodded. "But I won't rest until we discover which of the inhabitants has broken the agreement. This can't be allowed to happen again."

"Perhaps, Master Heath could help?" he suggested with a glance to the man striding across the lawn.

Chapter Thirty-One

The woman standing before Heath seemed transformed. Gone was the brash front that hid her self-doubt and the uncertainty in her gaze. Instead, she seemed invigorated, the magic in her eyes finally sparkling as she made eye contact.

"Killing vampires suits you, Cathy," Heath said before bending down to retrieve a curved blade from the pile of ashes. It was cold to the touch, the vampires disintegrating without the need for intense and burning heat.

Her eyes widened. "Oh, well, I wouldn't say that!"

"You didn't enjoy it?"

"No!"

"She quickly became proficient at the task, Master," Argenon said with a smile towards Cathy. "She is a worthy successor to Mistress Hyldreth."

"And how many did you find in the cellar?" he asked scanning the piles.

"Five," Cathy replied.

"Five? Then you have caught the situation just as it was about to tip into disaster. Five new vampires without the harness of self-restraint would have resulted in carnage."

"Indeed, Master. A veritable plague!"

"That's what I wanted to talk to you about," Cathy said. "We can't let it happen again."

"I agree."

"So ... I was hoping that you could help me discover which one of the vampires is breaking the agreement. I've taken a look at the contract. Breaking its terms gives us the right to termination."

"Termination of the contract?" Heath asked.

Cathy shook her head. "Termination of the agreement breaker."

"I don't think that is something I can help with," he said, fingering the blade, "much as I'd enjoy that."

"Lord, I suggest that we listen to Mistress Catherine. We won't be able to rest until the situation is under control and that cannot be gained until the rogue vampire is dealt with."

"Again, I agree, but Catherine is the only one permitted to terminate the vampires. What use am I?"

"You can track them," Cathy stated. "When they leave the Hall to feed, track the ones that stray from the estate. Those are likely the culprits."

Heath cast Argenon a quick glance. Tracking them would mean leaving the estate as the beast.

"It could be done, Lord," Argenon said with encouragement. "I have discussed it with Mistress Catherine and suggested that she cast a charm of protection about you."

"And I thought of a cloak to hide you," Cathy added.

"How will a cloak hide me?" he asked whilst throwing Argenon a challenging frown; the man knew that leaving the estate after twilight risked discovery and a cascade of destructive events.

"It could make you invisible ... if I find the right charm in my aunt's grimoires."

"You don't have your own?"

She shook her head. "My mother passed on very little of the craft to me. Aunt Hyldreth's grimoires are ... will help me begin to learn."

"An invisibility cloak," he mused. "It sounds outlandish, fantastical."

"But it could work and if it does it would protect you from being discovered by the vampires."

Being discovered by the vampires is not what I'm afraid of, Heath thought. Controlling the Beast's primal urges as he followed their scent into the towns would be his greatest trial. But what was the alternative? Daily slaying sessions for Cathy? No! That would be too cruel. "Very well," he replied. "If you can promise me safe passage, then I shall do it. I shall follow the shadow walker."

A large smile broke across Cathy's face. "Thank you!" she said.

"I am happy to help," he replied noticing the nod of approval from Argenon.

"But there's one more thing," she said.

"Oh?"

"Yes, the books ... they're written in runes, and Old English-"

"Old Norse," Heath corrected. "With the later booklets being English of the Middle Ages. At least, that's what your aunt told me."

"Oh! Well ... whichever language they're written in, I don't understand it so-"

"You can't read the spells?" he asked unable to keep the tone of surprise from his voice.

"Or the hexes, Lord," Argenon added. "Or the instructions, or the charms, or the wisdom. In fact, very little is accessible to Mistress Catherine due to her lack of schooling, so we were hoping that you would assist?"

"Me?"

Argenon nodded, a broad smile breaking across his face. "Yes, Lord. If you could help Mistress Catherine search through the books for the magical texts and translate them …"

"Then we can catch the vampire!" Cathy said.

"And then we will know which of the creatures to slay," Argenon added with relish.

"Calling it slaying sounds so harsh!" Cathy complained.

"What do you want to call spiking the creature through the heart then leaving it in the sun to disintegrate?" Heath asked.

Cathy wrinkled her nose in a girlish fashion. "Erm … dispatch?"

"That sounds as though you are reporting the news and is weak," said Heath. "Execute?" he suggested.

After several moments Cathy agreed. "Execute," she repeated. "It does sound more professional."

Argenon huffed. "I much prefer slay," he grumbled.

Heath laughed. "You always were bloodthirsty," he said, wishing he hadn't spoken as Cathy swivelled to Argenon in surprise.

"He's joking."

"I am," Heath lied. Cathy knew nothing of their past, and that was a situation that couldn't change, at least not until the child had been born. At that point, he would be honest, if questions were asked.

"Will they retaliate?" Cathy asked. "If we execute the vampire? I mean if he's one of the original vampires ... will we annoy them?"

"There's no honour among them, but if they believe themselves to be in danger from us ... then I suppose that could be the case."

"Then what do we do to stop that?" Cathy asked with a note of fear in her voice. "Can they get into the house?"

Argenon shook his head. "The problem is not if they can come into the house, it is being terrorized by them. None of the household will feel safe. We cannot let that happen."

"What did Aunt Hyldreth do after the last outbreak? How did she prevent it?"

Argenon tapped a finger to his lip. "I think the answer may lie in the tool bag, Mistress."

Cathy turned to the leather bag beside the sofa.

"Check the pockets inside."

Cathy delved within the bag, searching each of the internal pockets and pulled out a sheet of paper. "It's a notice of sentence," she said reading the top line. She scanned the text. "It details the crimes committed and the sentence passed.

"Excellent!" exclaimed Argenon, "I suggest that we write one ourselves and pin it on the cellar door, on the inner door, of course."

With the document as a template, Cathy began to make a new copy.

"Make sure to write that they have been terminated as per the contract and have been dispatched by the slayer to the Ever After, or thereabouts."

"Why 'or thereabouts'?" Cathy asked.

"Because we don't know if he will go to the Ever After."

"Unlikely," replied Heath.

"Yes, I agree. If there is any justice, then he will be dragged down to the belly of Hel."

"But is that fair?"

"Fair?"

"Yes, if he was bitten and turned into a vampire, then he has little control over his desires. Does he even have free will anymore?"

"What's your point?"

"Well, if he is driven by his undead desires, then is he really responsible?"

Heath sighed. "I believe ... I suppose that when we dispatch the vampire it will release his soul from damnation and allow it to travel to the Ever After."

Cathy gave a relieved sigh. "Yes! That sounds ... just. It's not fair to punish the innocent for crimes they would never have committed if they hadn't been turned into vampires."

Heath grew thoughtful. Cathy's words soothed him, oiling the chaffing in his soul. The heinous acts he had committed since being cursed to live and behave as the Beast could be forgiven. *Yes, but not the ones you committed before.* He gave a heavy sigh and turned to the window. The last rays of sun spread their warmth across the garden, but twilight and the forest beckoned and the chaffing in his soul grew sore.

"There!" Cathy declared and held up the paper. "It's finished. I just hope they accept the judgement. They will, won't they?" she asked with a note of uncertainty.

"They realise how vulnerable they are—during the day. It is why they agreed to the contract in the first place. Hyldreth gave them shelter as long as they promised to do no harm. If they revolt, then punishment will be swift. Yes, put that at the end."

"But I've already signed it," Cathy complained.

"Add a nota bene beneath your signature," Argenon urged. "Say ... now, write this down," he motioned to the desk. Cathy lay the paper flat and picked up the pen. "Write it thus, 'Should any member of the compact disagree with the judgement, heretofore mentioned, and take action against the accusers and/or executioner, punishment will be swift and bloody!"

"See," laughed Heath. "I told you he was bloodthirsty."

Chapter Thirty-Two

It was quickly determined that their time was best spent scouring the grimoires for suitable spells to give Heath protection against the vampires when he followed them that evening. Unknown to Cathy, a spell of protection was redundant, but a shield of invisibility would mean that he could walk the streets without being seen—essential if he was to be successful. Not only would it hide Heath from the vampires, but the townsfolk too. The hideous beast he became after twilight would be a terrifying sight and instantly agitate the population into panic. Over the centuries there had been numerous occasions when he had been spotted in his cursed form, there was even a local legend that they used to promote tourism to the area, but it was largely ignored. A sighting, particularly with photographic evidence, would only encourage it and make life at Witherwood difficult once more.

Heath turned another page of the largest grimoire over, scanning the text, disappointed to find yet more recipes for the treatment of warts, rashes, and pustules. After another half an hour of reading, he was about to take a break, when he found a spell labelled, 'A charm to bewitch a cloak and hide the wearer'. He read it in old Norse and then translated it for Cathy.

"It sounds perfect!" she said with a note of relief and leaned over his shoulder to look.

When she placed a hand on his shoulder and her body brushed against his back, he experienced her touch like a shot of electricity. The primal urges he wrestled with, the need to take her and make her his, began to surge. The full moon was close, and as it approached, the beast within grew dominant. He clenched his jaws, swallowing down the desire to turn and take her in his arms, feel her gentle curves beneath his hands, and allow his fingers to knead her flesh, his lips to explore her warm and dark places. An image of her beneath him in their marital bed flashed in his mind and he stood abruptly and took a step away from the table, the desire to take her overwhelming.

"Oh!"

"I need to stretch my legs," he said, unable to think of a valid excuse as to why he had almost jumped from beneath her touch. He walked to the fireplace as though to prove his point. "If you have a pen, I shall read the charm to you, and you can write it down."

"Good idea," she said looking a little perplexed. She held up a pen and a notebook. "Ready when you are," she said.

"Good," he replied.

He remained by the fireplace, mesmerised, his thoughts anchoring him to Cathy, the image of her naked in his bed keeping him prisoner.

"Shall I bring the book to you?" she asked when he made no effort to move.

"The book?"

"My aunt's grimoire - the spell - for the cloak?"

"Yes! Of course," he managed then strode across to the table and lifted the book before standing at a safe distance from the woman. He gave her a secret glance as she readied herself to begin writing down the spell. Had the witch cast a spell on him? He felt the call to bed her from every organ of his body. To feel her soft flesh against his, the warmth of her legs as they wrapped around his-

"Are you ready?" she asked, breaking into his thoughts.

I am ready for you, the beast growled. Their eyes locked as he struggled to hold himself still, the urge to throw down the book, and take her in this very room intense. "Yes," he managed. "I shall begin. But I need more light," he lied and walked to the window. "That's better," he said with relief at the distance between them. He reread the charm then began to translate. Cathy wrote as he spoke, asking him several times to speak a little slower. When the charm was complete, he scoured the remaining text on the page for any other relevant information and translated that too. "That is all," he said and closed the book. "If you will excuse me, I have business to attend to on the farm. I will ask Argenon to assist you for the remainder of the afternoon."

"Yes, sure," she said with an amused smile.

He left the room without further comment and breathed an enormous sigh of relief as the door closed behind him, separating him from Cathy. Frustrated desire rode through him, a turbulent river that wouldn't be quelled, and he took the steps to his apartment at a run where he paced the rooms with dissatisfaction. "Bewitched!" he said as he poured himself a glassful of whiskey. "The woman has bewitched me."

Mercurio flapped his wings and cawed.

Startled, Heath swivelled to the bird, spilling amber liquid on the floor. "Bird! What do you think you are doing?"

Mercurio scoffed. "Me, Lord?" he said. "Why nothing, but I can see that you are in a flap."

"A flap! You make my torture seem trivial. I find you insulting."

Mercurio laughed. "Mistress Catherine has you in a tizzy, then."

"The full moon approaches, nothing more."

"As you like," the bird said with a sigh and turned back to looking out of the window. "Twilight fast approaches, Lord. And another day will dawn where I am trapped in this form. When are you marrying the witch? The wait is beyond endurance!"

"Patience, old friend," said Heath with empathy. That his friend suffered alongside him ate at his conscience. "The marriage will take place soon."

"I fear ... I fear it will never happen."

Heath sighed. "I will do everything in my power to make it so."

"And ... then the child."

Heath took a mouthful of whiskey, enjoying the fiery liquid as it ran down his throat. The beast soothed, he laughed. "And I shall enjoy every moment of making that child."

Mercurio huffed. "When I am set free, I shall find a wife for myself. A solitary life is no good for any man."

"Indeed, it is not, Mercurio. You have suffered, I recognise that, but we are so close to breaking the curse ... just a little longer ..."

Heath poured another glass of whiskey, the alcohol helping to numb his senses, dulling the intensity of the beast's need to take control. This evening would be a trial and he would have to use every ounce of his energy to keep the primal urges of the beast to hunt and kill at bay as he followed the vampire into town, or wherever it travelled to hunt. Moving from window to window, he scanned the garden, trees, and fields. The Hall's lands stretched to the horizon, and he was thankful for the acres of forest where he could relax and allow the beast's energies to be sapped when he was no longer able to keep them under control.

A knock at the door announced Argenon's arrival. In his arm he carried a bundle of cloth.

"Your cloak, Lord," he said and presented the cloak to Heath.

"It worked?" he asked in surprise.

"That we do not know. Mistress Catherine cast the spell exactly as was written. She claims to have felt the energy of the spell, but the cloak did not disappear."

Heath huffed. "Then what shall I do?"

"Try it on!" cawed Mercurio.

"And what difference will that make?" Heath asked with irritation. "If the spell has failed ..."

"It might work, but you will never know if you do not try!" said Mercurio with exasperation.

Argenon nodded his agreement and held out the cloak.

"Very well." Heath took the cloak and swung the fabric behind him, hugging it to his shoulders, and covering his head with the hood.

Mercurio cawed. Argenon sighed.

"What a waste of effort!" Heath snapped. "We have failed."

"Nay, Lord. It works. See for yourself in the mirror."

Heath turned to the mirror. Where the cloth covered his body and face only the room was reflected. Part of his nose and one eye were visible. "Hah!" he said, pulling the cloth closer to his face. A finger appeared where it grabbed the cloth. "Hah!" he repeated then laughed. "Amazing! I am no more. Look, Mercurio," he said pulling down the hood. "Now you see me," he pulled the hood back up, "and now you don't!"

Mercurio cawed. "Very good, Lord," he said with a resigned and sarcastic tone.

"Quite incredible," said Argenon throwing a frown at the bird. "Mistress Cathy's magic is powerful. Hyldreth would have been proud."

"Indeed, Argenon." Heath swung the cape, watching his barely seen reflection in the mirror, noticing the parts of his body that appeared when the cloth fell away. "And how long will it last?"

"Of that, we have no idea. I read the spell myself, and the notes surrounding it, and there was no mention of how long it will be effective."

Heath narrowed his eyes. "So, if you read it, why did I have to endure an afternoon of scouring through those books?"

"I thought that you might enjoy the company, Lord," Argenon replied with a barely suppressed smile.

With a huff, Heath shrugged off the cloak and let it drop to the chair. "Twilight approaches. I shall eat and then make my way to the vampire's quarters. Keep Mistress Catherine entertained. I do not want there to be any chance of being discovered. The curse will be broken soon, I can feel it. Nothing can get in the way of our marriage. Do you understand?"

"Yes, Lord. I will ensure that Mistress Catherine is kept busy this evening."

After a meal of cold meats and bread eaten in his room, Heath once again put on the cloak, disappearing before the mirror, satisfied as the dark hairs and huge canines disappeared within its hood.

Chapter Thirty-Three

Twilight had fallen away to night when the first of the vampires emerged from their lair. There were seven caskets in the cellar, and seven vampires emerged, confirming that Cathy had 'executed' all of the newly turned creatures. Each creature, hidden by the night, floated as a shadow. Six headed towards the field where the herd was kept. They moved slowly, shadowy spectres hanging in the air, almost invisible against the sky. As the rogue vampire floated in the opposite direction, Heath, invisible within the cloak, turned to follow.

The creature's scent was intense, and when its form was lost among the trees, Heath followed it with ease, sniffing out the sticky particles as they rode the breeze. The moon had risen to its highest point when they arrived at the town. Pulling his cloak tight against his body, he crossed roads hidden from the townsfolk as they walked their dogs or strolled from pub to pub.

The creature made its way to the centre of town. The scent of cooking wafted in the air, rich with the aroma wafting from the shops where food was being prepared. Groups of children hung about the streets, laughing, calling, and shouting to one another. A small group threw a ball across the road, stepping back as a car passed by. The vampire hovered, watching the groups, its form still hidden in a haze of dark mist. Like Heath's cloak, the mist hid the creature from the people.

It moved to hover above a group of girls sitting on a bench, each with a mobile in hand, they pouted as they held the device in front of their faces. When one of the teenagers left the group and waved goodbye, the creature followed.

Heath sprinted across the road, vaulting over a passing car, his claws landing on the boot with a metal-scraping thud.

As the teenager crossed the road, the creature followed, lowering to the pavement and revealing itself to walk behind, increasing its speed until it was by the girls' side.

Heath stalled. The creature was female, and apart from its blood-red eyes and pallid skin, could have been the teenage victim's classmate. He watched as it lured her to the darkest shadows and took its first bite then followed as it dragged the girl to an area of scrubland to feast.

Chapter Thirty-Four

The following morning, after bathing and ridding himself of the Beast's stench, he dressed and made his way downstairs. He found Cathy in the drawing room.

"You're back!" she said as he knocked on the door. "Come in! Did you find it?" she asked before the door closed. "Where did it go? Did it hunt? Has it turned someone else?"

He managed a smile and held up a hand. "It is early, Catherine. What little sleep I had, was poor. One question at a time, please."

"Sorry!" she said. "I slept badly too. I was so worried that the cloak would fail, or that the protection spell wouldn't protect you."

He raised a brow at the depth of her concern. "As you can see, I am unharmed. Your magic worked."

A broad smile spread across her face and iridescent sparkles returned to her iris.

"I followed the vampire into a town about five miles from here. It lured another young woman."

"He bit her?"

"Drained her and left her for dead in scrubland. She will find her way to the Hall tonight."

"So ... what do we do now?" asked Cathy.

"We must execute the vampire before nightfall and then deal with the woman tomorrow morning, before she has a chance to begin hunting."

"I understand," she replied without enthusiasm.

Heath stalled and then a knock at the door announced Argenon.

"Good morning, Mistress. I trust I find you well?"

"Very well, thank you, Argenon," replied Cathy.

"I was just about to tell Mistress Catherine what I discovered about the rogue vampire."

"Ah! Then I have arrived at a good time."

"What have you discovered?" questioned Cathy, the smile now gone.

"There's something you need to know about the vampire I followed."

"What is it?"

"The vampire was a young woman."

"Not the man with the beard? I was so sure it was him. I thought he must be collecting a harem."

Heath shook his head, unsure how to break the truth to Cathy.

"You think it was Fion, don't you," Cathy said as though reading his mind.

"I can't be sure," Heath replied. "We were always absent from the Hall during the summer—as a kindness to you aunt."

"So it might not be her?" Cathy asked with a lilt of hope.

"It could be one of the other vampires, yes," Heath agreed. "We believe one of their number is a younger woman although Argenon thinks that she was above twenty when she was taken."

Cathy sagged. "And Fion was just a teenager, fourteen years old."

"The vampire I saw in town looked to be of that age. I'm sorry, Cathy."

Cathy grew silent.

If Fion was the rogue vampire, then it had become Cathy's duty to execute her own cousin. Heath placed a hand on her shoulder. "I really am sorry, Catherine," he said with sincerity.

"It will be a kindness, Mistress," Argenon explained. "As a vampire Fion is cursed to walk in the shadows for eternity. Releasing her will allow her soul to pass to the Ever After."

Tears glistened in Cathy's eyes. "But you said that you were unsure where they went!" she accused. "When I asked if they would pass to the Ever After you said, 'Yes, or thereabouts'. Where is 'thereabouts', Argenon?" she said with passion. "Is it Hel? Is that where her doomed soul will go?"

Heath placed a hand on Cathy's shoulder. "The truth is that we don't know what will happen after she passes. We can only hope that she is taken to the Ever After."

"But what if it is Hel? I can't send her there!"

"But if she has gone rogue then she will turn this place, this entire area, into a living hell!" Argenon said with a touch of anger. "I am truly sorry, Mistress, but we simply cannot allow her to remain free to slaughter at will."

"It is not only hunting that Fion is about, Cathy," Heath said as he held her shoulder in a firm grip. "She is recruiting. She is increasing their numbers and those new recruits will be desperate for blood. The newly turned have yet to learn restraint and hunt with abandon. Vampirism will spread like a plague."

Argenon nodded, his face grave. "Mistress, this is a responsibility that you cannot shirk."

"I am not shirking it!" Cathy replied with passion. "But for the love of ... of all that is good in this world, you're asking me to kill my cousin." A sob rose in her chest, and Heath pulled her to him.

"I understand," he said, his voice soothing.

Cathy pushed Heath away, sagging a little. "I'm sorry. It's just ... I cannot believe this is happening. I knew that something terrible had happened to Fion, and I swore to discover who had harmed her, *and* seek justice, but this ..." She caught her breath, holding back the emotion. "This is so, so cruel!"

"If I may suggest ... let us first confirm the identity of the vampire Master Heath saw in town. And then we can discuss how we are to resolve the situation."

Hope returned to Cathy's eyes. "Maybe it's not Fion!"

"Yes," agreed Heath. "It is possible that the vampire I saw is not the cousin."

"Mistress. Will you accompany us down to the cellar to confirm her identity?" Argenon asked.

"Yes!" agreed Cathy with enthusiasm. "Let's go down now."

Heath grimaced at the hope in her voice; the rogue vampire's face had been strikingly similar to Cathy's.

Chapter Thirty-Five

Cathy followed the men through the house to the west wing where Argenon unlocked the door and held it open for her to step through.

"If we are only confirming the identity of the vampire, why have you brought the bag of tools?" she asked as she stepped over the threshold and noticed the bag at Argenon's feet. She had been so involved in her own thoughts that she hadn't seen him pick up the bag as they'd left the day room.

"Well ..." he shared a look with Heath. "I ... I had presumed that we would carry out the job once we had confirmed the identity," he said with a questioning frown. "It is already midday ..."

"No!"

"But ... the vampire must be dealt with if we don't-"

"I ... I need time," insisted Cathy.

"But, Mistress, if you don't dispatch her today then she will rise again tonight and continue to hunt."

"Slaughter and recruit," added Heath.

Cathy sighed, holding back emotion. "This is all too much!" she said. "I'm not made of stone. I just can't-"

"Very well," Argenon nodded. "I understand." He placed the bag of tools in the corridor. "We shall confirm the identity, and then discuss how to proceed. Perhaps after a cup of tea things will be a little clearer."

"Tea!" said Heath with a note of exasperation. "You have become obsessed by drinking tea."

"I find it a soothing drink, Lord. It helps clear the mind."

Cathy sniffed back a tear. "Tea would be nice," she said.

Argenon gave a quick and triumphant glance at Heath. "There, you see. All will be well."

The door closed behind them with a soft thud, and they made their way to the cellar.

Light from the uncovered side windows fell across the boxes set out in neat rows between the brick pillars. Less fearful than her first encounter with the cellar, Cathy took her time moving among them. There were seven almost identical boxes. Unnamed and without any indication of their contents it was impossible to know who lay within.

"Where are you?" she whispered as she walked among them. Trailing a hand across one box, she gasped, pulling her hand away as thought burned.

"What is it?" Heath asked.

"The box!" she replied. "I know who's in it—at least, I think I do."

"You received a vision?" asked Argenon, a glimmer of interest in his eyes.

"I saw a man. He was looking into a mirror, a razor in his hands, about to shave. I felt his fear. Something was in the room with him."

"The moment he was taken," Argenon said. "Hyldreth said she believed you have the gift of sight."

"A volva?" questioned Heath with a worried frown.

Argenon nodded his head. "Yes, Lord, but unproven and heavily suppressed."

"Ah! Good," he replied.

Oblivious to Heath's concern, Cathy stroked the box she had opened where the large and bearded man lay. Again she was assaulted by a memory that was not her own. "It's the same man I saw in the box," she said. "He was a farmer. The vampires fed on his family. He put up a fight, but," she shuddered, "they were overwhelming."

"Fascinating!" said Argenon with real interest. "We can take a history of these people and finally understand who they are."

"I'm going to start opening them up," said Heath with impatience. He began to lift the lid of the farthest box. "Being down here in this dank cell does not sit well with me."

The box held another man, this one far younger and slimmer than the bearded vampire. Heath continued to the next box and Cathy waited, unnerved by the visions of the vampires' final moments before being dragged into the world of the undead. He lifted the lids on three more before pausing with one open and beckoning to Cathy. "Is this your cousin?" he asked.

Cathy stepped to Heath's side and looked down on the vampire. "It is!" she said unable to hold back the shock. "It's Fion."

Fion lay deathly pale, her lips tinged blue. Unlike Cathy's almost raven-coloured hair, Fion's had been flaxen. 'Like chalk and cheese' her mother had often said of the pair although there was a resemblance. They shared the same slender figures, both being about the same height.

Untouched by time, Fion lay completely still without a flicker beneath her eyelids or a rising of her chest. Cathy reached in and stroked her cheek but flinched at the icy coldness of her skin. As she withdrew her hand, Fion's eyes flickered then opened.

Cathy took a step behind Heath.

Blood-red eyes stared, and the creature hissed but made no effort to move.

"It can't harm us, Cathy," Argenon said as he moved to the end of the box.

"She ... it's a she! And her name is Fion." Cathy took a step back towards the box.

"Yes, sorry. Fion can't hurt you, at least not until twilight gives way to night."

"We can't trust her anymore," Heath said. "If she is leaving the estate to hunt, what assurance do we have that she won't turn on us?"

"None, my Lord, which is why she must be dealt with."

"Cathy?" Fion's eyes locked on Cathy. "Cathy?" she repeated.

Startled to hear her voice, Cathy remained silent, forcing herself to remain beside the box.

"I knew it was you," Fion said. "I sensed you. I knew you would come to save me."

Tears pricked Cathy's eyes.

Fion held out her arm. "Help me, Cathy."

Heath blocked Cathy's attempt to reach for Fion's hand. "No! She cannot be trusted."

"I knew you would come. Have you come to find me? I heard your promise, Cathy."

Cathy nodded, wiping away a tear. "I have," she managed. "I promised to find out what happened to you and bring your killer to justice."

"Let me see you, Cathy. Come closer."

Mesmerised, held captive by the gleaming red of Fion's eyes, she leant forward.

"I am so lonely, Cathy. Come with me. Let's play in the garden like we used to."

Cathy took another step closer, sinking into Fion's gaze.

"We had so much fun."

"We did."

"I'm lonely, Cathy. Stay with me."

Heath pushed Cathy back. "Nay, woman! You cannot trust her."

Fion hissed.

"Hold your tongue, devil," Heath said and closed the lid.

Cathy struggled against his arm. "Open it!"

"No," he replied. "That thing in there is no longer your cousin. It is an evil being. She was casting her foul magic against you. Pulling you to her. Did you not feel it?"

"I wanted to be with her," Cathy admitted.

"And she would have taken you too." He turned to Argenon. "Fetch the bag."

"Cathy!" Fion called from within the box. "Be with me, Cathy. I am so lonely."

Fion's plaintive cry sank into Cathy's bones and the thought of her cousin spending her days in the darkness of the box and the dankness of the cellar chilled her.

"I can't stand this," she whispered as Fion continued to call, her voice mournful. "She's so lonely."

"That may be true, Catherine, but what is done is done. We cannot bring her back to life to live among us."

"Do you think that's why she bit those girls?"

"Because she is lonely?"

"Yes. Perhaps she just wanted some friends."

Heath shook his head, a deep frown at his brow. "I understand your pity for her, but you must hold on to the knowledge that she is of the undead now. If she rises tonight, she will kill again and increase their numbers. We cannot allow that to happen."

Cathy shivered, rubbing her arms as Argenon's footsteps were heard on the staircase.

"I have it," he said, breathless as he held out the bag.

Minutes passed as Cathy retrieved the tools from the bag then crouched beside it, dreading the moment when Heath opened the box.

"Come to me, Cathy!" Fion sobbed. "I'm all alone. It's dark, Cathy. It's dark all the time and I miss you."

Heath placed a heavy hand on Cathy's shoulder. "It is the kindest thing," he said. "She's living a tortured life, her soul chafing through every moment of her undead existence."

Cathy rose to stand, mallet in one hand, stake in the other.

"Ready?"

Cathy nodded.

Heath opened the box, removing the lid entirely.

"Cathy!" Fion gasped and held out her arms in an embrace.

"Set her free, Mistress," Argenon urged. "Save her!"

Cathy held the spike over Fion's chest and as she held the mallet ready to hammer it down, the vampire covered her hand with her own. "Set me free, Cathy!" she whispered, her red eyes staring into Cathy's. "Send me to the Ever After."

Cathy held her gaze, her heart breaking for her cousin, horrified that Fion was still present within the undead creature. Tears blurred her eyes. "Oh, Fion ... I will." With Fion's cold hand gripping hers, Cathy hammered the spike into her chest.

Chapter Thirty-Six

Over the following days, Cathy recuperated from her experience, reliving each moment, and grieving for Fion. Throwing herself into her new role as Housekeeper helped to make each day a little more bearable. She particularly enjoyed helping out on the farm and joined Ellette's children as they collected eggs and even tried milking a goat. Her old life became like a distant and unimportant memory whilst her sense of being exactly where she belonged grew. Witherwood Hall and Heath were her future, and she woke each morning a little more joyous to explore the house and the estate. Heath, whilst still taciturn and brusque began to sit with her at lunch and requested that she accompany him on his daily survey of the estate. Together they noted the improving health of the cows, readied the sheep for tupping, and checked the estate's boundaries. Her amateurish efforts at riding improved and Heath praised her efforts. He also wanted her help to develop and market a range of goats' cheeses, a project she was excited to work with him on. As the days passed, she began to realise how committed to the Hall he was and suspected that behind the brusque exterior was a man yearning to be loved. Her affection for him grew and she began to look forward to their wedding day with excited anticipation.

Argenon had arranged that the wedding take place on the day before Freysblöt when they would sacrifice one of the goats to Freyr to celebrate the harvest. Cathy, urged by Argenon, had invited her coven sisters to the ceremony, and it had been arranged that Lexi and the girls take rooms at the local pub, the *Wolf & Lamb*.

On the day before the wedding, text messages from Lexi had flowed all morning, updating Cathy on their progress, and then their arrival at the pub. Excited to see Lexi again, Cathy set off to the pub.

Lexi, Sasha, Judy, Naomi, Abby, and Carole were still in the carpark when she arrived and squealed with excitement as they flocked around her. A couple in the beer garden, watched with interest.

"I can't believe you're going through with it!"

"What's he like?"

"Is he hot?"

"Please tell me he is drop dead gorgeous!" exclaimed Sasha. "And the house. Tell me the house is amazing!"

Cathy laughed, buoyed by her excitement. "Well," Cathy teased, "I wouldn't kick him out of bed and the house is just incredible. I can't wait for you to see it."

Lexi hooked her arm through Cathy's. "Let's book in and talk upstairs. It looks like there are mice at the crossroads," she said, gesturing to the couple who were glancing their way but pretending not to listen.

"We don't want everyone to know that the lady of the manor is a mail order bride," she whispered then gave Cathy a nudge with her elbow.

"Oh, stop it!" Cathy said. "It's not like that."

"No, it's worse, you're being bought."

"I am not," Cathy said. "Heath has not bought me! No money has been exchanged."

"What I think is hilarious, is that he's called Heathcliff and you're Cathy. Like in Wuthering Heights."

Cathy laughed. "They're both common names. And anyway, he's Heath, not Heathcliff."

"Same difference."

Lexi grabbed Cathy's arm. "It's just too much," she exclaimed. "Isn't that guy you met called Ed Linton?"

"Yeah," Cathy said with a frown. "What of it?"

"The guy Catherine married in *Wuthering Heights* was called Edgar Linton!"

"This is too funny!"

"Is she already cheating on her fiancé?" quipped Naomi.

"No! I am not," Cathy snapped.

"You know that Cathy left Heath for Linton, don't you?"

"Don't be silly. This is not the plot of a novel."

"Maybe this is the novel," said Abby. "What if Emily Brontë was a volva? Maybe she wrote about you."

"Don't be silly," Cathy said. "It's just a coincidence. That's all."

"She died," declared Abby.

"Who died?"

"Cathy. In the book, she died, and Heath was left heartbroken, forever waiting for her ghost to return."

"Well, that's not going to happen," declared Cathy. "I'm marrying Heath tomorrow," she said as they entered the pub. "And it's going to be a wonderful day-"

The flow of chatter came to an abrupt halt as Cathy noticed Edgar Linton standing at the bar. He raised his glass as she stepped through the doorway, and she gave a tentative smile in return as the girls dumped their bags on the floor. Sasha headed straight for the bar to enquire about the rooms.

"Wow! This place is amazing," exclaimed Naomi. "It's like a real old-fashioned pub," she said. "And the locals are pretty hot too," she said in a lower voice whilst watching Edgar Linton at the bar. "Does he know you, Cathy?" she asked as Sasha caught the attention of the barmaid. "Or is he just happy to see us?"

"Oh," Cathy replied, trying to sound nonchalant. "That's Ed."

"The guy you had a date with?"

"Shh! Yes, and it wasn't a date. He just asked me out for a drink. It was my first day here, remember."

"Sure," replied Naomi. "So ... he's up for grabs then?" she asked with a raise of her brows. "Is he coming to the wedding?"

Cathy managed a laugh though her emotions were flipping. Ed seemed even more attractive than the first day she'd met him, and she could understand why Naomi was so interested, but there was no way she could invite him to the wedding, even if he was the only person in the village she knew. "Be my guest," she replied with an offhand laugh. "He's all yours but we're keeping the wedding cosy."

"Can't he be my plus one?" Naomi asked, her gaze now locked to Edgar's as he noticed the attention.

"No!" Cathy replied, her cheeks beginning to sting.

"Shame," Naomi replied. "I may just have to cast a spell or two," she said with a raise of her brows.

"Just talk to him," Lexi advised. "And here's your chance," she said as he placed his glass on the bar and headed towards them.

"Good afternoon, ladies," he said with a broad smile and a particularly long look at Naomi. "Can I get you a drink?"

"No, thanks," Cathy replied.

"Yes, please," Naomi said.

"We're just booking in," Lexi explained.

"Then let me help you," he said reaching down for Naomi's bag.

"Why, thank you!" she said with an exaggerated and girly voice, pouting her lips and pushing out her chest just a little.

"She is awful!" laughed Carole as the pair walked towards the staircase.

"He is attractive, though," Lexi said whilst casting a glance towards Cathy.

"He is," agreed Cathy, "but Naomi is welcome to him. I'm spoken for."

"You are," agreed Lexi. "And I can't wait to meet him. He sounds delicious!" she said and followed after Carole.

"I'll meet you down here," Cathy said.

"Get the drinks in," Lexi shouted back. "We'll be back down soon."

Happy to see her friends, but in a torment of emotion, Cathy ordered the drinks then claimed a table in a snug corner of the pub. Taking a relieved sip of wine, she nearly choked as Ed reappeared. He returned to the bar, bought another pint, then walked with purpose and sat beside her, shuffling close on the bench. Too close!

"So, Cathy, how are you finding Witherwood Hall?" he asked, slipping his arm across the upholstered back of the bench.

Heart pounding, excruciatingly aware of the closeness of his body next to hers and the waves of desire that buffeted against her side as a pulse of energy, she took another sip of wine. "I love it," she replied.

"Naomi, tells me that you are to be married. It must have been a whirlwind romance. I thought you were the housekeeper."

"I am. It was. I mean-"

"He whisked you off your feet, then," he stated.

"We hit if off straight away."

"Yet marriage, after a couple of weeks?"

"Oh, it's longer than that."

"Naomi mentioned something about an arrangement?"

Cathy's cheeks seared. "What arrangement?" she asked, attempting to feign ignorance.

"That you have with Heath."

"We're to be married tomorrow."

"The eve of Freysblöt?"

"Yes."

"And did you discover how your aunt had died?"

No! "Natural causes. She was old."

"Ancient," he said. "And your cousin?"

Cathy twisted to him in surprise. "What do you know of my cousin?"

"Only that she disappeared under strange circumstances."

Cathy shivered, as the energy from Ed began to envelop her. Suddenly she felt a little distant within herself and the desire to be close to him, feel him hold her to his flesh became intense. Her glass became opaque, hiding the liquid within and the pub became as though seen through a misted lens, darker at the edges. Heat began to rise between her legs as desire took hold. "Why don't you come home with me tonight, Cathy?" His voice was velvet, and she wanted to taste his lips upon hers. "Come home, Cathy. Come home with me. We can spend an eternity together. I can love you, Cathy. Give you everything a man can give to a woman." His voice was inside her, in her head. He leant into her, his nose pushing at her hair, his lips brushing against her cheek. "I'll take you in the night, Cathy. My lips will caress every part of your body, even your most secret places," he whispered. His voice tugged at her desire, coaxing her to agree. "Come home, with me Cathy. Be my bride, not his."

"Cathy!" Heath's voice jolted her from her stupor.

Still heady with the desire flooding her veins, she looked up as though drunk to see Heath standing on the opposite side of the table.

"Heath!" Ed exclaimed as though greeting a long-lost friend. "It is so good to see you."

"What are you doing, Cathy?" Heath asked.

"I ... just ..."

"Why, she's having a drink with a friend," Ed replied.

"I was not speaking to you, Linton! And you are no friend of hers."

Ed laughed. "Oh, but I will be."

"By the god's but I will put you in the ground, Linton!" raged Heath and reached across the table, grabbing Cathy's arm.

"Oh, but you mustn't be so selfish, Heath. Afterall, we have shared your other brides, have we not?"

"Damnable monster!" Heath hissed as Cathy's friends returned to the bar.

Chapter Thirty-Seven

The door slammed behind Heath with a crack, and he strode into the Hall using every ounce of self-restraint he had to curb his rage. Linton had smiled superciliously at him as Cathy's friends had returned after visiting their rooms, and he had continued to fondle her shoulder as they flocked round. One of the women, a dark haired and lascivious creature, had slipped beside him, a flicker of jealousy obvious as she'd noticed Linton's arm across Cathy's shoulder, but she had only laughed and made a quip about Cathy being quick off the mark—as usual. Ed had laughed whilst holding Heath's gaze, goading him to react, mocking him. Heath had wanted to let the Beast free and launch himself at Linton, sinking claws into his psychotic flesh and ripping out his cold and beating heart.

"And one day, I will," growled Heath as he walked Cathy to her room. That she had been under his influence was obvious from her glazed eyes as she'd responded to his call. He'd caught them, Linton with his hand groping her shoulder, nuzzling against her neck, whispering his poisonous words. Was this how it had been with the others? Linton seducing his brides, pulling them away from Heath with his toxic charm. They had changed, he remembered.

The closer their wedding day grew, the more distant and glassy eyed they had become, until they'd simply disappeared. After the second bride had disappeared, he had come to recognise the signs and the pattern. His first runaway bride, Agata, had caused him deep despair and grief. He thought her kidnapped or murdered and scoured the countryside with his men day after torturous day. When Linton had flaunted her at a gathering several weeks later, he had been relieved but enraged by the deception.

Instead of making a scene, Heath had been polite to Cathy's friends, introducing himself formally, then left with Cathy, explaining that there was much to do in preparation for the wedding and invited them to supper at the Hall. He'd put on a good display, of which Argenon would be proud, even hiding his hatred of Linton, but his rage was growing with each second, and his efforts at subduing it weaker.

As they stood in Cathy's sitting room, she pulled her elbow from him.

Be nice, Lord!

"Catherine-"

"I'm so sorry!" she blurted.

The emotion in her voice took him by surprise, he had expected anger at being removed from her friends' presence.

"You have nothing to feel sorry for," he replied, holding back the angry words he wanted to shout.

"Ed ..."

"Edgar Linton is a conman, Cathy. A trickster. He uses his powers to seduce women. Whatever you felt whilst you sat beside him was a lie."

She sighed as though a weight were being lifted from her shoulders. The anger left him. Linton was playing a game, allowing rage to fester would be letting him win. He turned to face Cathy and cupped her chin. "Tomorrow, I make you my wife, Mistress Earnshaw," he said with a gentle voice.

"I am looking forward to becoming your wife," she replied, the remnants of Linton's spell gone from her eyes.

"For that I am glad," he said. "Tonight, to celebrate your last hours as a free woman. I have invited your friends to celebrate with you."

"Here?"

"Yes, here, in your home. Ellette and Tatwin will see to everything. All you have to do is prepare yourself and then enjoy the company of your best friends."

"Will you come?"

"And see my bride the evening of our wedding? No," he laughed.

"Just for a short time," she pleaded.

She seemed so small and fragile in that moment, a tiny doll he wanted to crush to him. His yearning for her pushed out the last of the rage and, unable to help himself, he slipped his arm around her slender waist, feeling her flesh pressing against his for the first time. His need began to consume him, and he felt the first stirrings of the primal beast driven by instincts he would become. He tipped her chin up. "Close your eyes," he said as he drew her close. For a moment her eyes flickered with fear and then closed. He leant down, pressing his lips against hers. They were soft, warm, and he began to sink into desire before pulling away.

"Good!" he said, hardening against the emotion. He gave a slight and formal bow then left the room. Heart pounding. Tomorrow she would become his wife. Only tonight stood in his way before she belonged to him completely and was out of Linton's reach forever.

Chapter Thirty-Eight

As the bedroom door closed behind Cathy, she fell back against it, unsure of what had happened in the pub. Ed had whispered sweet words into her ears as he'd nuzzled against her neck. She'd sensed their intoxication even without understanding the language in which they were spoken and begun to sink into a warm place. But stronger than the fear was the need to leave with Ed. He whispered of taking her home forever, and making her his, and words that weren't hers but seemed to well from inside, answered his call with 'Yes!', whilst another part of her screamed 'No!' The intoxication was intense, and she was about to leave with him when Heath had walked through the door. Dangerous energy, dark and violent, had filled the room.

The bedroom door felt solid beneath her fingers, and she gripped the handle to reassure herself it was real. Heath had driven them home, and the feeling of not quite being part of the world had thinned. Had Ed drugged her?

As calm returned and the feeling of unsteadiness finally left her body, she noticed that her bed had been freshly made and that there were a number of items laid on the pillow. The largest was a bulky package wrapped in tissue paper and beside it was a small box and an envelope. She picked up the envelope first. In dark ink, written in an old-fashioned hand was 'Mystresse Earnshawe' and it was sealed at the back with a blob of wax which also secured the ribbon that was wrapped around the envelope. She pulled the ribbon, breaking the wax and opened the letter. Inside was a single sheet of paper containing a note written in the same hand. 'To my bride on the eve before our wedding. May our union be fruitful. I hope that you enjoy this last night of freedom and that my gifts bring you pleasure. Most sincerely, Heath'.

She turned to the bulky package. Removing the paper revealed a silk dress in a delicate pale green. With long full sleeves it had a fitted bodice and a full skirt but sat off the shoulder. "It's beautiful," she whispered as she held it against her body. The large box revealed a pair of heeled sandals that matched the dress perfectly. She turned to the smaller boxes. The larger one, a flat square, contained a necklace of emeralds whilst the smaller box contained a ring of gold filigree with a large emerald at its centre. She slipped it onto her finger and held it to the light, mesmerised by the way the gems face's glinted in the sun. The spell was broken by the ringing of her phone.

"Hi!" she answered, unable to keep the happiness from her voice, and held her hand back into the light where the sunlight played with the creatures.

"Well, that was short and sweet!" Lexi quipped. "Seems like your groom wants to keep you all to himself," she laughed.

"Oh, I am so sorry about that. Heath needed me back here to help get things ready for this evening," Cathy replied, repeating Heath's words at the table.

Lexi laughed. "I think Ed had a little to do with it too."

"What do you mean?"

"Well, he was all over you, I don't think Heath was very happy about that. Can't say I blame him."

"Me neither," replied Cathy. "He was a bit overwhelming," she managed a laugh.

"The guy's a player, Cathy. You know the type. And you'll never guess, or rather you will, but he's turned his attention to Naomi now." Cathy was surprised at the surge of jealousy she felt as Lexi continued to describe how Naomi had moved in just as soon as Cathy had left. "And she left with him!"

"What?"

"Yeah," Lexi laughed. "He's gone to show her his collection of swords or something."

"That's one euphemism for it," Cathy replied, managing a laugh. Naomi's addiction to men was well known. Her relationships never lasted very long, but as soon as one ended, she was on the lookout for another. "I guess they're well suited then," Cathy said then grew quiet.

"You okay?"

"Yeah, just … well everything is moving so fast," she said. "It doesn't seem real."

"You're on an amazing journey, Cathy, embrace it," replied Lexi. "Heath seems like a nice guy."

"He is," replied Cathy.

"We were just wondering what's been arranged for this evening? Heath invited us over, but didn't specify a time …"

"He said that he would join us on the terrace for drinks before dinner."

"So, six o'clock?"

"Yes, that would be perfect," Cathy replied.

"We'll be there."

"And ... can you call Naomi to check on her?" Cathy said with a wave of concern. Heath had called Ed a conman, and for all Naomi's brazen manhunting, she was just desperate to be loved and that made her vulnerable to predators.

"Sure."

Cathy spent the remainder of the afternoon bathing and preparing herself for the evening, whilst down on the terrace metal and glass clinked as Ellette, Tatwin, and their children decorated the tables. Flowers were picked from the garden and presented in abundant displays whilst jars filled with water from the spring were hung in numerous places.

With ten minutes left before her guests were to arrive, Cathy slipped into the silk dress. It fit her perfectly, emphasising the slenderness of her waist and the gentle rise of her breasts. She twirled in front of the huge mirror, the lowering sunlight catching the emeralds at her throat. For a second, the memory of her alcohol sodden face when she'd reached her lowest point and reached for the pills from her bathroom cabinet reflected back at her and she slowed, her joy evaporating to be replaced with wonder. Her life had turned upside down. Only weeks ago she had been willing to take her own life, broken by her own stupidity, but now she was on the verge of falling deeply and profoundly in love, and creating life. The thought terrified her.

The fairy with the mop of copper hair swooped down and chittered, landing on the mantlepiece. It was quickly followed by another and then several more. Each chittered excitedly and then two swooped down carrying a flower.

They hovered with the flower and, as she took it from them and placed it in her hair, there came a knock at the door.

"Come in," she called.

Ellette entered and with a small bob-curtsey, said, "Your guests are here, Mistress."

Chapter Thirty-Nine

Dressed in her new silk dress, emeralds gleaming at her throat, the flower in her hair, Cathy descended the wide staircase of Witherwood Hall. The chatter and tinkling laughter of her friends as they waited for her on the terrace filtered through the house but as she took the final return to the entrance hall, she became oblivious to the noise as she noticed Heath at the bottom of the stairs. Even with his back to her, he exuded a sexual energy that was impossible to ignore.

He wore a dark navy evening suit that his broad shoulders filled perfectly but it was when he turned, and his eyes lit up and locked to hers as he watched her descent, that she felt a bond between them lock. Images of them standing before an altar in the forest, their hands bound together with a silken rope sparkling with the magical dust grew vivid as he held out his hand to take hers as she took the final step.

"You look beautiful," he said.

"Thank you," she replied. "You look very ... handsome."

"The dress fits you perfectly," he said holding her at arms' length then held up her ringed hand. "And you are wearing my ring," he said with a smile of satisfaction. "Do you like it?"

"I ... it's beautiful. I don't think I've ever seen one like it."

His smile broadened. "It is unique, very old."

"It looks antique."

"Oh, yes, it is definitely antique."

They stood together for several more moments, his hand holding hers. "Shall we greet your friends. Unfortunately, I cannot stay long."

"Well, it is bad luck for us to see each other the evening before our wedding anyway."

His mood darkened for a moment before the smile returned. He offered his arm, and they walked outside together.

Two large oblong tables had been dressed with colourful posies in glass jars, each filled with sparkling water, the golden particles shimmering.

"Oh! Cathy, you look beautiful!" Judy said as they stepped out onto the terrace.

"Stunning!" Lexi agreed as Ellette offered her a wine-filled glass. She took it with a polite thank you.

Glasses were filled, and Heath took control of the conversation, apologising for taking Cathy away from them earlier, and welcoming them to Witherwood Hall. The women hung on every word, and unlike the arrogant and taciturn man he so often presented, he was the perfect affable host. As he continued to talk, she watched her friends, noticing how each of them was captivated, warming to him, their doubts about the marriage evaporating. Cathy's anxieties ebbed. Coming to Witherwood had been the right decision and agreeing to marry Heath, crazy as it seemed, was perhaps going to turn out to be the best of her life.

As the evening progressed, and the girls hogged Heath's attention, Lexi drew her to one side.

"He's nice, Cathy."

"Nice is not a word I'd use to describe him," Cathy laughed.

"Well, you know what I mean. He could have been some ugly troll or arrogant twit, or an old man."

"I guess."

"Honestly, I thought you were making a huge mistake – lost the plot after what Dan had done, but," she cast a glance towards Heath as he laughed and chatted with the girls, "I think it could be the best thing you've ever done."

Despite the prick of pain that the mention of Dan's deception brought, she managed to hold back her emotion. "I feel joy, Lexi. Honest to goodness joy at the thought of living at Witherwood Hall and being Heath's wife."

Lexi slipped an arm across Cathy's shoulder. "I wish you every happiness, Cathy. You deserve it."

"I'm not sure about that," she said with a touch of bitterness. "I was selfish, but ... but I think the gods have given me another chance. I can be happy and make someone else happy too."

"He's gorgeous!" Judy said as she joined them. "You are so lucky, Cathy."

As the other women filtered away, only Naomi was left talking to Heath. As usual, she was being her touchy-feely self, gripping Heath's arm and squeezing his bicep and no doubt flattering him about his strength.

"She's at it again!" Judy said before taking a sip of her wine.

"She's shameless," Lexi replied as Naomi stood on tip toes and placed a kiss on Heath's cheek.

"Aren't you bothered, Cathy?" Judy asked.

"No, Heath's marrying me tomorrow and I know what Naomi's like. She's a terrible flirt."

Heath laughed at something Naomi said and then she rose once more on her tiptoes to whisper in his ear. He bent down to listen, looked momentarily surprised, glanced over at Cathy for a nanosecond then led Naomi to the group, his hand resting lightly on her slender back. She seemed to glow with excitement, or lust, and gave Cathy a challenging glance whilst stroking Heath's arm. She seemed tipsy already and Cathy suspected she hadn't stopped drinking since they'd arrived at the pub.

As the last rays of sunlight began to ebb and after taking Cathy's hand and kissing it in gentlemanly fashion, Heath wished them a good evening then withdrew from the party. Naomi watched him leave, mouth slightly agape, then turned with raised eyebrows to the group of tipsy women. "Oh my goodness! Cathy, he is gorgeous!"

"How did it go with Ed?" Lexi asked, deftly changing the subject. "He's asked you out, hasn't he?"

Head fuzzy with champagne, and with Heath gone, Cathy relaxed, and listened as Naomi told them exactly how she wanted to get to know Ed better.

"You are terrible!" laughed Judy.

"Well, a girl has got to live! I intend having a lot of fun before I get old and saggy."

"Gross!" Abby laughed. "I'm sure you'll be a very attractive old cougar."

"Well, I don't intend being left on the shelf, darling," she said. "I'm searching for love and a ring on my finger, but I'll settle for the ring." She held up her hand. "We're not all as lucky as Cathy," she said. "We can't all have a gorgeous husband and fabulous home gifted to us in a dear old Aunt's will." She cast a glance to Cathy, then took another swig of champagne.

"No, we can't," Lexi said with a light frown that quickly disappeared as she caught Cathy's eyes.

"Perhaps you should go steady on the champagne," Judy suggested as Naomi took a bottle from the table and began to refill her flute.

"Or maybe I shouldn't."

"Naomi," Judy whispered, "it's Cathy's party. Don't spoil it."

Naomi drank another mouthful of champagne and threw Cathy a smile laden with spite. "Of course I won't," she replied then pulled her mobile from her pocket as it began to ring.

"What's wrong with her?" Cathy asked as Naomi walked away from the group, mobile to her ear.

"She's had too much to drink," Lexi explained.

"Sure, but she's not usually so … mean. She was looking daggers at me."

"She's jealous."

"Jealous? Of me? But why on earth would she be jealous of me?"

Lexi gestured to the beautifully lit terrace, the gardens beyond, and the majestic Hall that towered before them.

"This," she said. "And Heath, and before that you had Dan, a beautiful home, and a fantastic career."

"Which I lost, along with my home, and Dan cheated on me with one of our best friends."

"I know that, but to Naomi it was a dream life. You threw it away, and now you've walked into a dream life even better than the last one. You know what she's like, Cath, always looking for Mr. Right and never finding him."

"She needs to stop looking so hard."

"And in the wrong places, I agree."

Cathy sighed. "She's gorgeous and so funny, when she wants to be, I'm sure she'll find a husband soon."

"Or die trying," Lexi laughed. "Maybe your Mr. Linton will be the one. He's asked her to meet up with him the day after tomorrow."

"He's not *my* Mr. Linton, Lexi! And sure, maybe they'll hit it off."

"I hope so, that means I'll have two of my coven sisters to visit up here." She slipped an arm across Cathy's back. "Tomorrow is going to be so amazing!"

As Naomi continued her conversation, she wandered into the garden, and Cathy turned her attention to her other guests. It was the perfect evening, balmy with a smattering of stars overhead, and just a wisp of cloud across the moon. The terrace lights began to glow within their glass jars, each filled with the magical dust that rose from the sacred spring.

"It's just so magical here, Cathy," Lexi said as they sat together.

"It is amazing," Cathy agreed. "It's so much more than I could have ever hoped for."

"Now tell me. I want to know everything about Heath. He is just as gorgeous and mysterious as this house!"

Cathy laughed and began to retell the story of the awkwardness of their first meeting, and how she'd turned down his offer of marriage. Minutes passed and she realised that Naomi was no longer on the terrace.

"Where's Naomi?"

"She went for a walk in the garden. I think I saw her walk down that pathway." Judy pointed to the overhung pathway that led to the woodlands.

"It's a bit dark to be walking in the woods," Abby said.

"She'll be back in a few minutes," Lexi said.

"I'll just go and see if she's okay," Cathy said.

"No, I'll go, Cathy," Lexi replied. "She's had a bit too much to drink and probably getting a bit emotional—wants a bit of space. You know what she's like."

"It's okay. I'd like to talk to her. Plus I want to know all about this date she's set up with Ed."

With the remnants of twilight and the golden haze of magical particles to light her way, Cathy stepped beneath the overarching trees and down the path to the gate. As she stood at the threshold, she heard a woman's giggle followed by a man's voice. She recognised the laughter as Naomi's but the man's was a muffled baritone dampened by the rustling of leaves as a light breeze swept through the canopy.

"She's arranged to meet Ed here!" Cathy whispered, remembering her own encounter with Ed in the woods.

As she walked further into the woods, the voices grew louder, and the couple came into view. The woman's giggle became a moan of desire. The man grunted.

Pushed up against the thick trunk of an ancient oak, Naomi clung to Heath, her bare legs wrapped around his naked hips as he thrust into her.

"No!"

Oblivious, Naomi moaned but Heath turned to Cathy, a broad grin breaking across his face as their eyes met.

Stumbling back through the woods, tears blurring her vision, Cathy reached the gate. Behind her the noise of Heath and Naomi's union grew faint but his smile was burned onto her memory. As she ran, a vortex of glittering particles gathered then swarmed, growing dense as it swirled behind her.

Lights glittered in the darkening sky, champagne flutes chinked, and her friends laughed, as Cathy reached the terrace.

"Get out!" she screeched. "All of you get out!"

The laughing stopped.

"Cathy! Whatever is the matter?

"I saw them!" she said turning to Lexi. She appeared as a blur, her eyes dark holes in her face. Cathy blinked away the tears and Lexi came into focus. "I saw Naomi and Heath ... they were ... they were having sex!" she blurted.

"Oh, Cathy!"

"I want you all to leave!" she shouted then ran from the terrace, leaving the house her only thought.

Ed had been right; Heath was rotten to the core.

Chapter Forty

After battling the beast, Heath returned to the house, bathed, dressed, and made his way to the breakfast room. The marriage ceremony had been organised to take place in the afternoon and unable to settle, he was on edge.

The breakfast room was empty and he rang the bell for Ellette before sitting down. Despite the queasy sensation in his stomach, he was hungry. Several minutes passed before Ellette and two of her daughters appeared.

"Has your Mistress been down for breakfast" Heath asked as Ellette placed a bowl of creamy porridge before him.

"Not yet, Master," Ellette replied.

"Are you serving breakfast in her room?"

"Nay, Master."

"Then, has she not woken?"

The elvish woman made an odd whimpering noise and Heath gave her his full attention. "Ellette, I sense that there is something amiss."

Mercurio tapped at the window.

"Let the bird in," Heath demanded.

One of the girls ran to the window and pulled up the sash. Mercurio cawed as he flapped through the rising gap, landing to perch on the back of a dining room chair and considered Heath with a beady eye.

Heath sat back in his chair, scanning both the bird and Ellette. "What is it?" he asked, no longer hungry. The very air seemed charged with tension. Neither Mercurio nor Ellette spoke, and the woman edged to the door. "You have something to tell me, pray, tell me!" he demanded.

Mercurio cawed.

"Tell me!"

"Mistress Cathy ..."

"Tell me!" Heath demanded, his heart suddenly tripping.

"She left the house last night and hasn't returned."

"What?" He banged a fist against the table, throwing a questioning glare at Mercurio. "Where is she?"

"She is with Linton," Mercurio cawed then flapped his wings as though to take flight. Ellette took another tentative step towards the door whilst the two children slipped out of the room behind her.

"Stay where you are woman!" Heath snapped. "Mercurio, tell me how! When I left Mistress Earnshaw last night all was well. She was happy but ... Why in the very hell is she with Linton?"

He stood from the table, forcing the chair back. "How did this happen?" he growled. He swung to Ellette. "How did this happen?" he roared.

Cowering, Ellette ran to the door, slipping out before Heath could stop her.

"Bird!" he shouted. "Tell me how this happened. This is my wedding day! Fetch me my bride!"

Mercurio flapped his wings then landed on the table, hopping down its length towards Heath.

"How did he steal my bride, Mercurio," Heath seethed, his rage barely held back.

"She went into the woodlands."

"And she saw?"

"Yes, sire," the bird snapped. "She saw!"

Heath groaned and slumped back into the chair.

"Was she ... did she find me ... horrifying?"

The bird cawed. "I heard her friends speak of it. They reported that she was 'traumatized' yet it is I who is traumatized. All our plans have been destroyed. How many years have we been set back now thanks to your ... your ... You have betrayed us all!"

Heath let out another defeated groan. "I have no control over it as well you know."

Mercurio let out an angry caw. "How could you do it?" he seethed. "You had to control yourself for one night!"

Heath shook his head. "The moon is growing so strong, but I thought ... I was sure that I was unseen."

"Hah! She saw and she was so horrified that she bid all her friends leave and then ran away into the arms of your enemy! You are a fool, sire. A damnable fool."

"A damned soul," Heath hissed through clenched teeth, forcing himself to remain calm with the bird. He was to be trapped forever by the curse, and he had consigned Mercurio to the same fate.

"Does Argenon know?"

"Not yet sire. He is late to rise this morning."

Mercurio hopped back along the table and returned to his perch on the back of the chair then glared at Heath. "I am surprised though, sire."

Heath frowned. "Surprised?"

Mercurio eyed him. "Yes, surprised."

Heath huffed. "Surprised at what exactly?"

"That you would allow your carnal desires to overcome you—on the night before your wedding to the woman who would set us free. It was foolish and I never had you marked down as a fool!"

Irked by Mercurio's insolence, Heath grabbed a spoon and threw it down the table. It narrowly missed the bird. He cawed but remained on his perch, considering Heath with disapproving eyes.

"And I am surprised that Mistress Earnshaw did not confront you."

"It would take a strong stomach and a heart of iron to confront the beast."

"Confront the beast? Are you blaming the curse for your lust?"

"My lust?"

"Aye, sire, your lust. It was the man that took Mistress Earnshaw's friend, not the beast, though rutting against a tree is beast-like." Mercurio stared with cold and challenging eyes.

"What are you speaking of imbecile?" Heath asked.

"Are you denying that you forced yourself upon the woman?"

"Indeed I am. I have forced myself upon no woman."

"Then she gladly accepted your advances?"

"There were no advances!" Once again, Heath pushed away from the table. "What are you talking about, Mercurio? Stop speaking in riddles."

"What riddles, sire? Mistress Catherine saw you with her friend in the woods."

"She did not! I have not seen them since taking their leave last night on the terrace."

"Then it was not you that ravished the woman?"

"Indeed it was not!"

"Then I do believe, sire, that dark magic has been used against you."

"Mistress Earnshaw thinks that I betrayed her?"

"I believe that is the case."

"And yet, I did not."

"And yet she is with Linton."

"Linton!" Heath growled. "It was Linton! He beguiled her."

"Fetch her back, Lord."

Dark rage whorled as a vortex within his belly. "I will and by all the gods, I will put Edgar Linton in the ground."

Armed, his sword sheathed at his side, Heath chose to ride to Linton's property and urged Sweyn to a gallop along the narrow lanes but as they drew close to the property the horse became skittish and then refused to go further. It strained at the reins as Linton guided it forward, pulling against him in an effort to turn back towards the Hall.

"Very well," Heath growled as the horse stood still in the road, unwilling to continue down the road, "I shall go on foot."

He tethered the horse to a low-hanging branch and made the rest of the journey on foot. With each step, his anger intensified, and by the time he reached Linton's gates he was ready to rip the man apart with his bare hands.

"Would that the beast came by day," he muttered, "I should claw Linton to death, and slice his guts with my talons and watch his innards slither to the floor." The thought of seeing his enemy suffer encouraged his grinding hatred and he almost grabbed for the iron gate to fling it open. "'Tis better to attack by stealth," he reasoned and drew back behind the enormous hedge that bordered the front of the property.

Making his way along the hedge, Heath stepped into the woodlands, hoping to find a break in the barrier. However, the further he followed it around the house, the higher it seemed to grow and when he reached the back it became obvious that the tangle of overgrowth was impenetrable. As he turned to retrace his steps, the hedge shivered, and tendrils of a curling ivy began to grow outwards. He brushed at the vegetation as he realised it was snaking towards him, but the tendrils threw out sticky suckers which clung to his sleeve.

"By the gods!" he huffed as he pulled out his sword and began chopping at the snaking ivy. Twigs seemed to reach for him each barbed with thorns, stabbing at his torso. He swung the sword, slicing through the bewitched vegetation, realising that Linton knew he was here and would do everything in his power to stop him entering the property.

"Cathy!" he called as a huge branch snaked towards him and began curling around his foot. He severed it with one almighty chop of his sword and ran back from the hedge. A crow cawed from the canopy above and then Mercurio was beside him.

"His sorcery is powerful, Lord. You will not penetrate it."

"I will kill him, Mercurio. I will slash and chop and hack his head from his shoulders."

A branch, barbed like a cat of nine tails swung out, narrowly missing Heath as he jumped out of its path.

"You cannot compete with his magic, Lord. It is dark, dark, dark!" the bird cawed. "Come home. You have lost."

"Never!" Heath shouted and swung his sword at the cat-o-nine-tails as it launched again. "Cathy!" he shouted, his breath coming hard. "Cathy!"

The battle continued until Heath began to grow weary and staggered back from the possessed hedge. It seemed to have grown even taller, its leaves darker. From somewhere behind he heard the cackling laugh of Edgar Linton. "She's my bride now, fool. I shall take her tonight, Lord of Wither Wood. I shall take you bride to my bed and lay between her legs."

"No!" Heath raged and swung again at the hedge with his sword.

Great lengths of vine shot from the leaves, each covered in long and spiney thorns and began to batter Heath. He staggered under their force, their sharp spikes ripping into his flesh. He fell to the forest floor, his cheek hitting the dark soil. It pushed into his mouth, and he grunted as a knot of wood, a carbuncle at the end of a rope-like branch thumped his side.

"Get up, Lord," Mercurio cawed. "There is no way to defeat him."

As the knuckle of wood swung for him again, Heath dragged himself out of its reach. "I can't let him win!" he seethed.

"He already has," snapped Mercurio.

Chapter Forty-One

After leaving the Hall, Cathy had thrown her sandals into the undergrowth and ran through the woods to the road that led to the village. Unable to bear the thought of seeing people, she ran in the opposite direction until she began to flag and slow. Darkness had descended and too tired to walk she slumped against a tree for support. The image of Heath and Naomi was scorched onto her mind and she had allowed the tears to flow, oblivious to the approaching car until it drew up beside her. It had been Edgar Linton.

"Why don't you stay for another night?" Ed suggested.

"No ... I should go back to the Hall. It was kind of you to pick me up, but I've got nothing with me."

"You look very nice in my shirt, although the trousers are a bit long, I admit," he laughed.

Cathy managed a smile.

"But seriously, you don't need to go back so soon. Stay here, I can buy clothes for you."

"Oh, no that's-"

"My house is large, Cathy, you can sleep in the spare room for as long as you need it—without concern of being disturbed." He smiled. "Don't worry, I'm a gentleman." He drank another mouthful of wine. "Unlike Heath."

"I wasn't suggesting that-"

Ed laughed. "I know, don't worry. It would be crass of me to make moves on a woman when she is so upset, easy, but crass."

"Well, it is late," she said glancing at her watch. "Really late!" she said with surprise. "I can't believe it's nearly ten o'clock!"

"Time flies when you're having fun," Ed replied.

She wanted to say that the past day had hardly been fun, but she knew what he meant—their time together had flown by. She had found him to be a good listener and his knowledge about the Hall, Heath, and her aunt fascinating. And the longer she sat talking with him, sipping wine, the less she remembered, the pain easing.

"It does," she replied. "And I do feel bad about asking you to take me back to the Hall at this hour-"

"Then I insist that you stay."

After another glass of wine, Ed walked her to the bedroom where she sank into a deep sleep, thankful of the oblivion.

Ed was a good host, and she grew oblivious to the fact that every mention of leaving, even going to the shops to buy food for a meal, was expertly deflected until she no longer even thought about leaving the house. He was true to his word and not once had she caught him outside her door or made an excuse to visit her room. He had been the perfect gentleman, apart from the times when she'd strayed to the front door, and then he'd seemed annoyed, but the annoyance had quickly slipped from his face as he'd led her to the kitchen or the living room or the garden, suggesting they play cards, or prepare the evening meal together with a glass of wine. Over the days, her heartache faded along with her memories of Heath, the Hall, and her friends.

One night became two, then two a week, and the longer Cathy stayed the less she thought about Heath or the Hall or her friends. Eventually, she didn't think about the Hall from one day to the next and Heath's face was a blurred and fading memory. She spent her days reading and wandering around Ed's large garden.

As the flowers in the garden faded and the trees began to drop their leaves, the skies grew dark and heavy, and a chill invaded the house. As with her mind, Cathy succumbed to a weakness of body. She no longer left her room, spending her days in silence, going through the motions of washing and dressing without thought, wearing the clothes Ed gave her without question or complaint, eating the food he prepared without comment. He visited her daily and would brush her hair, then lay beside her and whisper about the days they would spend together, how she would be his bride forever.

As the first frost of winter spread its glittering breath across her bedroom window she lay as a shadow and something tugged at her memory, bringing her conscious mind back for a fleeting moment. She lay in bed unmoving. The bedside clock ticked and as its hands moved towards three am she heard the noise that had been haunting her dreams and behind it a voice ringing with pain. 'Cathy!' it called. 'Cathy! Come home.'

A name wafted at the edge of her memory, a face tugged at her thoughts. She struggled to remember. It was as though the name was on the tip of her tongue, just out of reach.

For several moments her thoughts became lucid. "Heath," she whispered but the memory was quickly followed by a galloping pain that pummelled her chest with its hooves and she sank back into oblivion.

'Cathy!' the man's voice called from within her darkness.

'Cathy!' a girl's voice called.

Cutting through the fog, the girl's voice was clear. "Fion!" Cathy whispered, her eyes opening. "Fion?" she searched the room, the voice had been so clear, so close.

"I'm here." The voice was followed by a tapping at the window and Cathy saw the figure of a girl floating.

"Fion!" she whispered in excitement. "It's you."

Stumbling from her bed, her legs barely strong enough to carry her, she walked to the window and placed her hands on the glass. The girl, Fion, placed her hand against Cathy's, their palms together but for the glass.

"It's you! It's really you."

"Leave this place. Return to Witherwood."

"I can't," Cathy replied. "Ed wants me to stay. He said we should be married."

"To be his bride, Cathy, is worse than death."

"He wants me here. Always. He said I should be his forever bride," Cathy replied.

"Yes, his forever bride. Forever and ever and ever."

The figure of the girl began to fade, and Cathy watched as she disappeared, thinning to nothing.

"Fion!" Cathy whispered, the cold making her shiver. "Fion!"

She's gone to the Ever After, Cathy. Come away, she's dead.

Sinking to the floor, unsure whether the vision of Fion had been real or a figment of her struggling mind, she pulled her knees to her chest and shivered, her fingertips tingling from contact with the frozen glass. Hadn't she come here in summer? Was it winter now? How could that be?

Pulling herself up, she rubbed at the misted glass and peered outside. The ground sparkled white with frost and leaves lay in darkened piles across the garden, the trees bare.

"Winter," she whispered.

As she struggled to collect her thoughts, trying to find the days that had become lost to her, nothing made sense and her memories were too vague to piece together. Legs trembling as her muscles began to burn with fatigue, she made her way to the dresser and the large mirror that sat above it. Staring back at her was a woman with a face she barely recognised. Hair hung around a gaunt face, her skin a waxy pallor. Dark circles sat beneath dull eyes and her lips were dry and cracked. A white nightdress of white cotton in an old-fashioned Victorian style with pin-tucked yoke and frilled collar, hung from her emaciated frame. At the corner of the mirror was a headdress of roses, dry, dusty, and faded with age. Beside it, hung from a peg on the wall, was an ivory silk dress with large and billowing sleeves, a fitted bodice, and full skirt. A memory returned of Ed speaking in low tones, his eyes holding a devilish glint, the magic within flickering like embers in a dying fire. 'You will be my forever bride, Mistress Earnshaw. Mine forever and ever and ever.'

The face staring back from the mirror opened its mouth as though to scream, but Cathy snapped her jaws shut, keeping the noise inside, the fog in her head clearing.

Memories returned. She had run from Witherwood, overwhelmed with the shame of being betrayed. Ed had found her on the road and taken her to his home. At first, he had been kind and understanding, and she had been lulled by his warmth and grown less concerned at her loss of freedom and oblivious to his neglect. Had he drugged her? Had he cast a spell against her?

She staggered against the chest of drawers, grabbing the edge to steady herself.

That he had cast a hex against her was the only explanation. How else would she not have noticed the passing of the seasons. Autumn was gone and the woman in the mirror was emaciated. "He's starving me to death!" she whispered in a moment of perfect clarity.

She glanced again at the window, remembering Fion's face as their eyes met through the glass. Whether she had been real or not, a figment of her imagination or a visitation from the Ever After, Cathy knew her presence was a call to wake from stupor, a call back to life.

Chapter Forty-Two

If Edgar Linton had cast a spell, it was broken and, despite her fatigue, she tried the door, surprised to find it unlocked. With morning light hours away, she stepped out into a dark corridor and began to make her way to the stairs. The house was large with a number of staircases. After several steps, she stopped to listen, searching the quiet of the house for signs of Edgar's presence. She had a fuzzy recollection of other people in the house and their faces were blurred to her, but she was certain of at least three other adults that formed Edgar's staff. With the house silent, she continued to make her way to the staircase. As she walked along the corridor, she heart a faint wailing. As she moved from one corridor and turned into another the murmur grew a little louder although still barely audible, like a breeze that brushes the skin with its warmth but is quickly gone.

Cathy felt the energy from the room before she reached the door. Like the noise it was barely sensed, riding an undercurrent, smothered by the waves of energy snaking their way along the staircase and slithering between her legs. She realised without understanding that the snaking energy was Ed's, and it filled the house with its presence. The smothered energy was coming from behind the door. Like the snaking energy it was something she had never experienced before but she knew, without hesitation, that she had to discover what it was.

The door opened into a moonlit bedroom with a four-poster bed, dressing table, and large wardrobe, intricately carved and inlaid with mother of pearl. It was not empty, and Cathy stood frozen, paralysed as she processed the scene. Sitting at the table was an emaciated woman, her arm raised, brush in hand, perpetually staring at her face in the mirror. Another woman lay in the bed, long and flaxen hair splayed across the pillows, the ties of a white bonnet tied in a bow beneath her chin. With bony arms crossed, sunken eyes closed, the embroidered covers were pulled beneath her armpits. Beside the window sat another woman. She wore her hair in braids, plaited in an elaborate style to the side. At her neck was a torc of twisted gold and a pair of brooches were pinned to the front of her shift-like dress. Before the wardrobe, one hand clutching the open door stood a fourth woman. Like the others, she was thin to the point of being skeletal. Her glossy black hair was dressed with ringlets either side of her face and she wore the full-length dress with short sleeves and high bodice of the late eighteenth century. Each woman remained perfectly still, caught in a moment of action. The energy in the room pulsed and the low wailing ran as an undercurrent through Cathy's senses.

Her first thought after the initial shock was that the women were mannequins but as she stood beside the woman at the dressing table, and looked at her in the mirror, Cathy noticed the same emaciated face that had reflected back at her earlier. The woman was real. She touched a gentle finger to her cheek, surprised at the softness of the skin and firmness of the flesh. A mannequin would have been cold and hard, a mould of plastic or even wax. The woman's skin was cold, but it was firm not hard. Cathy retracted her hand with a shiver. The skin was cold—too cold for life, but that the woman was real was beyond doubt. As she inspected each woman, another realisation grew—they were each from a different century. The woman at the table had jewellery and clothing that marked her out as from the Renaissance period, the woman in the bed from the medieval period, the jewellery of the woman in the chair, from the brooches and the torc around her neck looked as though she could be a Viking or Anglo-Saxon, and the woman standing in perpetuity at the wardrobe could have stepped out of a Jane Austen novel. All were young. All beautiful. All emaciated.

"Who are you?" Cathy whispered as she stood in front of the seated woman. The wailing intensified, wafting in woeful waves. Cathy took her ringed fingers in her own, watching her eyes. "Who are you?" she repeated. The woman's face made no movement, her eyes gave no hint that she had heard, yet the low and sorrowful wail continued. "They can't be real women, this ... they must be some sort of mannequin. Something made of modern materials would explain the texture of the flesh," she murmured, turning the evidence over in her mind.

Sure, but why would he order mannequins who look so emaciated?

It's what gives him a kick?

'A forever bride, Cathy. You will be a bride for ever and ever and ever.'

"Forever bride," she repeated then glanced at each of the women. "Is that what you are? His forever brides?" The wailing intensified and a gust of cold air brushed against Cathy's bare feet.

Replacing the cold hand of the woman to the arm of her chair, Cathy once again gazed into her eyes. They were glassy but retained their bright blue colour. Dust had settled on the lashes and a spider had woven its web between her head and the back of the seat. She brushed it off and picked up a lock of the white-blonde hair. It felt real. "But it could be real, even if she's not," Cathy whispered. Once again, Cathy took hold of the woman's hand, pushing down the revulsion she felt at the coldness of her flesh, and scrutinised it. If it were a fake, then the hands would tell her. She turned the hand palm up. Each fingertip was whorled with prints and a scar ran the length of the palm. "A defensive cut," she said. The wound on the woman's hand was healed. "So ... whatever happened to you, you lived," Cathy said. She turned the hand and considered the nails. Each was nicely shaped, but not perfect, and several had skin tags. "If it is a mannequin, would they have gone into such detail?" *Unlikely*, her inner voice said. Then she's real. "Okay, so if you're real, how do you look so alive?" *Magic, Cathy! Dark, dark magic.* Cathy considered the hands for a moment more, noticing more imperfections and another scar across the base of the thumb on the other hand. "So Edgar Linton is a psycho," she said then clamped her lips together as the words filled the room.

Fion's voice filled her mind. 'Leave, Cathy. Leave now or forever be his bride. Forever and ever and ever.'

"Fion!" Cathy whispered as the young girl's voice rose all around her. "Where are you?"

In the Ever After, Cathy. Come away.

Another shudder ran through her as she remembered his face and how he'd hinted at Heath's dark past. "Projection," she said. "What if it is Ed that has the dark past?"

You think? He's drugged you for the past months, nearly starved you to death, you've found a roomful of mummified women posed as though they're still alive and you're wondering if he's the dark one?

"Okay, I hear you," she replied to her thoughts. "Ed's a bad man!"

'Leave, Cathy,' Fion whispered in her mind. 'Run!'

Chapter Forty-Three

The bedroom door clicked shut behind her and Cathy made her way to the back of the house where she let herself out and crossed the garden to the woods.

Overhead, lightning brightened the sky and was quickly followed by the crash of thunder. Blown by an angry wind, the rain fell as sharp droplets. The leafless trees gave little relief, and her nightdress became sodden, clinging to her skin. Clouds blew across the moon, hiding its light, and the way grew dark.

Turn on the light, Cathy

The voice seemed to come from behind and she turned to see, but nothing stood in the dark spaces between the trees.

Read, Cathy. Read the pages. Turn on the light.

The voices nudged at her memories, and she remembered reading Aunt Hyldreth's grimoires, searching through the charms, spells, and hexes. She shivered as another gust of wind blew through the trees, chilling the nightgown's wet cloth. Her teeth chattered.

Think, Cathy. Remember. Turn on the light.

A book opened in her memory. 'Hyldrethe ownes thys booke' was written on the front page in dark brown ink whilst beneath it was the date '1726'. The pages turned as though by an invisible hand. 'A charme for a witches inner lyte' was written at the top of the page.

Read! Recite!

Holding out her palm, Cathy began to recite. No light appeared on her palm and, as she reached the end of the charm, she grew despondent. "It doesn't work!" she whispered, letting her hand fall to her side.

Believe! Recite!

"It doesn't work!" she said with more force.

Believe! Recite! The voice repeated.

Once again Cathy raised her palm and began to recite, this time forcing herself to believe in its power. As she reached the middle of the charm, a tiny pinprick of light appeared in her hand. Encouraged, she continued, the light growing with each word until an orb of soft yellow light hovered above her palm.

Behind her, a twig cracked as though snapped underfoot and she swung to scan the trees and the dark spaces between them. The light did little to illuminate the space and she quickly realised it would be of little help unless it could grow in size and intensity. "Grow," she whispered. "Grow." The light hovered and pulsed, but the intensity of its yellow light remained the same.

Beorhtnan

"Grow," she repeated ignoring the voice.

Beorhtnan, the voice repeated.

"Brighten," Cathy said. The light pulsed and grew a little brighter.

Beorhtnan

"Beorhtnan," she copied. The light began to glow, increasing in brightness as it pulsed. "Beorhtan," she repeated. The light grew bright, now the size of a football. The darkness retreated, the trees close to Cathy visible.

Deorcian, the voice whispered.

"Deorcian," Cathy repeated.

The light shrank and grew dim. "Hah!" she exclaimed. "Beorhtan," she said, afraid of how quickly the space around her had grown dark. Once again, the light brightened and grew to the size of a football.

Another flash of lightning was followed by a mighty clap of thunder and the wind whipped at Cathy, causing her to shudder, but the light from the ball gave off warmth and, with her path ahead illuminated, she made her way through the woodlands towards the Hall.

Time passed and despite her elation at escaping Edgar's house and discovering her ability to create witch-light, her energy began to fade, and she slowed, leaning up against a tree to rest.

"So, are you returning to Heath?"

Startled, Cathy swung to Edgar, the witch-light, thrown from her hand, extinguishing. The clouds had shifted from the moon and Edgar stood before her, lit by its silver light. Dark shadows hung about his face.

Rain trickled down Cathy's forehead, blurring her vision. She blinked it away, focusing on Ed. "Yes," she said, and sagged against the tree, her thoughts scattered.

"Then let me take you to him."

He spoke the words with such sincerity, and soothing tone of concern, that she allowed him to take her arm and lead her through the woods.

"I was worried for you, Cathy, when I found you gone," he said as they walked. "You only had to ask, and I would have driven you back to the Hall." Steel fingers gripped her elbow, and there was a tightness to his voice. "But, if my generosity is not sufficient, and you prefer to walk through the freezing rain as Thor roars above us, then I must apologise for being a poor host."

She stumbled forward as he continued to talk, supporting her as she staggered, her energy waning as rain turned to sleet. The cold seeped through to her bones. He tugged at her arm as she faltered. "Come along, then. Let us go to him."

Gone were the honey-like tones, replaced by words with a spiteful edge.

Time slipped and the trees passed in a blur as Cathy dipped below consciousness, Ed at her elbow, her feet trailing as though she were floating.

"Here." He released her elbow and she dropped to the floor. Ahead were yet more woodlands.

"You said you were taking me home," she said struggling to stand. "I want to go back to the Hall."

"I said I would bring you to him. Heath," Ed replied.

Cathy scanned the area but despite the moon's light could see nothing other than the darkness that filled the spaces between the trees. "He's not here," she complained. "Which way is the Hall?"

"Wait," Ed replied. "Good things come to those who wait, Mistress Earnshaw."

Still unsteady, Catherine swayed and once again Ed took her arm. A branch snapped underfoot within the darkness and a creature growled. The growling was followed by the sound of snaffling as though something was eating greedily. Cathy stiffened. "What is it?" she whispered. Ed brought a finger to his lips then waved a hand through the air. A pulse of energy pushed against Cathy and the space around them grew light, the darkness pushed back as though a spotlight had been turned on in the theatre. The scene that greeted her was one of horror. Sat on its haunches was a hair-covered creature. It resembled a large and muscular man, but its face was distorted, its jaw more wolf-like, its eyes amber. At its feet lay a half-eaten deer and, in its hands, it held a leg. Blood dripped from a mouth filled with fangs and sharp teeth.

Cathy took a step back.

"Do not worry. I cast a protective spell; it cannot see us."

"What is it?" Cathy whispered, her mind struggling to process the scene.

"It's a monster, Catherine."

"It's a ... it looks like a wolf!"

"And a man," Edgar replied.

"A werewolf? But they're just ... they don't exist."

"Ah, but now you know that they do. There is even a legend in these parts. Have you not heard of the Beast of the Wither Woods?"

"I've heard of it, but don't know-" She stopped as the creature turned towards them, casting large amber eyes their way. "It can see us!"

"Nay, but it can perhaps smell us."

Cathy yelped as the creature stood. At full height it towered even above Edgar and sniffed at the air as it approached. Cathy grew fearful and moved behind Linton. "Stop it!" she said.

Edgar chuckled. "But now that he is so close, do you not recognise him?"

The creature, growled and once again sniffed at the air, scrutinizing the space, standing only feet away from Cathy, before it returned to its kill.

"Recognise it? No."

Edgar laughed. "Then let me introduce you. Mistress Catherine Earnshaw, meet Lord Heath of the Wither Woods." His laugh turned to a cackle and then he pushed her forward.

As she stumbled in the dark the beast snapped its head to look.

Chapter Forty-Four

"Cathy!" Heath growled, the word passing roughly over his contorted vocal chords.

She stood before him, a quivering and dishevelled wreck. Emaciated and bedraggled, the sodden nightgown translucent against her body, outlining the slender curves, sticking to hipbones. "Cathy," he repeated, unsure if the vision were real or a spectre.

Linton's cackle broke the spell and the rage that whirled within him erupted as the man hovered in the shadows. Cathy screamed as Heath roared and bounded forward.

"You!" he raged, claws bared and ready to slice into Linton's chest, knocking Cathy aside as he launched himself at the fading figure. As he landed, claws sinking into the dark forest earth, the apparition disappeared.

Panting, he swung to Cathy, the need to rip and destroy savage. She lay sprawled on the ground. The urge to pounce and tear into her flesh, taste her blood as it trickled down his throat grew overwhelming. He roared, venting his rage, and dug his talons into the tree at his side, anchoring himself to the wood.

"Go!" he raged as she dragged herself from the floor. "Go!" he shouted, wrapping his free arm around the tree as he fought the primal urges that had ruled him since being cursed. As she staggered back, her nightgown smeared with dark forest earth, he willed the man that he had once been to dominate the beast. "Cathy!" he rasped. "Go! Go now before I lose all control."

"Heath?" she questioned and took a step towards him.

Her voice was weak, and his anger surged. That she had been abused since her disappearance was clear from the thinness of her body and the hollows beneath her eyes. "Linton," he growled. "Linton did this to you."

Cathy took a step closer, her hand outstretched. "Heath? Is it really you?"

The urge to capture her, to ravish and then devour her, waved through him.

"Go!" he roared.

She flinched.

"Run!" he growled. "Run for your life!" He followed his warning with a snarling roar.

She flinched but didn't turn to run and rage overwhelmed him, his free arm slicing through the air and catching at her nightdress, ripping the fabric. He dug his claws deeper into the bark. "Go now, Cathy. Before it is too late."

Overhead lightning brightened the sky as she turned to scramble away. Thunder quickly followed and the freezing rain blew against him, sinking beneath the hairs of his monstrous form and into his skin. He submitted to the pain as a man tied between posts and whipped. It was a punishment he had to endure, as was the curse. Mercurio cawed from the tree above then flapped his wings, his form illuminated by a flash of lightning as he launched from the branch and disappeared into the night.

Time passed slowly but as the darkness gave way to grey and the sun finally began to rise, he sagged against the tree, his form once more that of a man's. Exhausted and naked, he made his way back to the Hall and Cathy.

The door to his rooms swung open as he strode through.

"Your bath is ready, Lord," Argenon said as Heath passed him.

Ignoring the man, Heath strode to the window. "She was in the woods last night," he said, casting a glance across the trees. An early morning frost covered the garden.

"She? My Lord."

"Yes, Mistress Catherine."

"She's alive?"

"Yes. Linton had her, I am sure. She looked starved—barely alive. I will bathe and go to her."

"But she is not here, Lord. Ellette would have mentioned it, I am sure."

"Not here?" he swung to Argenon with a frown. "But she was in the woods. I ... I told her to run ... to save herself."

"You did not ... hurt her then?"

Heath shook his head. "No."

"Give thanks to the gods!"

"If she is not here, then she is still out there," he said returning to the window and looking out across the woodlands. In the distance dark clouds had begun to gather, a promise of more rain to come. Cathy's terror-filled face and emaciated frame, so clear to see through the thinness of her wet nightgown, rose in his memory. "Argenon, bring me my clothes. There is no time to bathe. Tell Tatwin to join me downstairs. Mistress Catherine is out there, and we must find her before she is lost to us forever."

"Yes, Lord."

Heath dressed with speed, pulling on his trousers seconds after they were handed to him. Downing the glass of stout that Argenon offered whilst counselling him. 'You always suffer more the closer we are to the full moon,' he had said. 'Drink. Replenish your energy.' He drank without question or complaint, recognising the truth. Becoming the beast stole more than just the night from him, but it was the days of the full moon when the curse overwhelmed him completely, and his reserves had been drained as he'd fought to retain control. Cold waved over him as he remembered Cathy's terror, the horror of his presence reflected in her eyes. He remembered his own terror that the beast would break the grip that anchored him to the tree and savage her as he had done the deer. The memory stalled him. She would loathe him. Reject him. Pain seared his chest as though an arrow had lodged in his heart, but he pushed it away, and reached for his boots, pulling them on with a firm tug. Cathy may reject him, but he would never be able to live with himself if she died out in the woodlands or up on the desolate moor. He had a second chance to protect her; he wasn't going to fail this time.

Within ten minutes, he had gathered a small group of helpers that included Tatwin and five of his children. Ellette had offered to help, but he had instructed her to stay behind with Argenon. She was to prepare Mistress Cathy's room, light a fire in the hearth, make sure there was enough hot water for a warm bath, and hot broth for sustenance. The children that remained were to perform a Sprinkling and reinforce the magic that surrounded the Hall to secure it from the depredations of Edgar Linton.

"Mercurio," he shouted to the bird perched high in the branches of the oak that straddled the garden from beyond the wall, "Fly high. Search the moorlands to the west, then return to search above the woodlands." The bird cawed and immediately launched from its perch, its wings black and unreflective in the grey light. He watched the bird soar, heading out towards the moorlands and the storm-burdened sky.

Thunder rumbled in the distance as Heath set off down the path to the woodlands. Ahead of him, Tatwin's sons ran to the gate opening it with solemn faces to allow Heath through. He sensed their excitement though, he felt it too. He was apprehensive at what he might find at the end of his journey but behind it there was the lurking hope that Cathy was alive and that she would accept him still.

Fool! Don't waste your thoughts. It is impossible that she would want you. She has seen you for what you are: a monster!

He pushed the biting thoughts away and focused on scouring the woodlands, ordering the children to spread out in a westerly direction. How close she had come to death last night was not something Heath wanted to dwell on. One more second of her questioning, pleading eyes would have been too much for him to take and the Beast would have overcome his resistance to its will.

Monster!

Wind buffeted his side as he continued into the woods and found the tree scored by the beast's talons. Scuff marks were evident in the ground where she had fallen – *you pushed her* – and he stepped over them to follow her path. Evidence of her flight was clear in the broken fronds of ferns and flattened grasses. He followed the trail, at one point losing it, but then picking it back up when he found a strand of white fibre snagged on a thorn. He imagined her running blindly through the forest, her way lit only by fleeting moonlight quickly covered by the shifting rain-filled clouds and grimaced. The thorns were long and sharp, spiteful to soft flesh, her gown no protection against them.

The morning passed and the darkened clouds shifted from the moorland to spread over the woodlands and the place became dingey, relief coming only when lightning shattered the sky overhead. As the wind began to whip the trees, the rain began, blown against his face in sharp and freezing spikes. He shivered, regretting leaving the Hall without more protective clothing, and continued to the edge of the woodlands. As he stepped beyond the treeline to the open space Mercurio cawed above before swooping down. Heath held out an arm for the bird to land.

"Tell me!" he said.

"I have found her, Lord."

"Show me!" he barked, throwing his arm out to force the bird back into the air. Mercurio cawed but soared back into the sky. Heath followed, running over uneven ground to keep up. When the bird swooped down and circled, he stalled, steeling himself against the worst. A hard lump formed in his throat as he strode forward, heart hammering against his ribs.

"She's here," Mercurio cawed. "Here. Here. Here."

Her figure was hidden by a rocky outcrop, and Heath scrambled the last few feet then stumbled to a stop. She lay slumped to the side, her arm still hooked over her knees as though curling up against the weather. Wet hair lay plastered over her face. Heath dropped to a crouch, pushing hair away from her eyes, mouth, and nose. Her skin held a bluish tinge, her lips dark at the edges. "Cathy!" he called. "Cathy! Wake up." Slipping one arm beneath her, he pressed his head against her chest and listened. Beneath him, he felt the faint beat of her heart.

"Is she alive? Is she? Is she?" the bird cawed.

"Yes!" Heath grunted as he scooped her into his arms. She lay across them like a broken doll, unresponsive and cold.

"Fetch Tatwin. Tell his children to run to the Hall and tell their mother to prepare the warming pans. Tell her." He choked. "Tell her I'm bringing their mistress home."

Without question, the bird flew back towards the woodlands leaving Heath to carry Cathy home. Cold in his arms, he could feel the thinness of her body beneath the wet cloth. "What did he do to you, Cathy?" He stopped for a moment, glanced down at her waxen face, hugged her close and whispered. "Don't leave me, Cathy. Please, don't leave me ever again."

Chapter Forty-Five

Cathy woke to whispered chatter and a dozen faces peering down at her.

"Ma! She's awake," one of the elf-like daughters of Ellette and Tatwin called.

The children parted and Ellette appeared, her concerned frown giving way to a smile as she gazed down at Cathy. "You're awake, Mistress," she said. "Bring me a glass of ale, Thora." The child closest to Cathy stroked her hair as her sister turned into the room. She reappeared after a moment with a glass half-filled with an amber coloured liquid.

"Drink," insisted Ellette placing a hand beneath Cathy's shoulders and helping her to sit.

Thora held the glass to Cathy's lips. The liquid was sweet and trickled down Cathy's throat with ease, spreading warmth as it made its way to her stomach. "Again," Ellette said whilst nodding her head. Again the glass was tipped to Cathy's lips, and she swallowed more of the liquid then lay back against the pillows. The 'ale' warmed her, spreading through her body until even her toes and fingertips felt its heat as a glow.

The children gathered back around the bed and Cathy felt a tiny hand clasp her own. Too tired to move, she lay in silence as they whispered to one another, stroking her hair, singing undulating and softly voiced songs, until she drifted back into sleep, unsure of what was reality and what was a dream.

Her dreams were difficult, filled with darkness and the worming roots of trees, flashes of Ed's face with its cynical smile, his eyes gloating at her pain, and something within the woods that remained hidden but tracked her as she ran.

She woke with a start to the same room, panicked that she would be back in the bedroom where she had lain for days that had become weeks, the nights blurring with the days, but she was in her own room at the Hall.

"'Tis me, Mistress Earnshaw," the child at her side said as she glanced about the room. "Mother bade me sit with you, until you woke."

"Thora?" she asked the blonde elvish child, remembering the girl who had given her the sweet drink.

"Nay, Mistress," she replied with a smile. "I am Inga," she said tapping her chest.

"How long have I been here?" Cathy asked, memories of drifting in and out of consciousness stirring.

"Three nights," she replied.

"Three nights," Cathy repeated then closed her eyes, already fatigued with the effort of speaking.

"I have ale for you. Mother said to offer it should you wake." She lifted a glass with golden particles swirling in the amber liquid. Cathy sipped it gladly, enjoying the warmth. "It is bringing you back to life," the girl said. "Mother made it with water from the spring."

"It's delicious," Cathy said enjoying the sensation of being caressed from within.

"It is working. The colour is coming back into your cheeks and your eyes are bright."

"They are?" Cathy asked, remembering the gaunt woman that had stared back at her with dull eyes before she had fled Edgar Linton's house.

"Yes. Master Heath came in to look on you earlier and he smiled when he looked down upon you. He thanked us for nursing you back to life."

Heath. The mention of his name made her heart beat a little faster. "He was here?"

"Every day. He sat with you day and night at first until Modor scolded him and told him to get some rest."

"He did?" Memories of Heath were confused and contradictory. She wanted to see him again but there was fear there too and pain, a pain deep in her heart.

"Yes," the girl nodded with enthusiasm. "I think he loves you," she whispered conspiratorially.

Cathy pulled herself up to sit, letting out a small groan as each muscle in her body ached. Images of Heath swam before her as she swung her legs over the side of the bed. Heath with Naomi in the woods, smiling at her. Heath barely recognisable snarling at her, one hand locked around a tree, screaming at her to run. Heath staring down at her, smiling as she gazed up at him, stroking her cheek and mouthing words she barely heard as she sank back into sleep. He had been here, she remembered him.

Nothing made sense.

"Inga, please help me to dress."

"I will run you a bath," the child replied.

It took time to bathe and dress and, alerted by Inga, Ellette arrived with a small bowl of soup, standing guard beside Cathy as she ate it, encouraging her to clean the bowl. Only when it was empty was she allowed to walk down the stairs and placed in a chair beside the fire in Aunt Hyldreth's room.

Exhausted, and frustrated at how little she could do, Cathy sat beside the fire, leafing through her aunt's softly bound and smallest grimoire, returning again and again to the page with the charm she had used to create witch light. It was exactly as she remembered it, even down to the small mistake corrected at the end of one line. Marvelling that she had recalled it so precisely, she continued to read, too tired to do anything else. As she read through the grimoire, her tiredness forgotten, she lost herself to the spells, hexes, and charms within its pages. Despite its size, it was packed with spells including fascinating notes on provenance, date that it had been scribed, and what other spells could be used in its place. One entry fascinated Cathy in particular, a spell to subdue a shadow walker. Written beside it in a smaller hand was a note that it had been used and found to be effective. The note was dated 1947. On another page was a spell framed in black ink and carrying a warning of mortal destruction. It carried the title, 'To slyppe to the Aether'.

"To slip into the aether," Cathy whispered and read through the spell. As she finished, a soft knock came at the door and then it was pushed open, and Heath peered into the room.

"May I come in?" he asked.

His gentle, uncertain, tone surprised Cathy. "Of course," she managed, scrutinising his face, remembering the dreams that had plagued her, dreams where Heath had morphed from a man to a beast. Images of a wolf-like creature sitting on its haunches ripping at the belly of a deer, steam rising in the frigid air, flashed in her memory.

Heath hesitated. "Are you sure?" he asked.

"Yes," she replied, pushing away the image. "I've been having ... difficult dreams and my head ... sometimes I can't tell if I'm awake or still asleep."

He took slow steps towards her then sat at the opposite end of the velvet sofa, perched on its edge. "It is good to see you looking so well," he said.

"I'm feeling a little better," she replied, beginning to feel self-conscious at the intensity of his gaze.

"Sorry," he said. "I didn't mean to stare. It's just that you were so ... I wasn't sure that you would regain your health."

"Ellette and the children have taken good care of me and ... Inga told me that you ... helped."

"Yes! I couldn't leave your side. For two days and two nights, I watched over you. I ..." The tumble of words came to a stop. "Forgive me ... we were worried for you."

They sat in an awkward silence until he said, "Cathy, what do you remember of the past months?"

"It's blurred. I remember running from the Hall and Ed finding me in the lane." A shudder ran through her as the faces of the mannequin brides returned to her memory. "Oh! Oh, Heath! He ... he ... he is a monster!"

For the next minutes she described what she had discovered at Edgar Linton's house. How she had woken as though from a drugged sleep, realised she was being starved and had no real will of her own, and how she had followed the wailing moans and discovered the women. "At first, I thought they were mannequins, but they were too perfect, or rather, they were too imperfect. No doll-maker, no matter how skilled could recreate them." As she described each woman Heath's brow creased and a darkness fell across his face, his jaw clenching.

"He will pay for this!" he seethed.

"It was horrifying, Heath and ... and I think that is what he had planned for me!"

She watched as he sat lost in his thoughts, his hands clenching and unclenching. "Do you know who they are?" she asked.

He nodded. "I do. I was betrothed to each of those women. Edgar Linton stole them away from me, just as he stole you."

"Stole me?"

"Catherine, on the night before the wedding, we held a party for your friends. Do you remember?"

"A little. But things have been so strange that I'm struggling to tell what is real."

He nodded. "On that night, Linton bewitched you. He made you believe that you saw me with your friend in the woods. It is what you accused me of before you fled from the Hall."

"I did!" she said as the memory revealed itself. Pain once again seared her chest. "You were with Naomi ... against the tree. You smiled at me as you ..."

"But it wasn't me, Catherine. It was Linton."

"But why? Why would he do that?"

"He is jealous."

"But that's insane."

"I think he is insane. The centuries have twisted him, and now he cannot bear to see me happy."

"I don't understand. Why would he do that?"

Heath looked across her shoulder to the window. "My first bride ... she had refused Linton's offer of marriage. When she accepted mine, he became enraged and swore vengeance against me. He accused me of stealing her from him and wouldn't accept that she had accepted me of her own free will."

"And did you marry her?"

Heath shook his head. "No, she disappeared the night before our wedding. Her name was Agata, a great beauty, the daughter of a great man. I think being rejected by her drove Linton to the edge, that and dabbling in dark magic."

"I noticed that he could cast spells. Is he a wizard?"

Heath shook his head. "No, he is a sorcerer. His powers run deep, but they are tainted."

With her thoughts still foggy, Cathy leant back against the sofa. "So, you didn't cheat on me?"

Heath leant forward, taking Cathy's hand between his own. "No," he replied, locking his eyes to hers. "That is the last thing I would do." Tears glistened in his eyes as he lifted her hand and kissed it.

Chapter Forty-Six

Cathy's recovery was slow, and the first blossom of spring drifted on the wind before she felt able to take on her full duties once more. Fearful of another bout of rule breaking by a rogue vampire, she checked on them each morning. So far there had been no sign of a repeat offence and she had come to the conclusion that poor Fion, struggling with her fate, and lonely too, had sought new friends among the girls she had attacked.

One of the projects she had been keen to complete was collecting the histories of the vampires and she had laid a hand upon each box, experiencing its energy, and seeing each story. None of the vampires had been taken since the end of the nineteenth century and only one of them was female which Cathy believed meant the teenage Fion was unlikely to have shared much in common with them. Fion often appeared in her dreams, walking beside her, running ahead, playing with the golden mist rising across the gardens, and it soothed Cathy's soul to believe that she had passed to the Ever After and not descended to the underworld of Hel or become trapped in some purgatorial plane between the aether.

As she recovered, Cathy began to help out around the farm, feeding the chickens and collecting their eggs, and hand feeding the lambs that had been rejected by their mothers. That morning she had stopped by the pigsty to check on one of the sows who was about to give birth and was stood watching ten greedy piglets suckling at their mother's teats when Heath stepped beside her.

"They're full of health this year," he said. "Mudlark has just birthed seven."

"Seven! She barely looked pregnant," Cathy exclaimed remembering the young sow named after her favourite pastime, wallowing in the mud.

"Aye, sometimes the sows do that," chipped in Aelfgar, one of Tatwin and Ellette's many sons, with authority, "especially when it is their first litter."

"You'll make a good swineherd, Young Tatwin," Heath replied then ruffled the boy's hair.

The boy grinned, pleased with the praise.

"So when are you marrying Mistress Catherine then?" he asked with a glint in his eyes. "Modor says you should do it this spring as spring is the best time to bring forth fruit."

Heath clipped the back of the boy's head with a soft tap and Cathy caught his self-conscious glance. She laughed as the boy giggled, covering his mouth with his hand.

"That tongue will get you into trouble!" Heath said. "Be off, before I cuff you again."

The boy darted away, dodging Heath's swooping hand, and disappeared around the corner.

"Ignore the mischievous imp, Cathy. He has the cheek of Loki."

Cathy laughed, as she felt the heat of a flush on her cheeks. "He's not wrong though," she said without making eye contact.

Heath turned to her, his surprise undisguised. "True," he agreed. Several moments passed as she felt his eyes upon her. She stared out over the suckling piglets. "So ..." he continued, "shall we ... wed, this spring?"

Cathy's heart fluttered. "Yes," she said whilst looking at her boots. "I'd like that."

Taking a step closer, and with a finger hooked beneath her chin, Heath tilted her head upwards. "Catherine?"

She met his eyes then closed hers and waited for his kiss.

It was soft, warm, and filled with the promise of passion.

THE HANDFASTING TOOK place the following week beside the sacred waters where Heath and Cathy exchanged vows of loyalty and life-long companionship as the golden mist undulated around their feet.

Heath knelt beside Cathy as the priest tied the cord around their joined hands. Argenon and the Hall staff stood behind whilst Mercurio watched with beady eyes from the hedgerow, cawing as Heath bent to kiss Cathy's lips. They were warm and soft, and he had to bite down the urge to scoop her into his arms and carry her off to his bed. Instead, he turned to the gathered crowd and accepted their congratulations, laughing as blossom collected that morning was thrown ahead of them as they made their way to the terrace where a table laden with meats, fruit, cheese, and bread waited.

The children chattered as they sat to the breakfast, filling their glasses with fresh juice, and helping themselves to fruit and cheese. The atmosphere was easy, and despite the undercurrent of need to be alone with Cathy, Heath felt relaxed. More than once he caught one of the children staring at Cathy or him then whispering among themselves and giggling into their hands. He felt no annoyance at being the object of their gossip and when Argenon raised a champagne filled glass to toast them both, Heath realised that the odd sensation he was experiencing, was happiness. Heath raised his glass with a broad smile then chinked it with Catherine's. Her smile, when their eyes met, caused him to swallow and his heart to flip and it was with a sense of rising dread that he realised, despite his efforts, she had crept into his heart. He raised the glass to his lips with a slight tremble in his hand and swallowed. The remainder of the breakfast passed in a blur of chatter, a speech of congratulations and hopes for conjugal bliss from Argenon, and the giving of gifts from Ellette and her children.

After drinking his last mouthful of champagne and, with the children running off to play in the garden, he thanked them for attending then took Cathy by the hand. Mercurio cawed from an ivy-covered arbour. Leading her from the breakfast table, he clasped her hand, and walked with her to the bridal chamber, heart beating hard.

Once inside, he lifted her into his arms and carried her to the bed.

Chapter Forty-Seven

Nine months later

Cathy arched her back, easing the ache from the heaviness of her belly, then closed the cellar door behind, her satisfied that the inhabitants continued to abide by the rules. She had begun to leave notes pinned to the top of individual caskets asking if there was anything that they required. The Will had stated that she was responsible for 'care and control' of the colony which she took as extending to their welfare as well as keeping them under control. Heath had found her efforts to engage with them amusing, but she had grown fascinated by the characters and secretly hoped to be able to meet them face to face one day. He'd grown dark then, refusing to entertain the idea, sure that it was far too dangerous for a woman in her 'condition'.

Since the pregnancy had been confirmed, Heath had become attentive to her needs but overly protective. No longer was she to ride with him in the mornings to check the herds and flocks, nor dig the vegetables from the garden, or take on heavy cleaning duties. When she had complained, he had looked hurt but insisted that nothing could get in the way of a healthy child being born. She'd relented in his presence but carried on as normal otherwise. More wonderfully, at least in the early days of their marriage, was that he seemed to want her. But as the pregnancy developed and her belly grew large, he became distant and the defensive and brusque man she had first met had returned. She secretly believed that he found her pregnant body unattractive and yearned for the birth and a return of the passionate man she had grown to love.

After locking the door to the west wing, she decided to take a walk in the woods to stretch out her legs and ease the ache in her back. During the pregnancy she had taken to walking before twilight, enjoying watching the changing colours of the sky. Today she felt drawn to return to the tree where she had discovered the staples and chains.

Frost trimmed the edges of fallen leaves and her breath billowed as white clouds as the gate clacked behind her and she stepped out of the garden and into the woods.

As she walked her progress grew slow and the pain in her back became deep and troubling. She stopped several times to catch her breath, the effort at walking whilst in pain becoming too much, but it wasn't until she reached the tree and a band of pain tightened across her belly that she realised she was in labour.

"It's coming," she said in wonder as the tightness eased. Looking back through the trees, she realised how far she had walked and berated herself for not realising the ache in her back that morning had been the first signs of the baby's impending birth.

With the pain gone, she turned her attention back to the tree, and the scratches she had discovered gouged down to the flesh beneath the bark. Once again, she splayed her fingers and covered each scratch with her own. The echo of the beast's energy surged, and she flinched at its rage, pulling her fingers away before replacing them back into the gouges. She closed her eyes, sensing the creature's pain. Another contraction began, the pain radiating out from her lower back but quickly enveloping her front as her belly tightened and became hard. She gasped at her own pain as it melded with the beasts. Heath's pain.

Since their marriage, she had not spent one night with Heath. During the honeymoon period they had spent hours together in bed, but he would always make his excuses and leave before twilight. Her memories of the time she had been kept prisoner at Ed's house were blurred and the escape from him, and being found, even more disjointed and mingled with dreams and nightmares. Discerning what was a memory and what imagination had become impossible and she had turned away from trying to decipher them and put her energies into getting back to health and then being Keeper of the Hall and Heath's wife. As the birth loomed, the dreams had returned, and she was back in the forest, emaciated and wet, dressed only in a thin nightgown, reaching out to a creature that hung in the shadows and wrapped its arm around a tree as though to anchor itself there. In her dreams she had yearned for it to step out of the shadows and wrap its arms around her.

"It was you," she whispered. "You are the beast."

"Catherine."

Startled, she opened her eyes and stared into Edgar Linton's just as another contraction hit.

"Stay away from me!" she gasped as the pain rode her.

"Why Catherine! What way is that to greet an old lover."

"Lover! We were never lovers. You imprisoned me!"

Ed laughed. "You were always free to leave."

"Liar!"

"Was the door locked when you left?" he asked.

"No ... but ... but you drugged me."

"Ah, I see."

"So rather than admit that you wanted to be with me and cheat on your fiancé you have concocted a story where you are the victim. Did you not enjoy our nights together?"

Cathy shook her head. "There were no nights together. We never ..." Cathy grew confused. She had no recollection of being with Ed other than the meals and walks they shared.

"Didn't we?" he asked with an arch of his brow and a gesture to her pregnant belly. "I see that you are carrying my child."

"No!" She grasped a length of chain, squeezing her hand around it as another contraction hit. Ed waited, the smirk on his face gloating. "This is Heath's baby. Not yours."

"No," he replied. "It's mine."

"Linton!" Birds launched from branches as Heath roared. "Linton! Move away from my wife."

"Certainly," Linton said without any hint of concern and took a step back.

As Heath reached Cathy's side he glanced at the chain in Cathy's hand.

"What have you done!" he snarled at Ed.

Raising his hands as though in surrender, he replied. "Nothing. I was merely taking a walk when I came across

Catherine. She appeared to be in pain. I asked if she required assistance. Nothing more."

"Liar," Heath hissed.

"No more so than you," he replied.

"Leave us, Linton."

"Ah, but there you see, I have come to collect what is mine," he said gesturing to Cathy.

"He thinks the baby is his, Heath. But it's not. I swear. It's yours," she said through gritted teeth. "You're the father."

"Of course I am the father," Heath snapped.

Ed chuckled.

"I know that he stole your other brides, but he didn't steal me. He never touched me. He didn't!" Cathy said.

"I know," Heath replied.

Cathy turned to Linton as another contraction began to radiate its pain across her lower back. "You've ruined everything for Heath in the past, but not this time. We're happy. I love him and not you. You stole his brides before, but not this time. We're married, Ed, and there's nothing you can do about it. Your jealousy won't destroy our happiness."

Linton raised a brow and locked eyes with Heath. "Is that what you told her?" he scoffed. "That I took your brides because I was jealous?" His tone was scathing. "Jealous?" he shouted. "No! I shall not let you lie. I took your brides to stop you breaking the curse."

"The curse that you laid upon me!" Heath spat back.

"Yes, and the curse that I wanted you to suffer for eternity."

"So it was you who cursed him to become a beast!" said Cathy then turned to the tree, overcome with pain at the intensity of the contraction.

"Yes," he said with a smirk. "And a beast he shall remain."

"But curses can be broken," Cathy stated, "and I shall find out how to break it. And then he will be free."

"He already knows," Linton said with a scathing glance to Heath. "Don't you."

Heath's jaw clenched and he remained silent.

"Heath?" Cathy questioned. "If you know, then we can break the curse."

Linton laughed. "Tell her Lord Heath of the Wither Woods."

"Heath?"

"Ask him why he was so keen to marry you."

Heath threw a scowl to Linton but avoided meeting Cathy's gaze.

"Go on then! Tell her!" Linton demanded.

When Heath remained silent, Linton said, "Very well, I shall tell her. The curse can only be broken if the first-born child of Lord Heath of the Wither Woods is forfeited to me."

Cathy clutched her stomach. "Heath! What is he saying?"

"What I am saying," continued Linton, "is that the child growing in your belly belongs to me—if the Lord is to be free of his curse."

"Heath! This can't be true."

Heath met her questioning gaze but quickly broke it.

It was true! Cathy sagged against the trunk. "Aunt Hyldreth's will," she said, the meaning of its words becoming clear. "That's why I could only have the house if I married you and gave you a child."

Linton leered at Heath. "Very clever, old friend. You dangled the carrot of the Hall and all its riches, in exchange for the fruit of her womb."

Cathy stared at Heath. He refused to meet her gaze. "The Codicil stated that I had to marry you and give you a child. Give!" she spat.

"And you agreed to the terms, Mistress Earnshaw," Linton said. "Didn't you."

The memories of her meeting with Heath and Argenon where he had asked her if she accepted the terms of the Will returned. Argenon had explained it to her. 'In short,' he had said as Heath watched her closely, 'you shall inherit the house if you agree to marriage to Lord Heath of the Wither Woods and give him the child.' The room had grown silent, and Cathy had realised that marrying Heath would be her last chance to have a child. Heath, she had reasoned, was a handsome man, and the child would inherit the Hall. 'Do you agree to the marriage and the gift of a child?' Argenon had pushed. 'Yes, I agree,' she had replied.

"Yes ... I agreed. But ..." she turned to Heath. "You can't let this happen! I didn't realise what the Will meant."

"And yet you agreed to the terms, witch," Linton spat with contempt.

"Heath! We can't give our child away. We can't!"

"It is the only way," said Linton.

Heath pulled back from Cathy, his face thunderous. Mercurio fluttered down from a branch and landed on his shoulder. "It's the only way to settle the debt."

"Debt? What debt?"

"I ... I killed his first born," Heath explained. "He demands retribution."

"He has to fulfil that demand. It is a matter of honour," Mercurio cawed.

"But the curse is retribution," Cathy gasped, riding the pain. "Isn't the curse enough?"

Linton glowered. "No curse could ever avenge the death of my child. Only the sacrifice of his child can appease the gods and bring me satisfaction. Blood for blood."

"Sacrifice!" Cathy gasped, clasping an arm around her belly. "No! You will never take this child from me."

"Then you condemn Lord Heath to live as the beast in perpetuity and prolong my own agony. You are selfish and wicked, Mistress Earnshaw," Linton hissed. "Selfish and wicked. You are a woman who would sell her child in exchange for riches. You do not deserve the child."

With the first urge to push overwhelming her, Cathy sank to her knees and began to sob. Linton's words seared her. She had sold her child!

You were tricked!

Cathy groaned as the urge to push increased, willing her body to stop. "You will not have this child," she growled. "Never!" As the contraction eased, and using the tree beside her, she pulled herself up to stand and then staggered away from the men, running despite the pain, reciting the spell she had discovered in Aunt Hyldreth's smallest grimoire. A spell framed in black and that carried a warning of mortal destruction. The page grew clear in her mind. At the top it carried the title, 'To slyppe to the Aether'.

"Leave her!" Heath roared from behind as she stumbled between the trees.

As she ran, reciting the charm to enter the aether, the forest around her began to close in and the noise of the men's fighting faded. Bright light blinded her, and she slowed to a stop, no longer able to see. In the distance a figure stood in silhouette and began to walk towards her, energy rising from its outline like heat rising from the road. Below her the forest floor had disappeared and she was floating.

The pain in her belly had eased and the sounds of the forest, of Heath and Linton, were gone. The figure continued towards her and then stopped, allowing the hood of its cloak to fall to its shoulders.

"Fion!" she said. "You are here!"

The girl raised her arm and pointed. "You must return, Cathy."

"But I can't. They want to take my baby."

"You must return. Staying will be a mortal death for you and your child. It is the path to Hel for you."

"I have to save my child."

"Return Cathy, or you curse your child to live within the aether motherless. Save yourself, Cathy. Go home."

Chapter Forty-Eight

Heath ran through the trees, searching for Cathy. She had disappeared as though scooped up by an invisible hand.

"Cathy!" he shouted. "Cathy!" A groan from ahead caused him to stop and listen then follow the noise. "Cathy!" he whispered as he caught sight of her crouched beneath the oak with its scored trunk. He removed his jacket and placed it beneath her head.

"What can I do?" he asked as another contraction took hold, her face held in a grimace.

"Fetch Ellette," she hissed.

"But I can't leave you!"

"I don't want you here. Fetch Ellette."

Taking a step back, scorched by her words, he turned to run back to the house, returning with Ellette.

"Help her," he said as Cathy growled.

"I will, Lord. I have much experience. She is safe with me," the tiny woman said then shooed him away with her hand.

Hanging back among the trees, Heath felt helpless as Cathy laboured. Listening to her cries of pain as his child passed out of her body was a torment but the look of hate she had thrown him seared his soul. He sagged against a trunk, his head turned away from the scene as he listened to her labour until the child's cry pierced the forest air.

Mercurio cawed, and launched himself from a nearby tree, landing beside Heath. "It is here, Lord! We are saved."

Ignoring the bird, Heath stepped to Cathy. The child lay bloodied in Cathy's arms as Ellette covered her legs with a towel. She passed him a blanket. "For the child," she said and gestured to Cathy.

He sank to his knees beside Cathy, placing the blanket across the naked child. "It's a boy," she said.

Ellette turned her attention to the child. "Let me wrap him in the blanket, Mistress," she said then took the child, snipped and tied the cord, and wrapped it in a neat swaddle.

"A boy," said Linton stepping beneath the oak's bowers. "May I be the first to congratulate the happy couple," Linton smirked.

"Leave us!" barked Heath.

Linton snorted. "Ah, but you should be overjoyed, for here is the end of your torment." He turned to Ellette. "The child," he said, "pass it to me."

Ellette held the child a little closer to her chest. "Nay!" she replied.

"The child belongs to me, woman," Linton insisted. "Pass it to me."

"Master?" she asked with a frown. "Say it isn't true."

"It is true, Ellette," Cathy said, her voice barely above a whisper as she lay exhausted against the tree. "I gave away the rights to my child when I agreed to marry Heath."

"But it cannot be allowed," Ellette said backing away from Linton's outstretched arms.

"She was tricked into it," Heath replied. "But it is the only way the curse can be broken."

Ellette looked with pity at the child and Mercurio flew down from the branch to the forest floor. "Give it to Linton," he cawed. "The curse must be broken."

"Linton is the curse," Cathy whispered, a tear slipping over her lashes. She began to speak quietly in an ancient tongue, her words disappearing beneath the baby's cries.

"Mistress? What shall I do?"

"Give the child to your mistress, Ellette," answered Linton. "I am not so cruel as to deny her a final goodbye."

Ellette held the child a little closer.

"Pass the child to Cathy," Heath said.

"How can you be so cruel?" she gasped. "To carry a child and lose it …" her voice broke with emotion. "Lord, there must be another way!"

Heath took the child from Ellette, hardening his heart against her, pushing away thoughts of Cathy.

"Give it to Linton, sire," Mercurio encouraged. "This will be our last day to suffer this curse." The bird hopped excitedly. "Centuries have we suffered."

"There is greater suffering," Heath said with a glance to Cathy. She lay with her eyes closed, her head turned away, but tears ran down her cheeks. She seemed to be muttering beneath her breath, her mind finally breaking.

With the baby held in his arms, Heath faced Linton.

Linton withdrew a knife from a sheath held at his waist. His eyes glinted, his smile gloating as his locked with Heath's.

"Edgar Linton," Heath began, "you demand justice for the death of your son. You have taken revenge against me, his killer, by cursing me to live as a beast and demanding a sacrifice. Now I seek release from that curse. Do you offer me that?"

A cruel smile spread across Linton's face as he glanced from Heath to the baby. "I do."

"Then, I offer a sacrifice."

Ellette gasped and Cathy heaved a sob.

"Take the child." Heath swung from Linton and placed the baby in Ellette's arms then turned to face his enemy. "I offer myself for sacrifice to appease the cruel gods of your dark heart."

Linton's eyes narrowed.

Ellette crouched beside Cathy and placed the child in her arms.

"Sire! You cannot do this," Mercurio said.

"It is the only thing I can do, old friend," replied Heath. "You shall be free of the curse, as shall I."

"But ... the child, the child is to be the sacrifice."

"My son ... is innocent, as is Catherine, and neither should carry the burden of my crime." Heath returned to Linton. "Do you accept this sacrifice? Will you take my life as I took you son's?"

Linton stared into his eyes. Malice shone back. "I do accept, and I *will* take your life," he said. "And I am ready to take it now." He held up the knife, the sharpened edge glinting in the sun.

Heath unbuttoned his leather tunic, throwing it to the ground, then removed his shirt. Bare chested he spread his arms. "I am ready," he said.

Cathy spoke in low tones, her words a mumble. *Under the eagle's claw - ever may you wither!* "under earnes clea, a þu geweornie."

Linton nodded and moved behind Heath, gripping a handful of hair to pull his head back.

Shrivel as the coal upon the hearth! "Clinge þu alswa col on heorþe"

The baby snuffled against Cathy as the cold blade of the knife was pressed against Heath's chest, the point breaking the skin. A droplet of blood welled at the cut.

Shrink as the muck in the stream. "Scring þu alswa scerne aPage," Cathy whispered.

The ever-present rage that whirled within Heath's core evaporated and a sense of peace enveloped him. "Take me," he sighed. "I am ready."

May you become as little as a linseed grain. "Swa litel þu gewurþe alswa linsetcorn," Cathy said in a stronger voice as Linton raised the dagger. Ellette squealed, hiding behind her hands.

And even so small may you become, that you become as nought. "and alswa litel þu gewurþe þet þu nawiht gewurþe!" Cathy screamed as the knife's point hit Heath's chest. "þet þu nawiht gewurþe!" she repeated.

Linton lurched as though he had missed his target.

The coldness of the blade's point grew warm, and particles of ash began to rise in front of Heath's face.

Ellette gasped.

The edge of the knife was aflame, the metal disintegrating as it burned, the flame devouring the metal as though it were a sheet of paper. Ash-like particles whorled in the gusts of wind that blew through the trees. The burning reached Linton's hand as he stood in paralysed confusion and swiftly rose to envelope his arm. Dust whirled as the wind whipped around him and Linton, his mouth agape in silent horror, disappeared within a vortex of embers and ash.

Heath remained still, amazed at the storm before him, then stepped beside Cathy and the baby.

"He's gone! How could it be?" Heath said, bewildered as the ash floated upwards.

"It is a miracle!" Ellette cried. "A blessing of the gods."

Cathy smiled though couldn't hold back a sob of relief.

"You don't seem shocked," Heath said, crouching beside her as she cradled the baby. He wiped at the tears on her cheek.

"I'm ... I'm amazed! ... I offered Linton as a sacrifice to the aether, to repay my debt, and it worked." Cathy held the baby close, kissing its cheek as more tears rolled down her face.

Heath slipped his arm across her shoulders and stroked the child's face, tears blurring his vision. "Then I owe you my life."

"If he's gone," asked Ellette, "does that mean the curse is lifted?"

"I think it does," replied Mercurio as he stepped out from behind a tree, a leafless branch covering his hips.

"It's good to see you again, old friend," Heath laughed as Ellette squealed. He flung his jacket across to the naked man, then returned his attention to his wife and son.

THE END

JOIN JC!

Stay up to date with JCs newest releases by signing up to her newsletter. You'll be the first to know what's coming up and receive an email to your inbox on publication day.

Sign up at the website: www.jcblake.com[1]

Or join here: JC Blake's Newsletter[2]

Other Books by the Author

Meet Liv and her fascinating aunts in this addictive series

Menopause, Magick, & Mystery

Hormones, Hexes, & Exes[3]

---

1. http://www.jcblake.com
2. https://dl.bookfunnel.com/pgh4acj6f8

Hot Flashes, Sorcery, & Soulmates[4]
Night Sweats, Necromancy, & Love Bites[5]
Menopause, Moon Magic, & Cursed Kisses[6]
Midlife Hexes & Gathering Storms[7]
Midnight Hexes & Hormonal Exes[8]
Midlife Curses & Lovestruck Shifters[9]
Harems, Hexes, & Hairy Housewives

Meet Leofe, the Poison Garden Witch, as she discovers her magical powers and makes life after divorce an adventure.

Deadheading the Hemlock[10]

A young woman is pushed to the edge of a breakdown in this supernatural murder mystery.

When the Dead Weep[11]

---

3. https://books2read.com/u/3yKEzv

4. https://books2read.com/u/baDnaa

5. https://books2read.com/u/31RGYl

6. https://books2read.com/u/meng79

7. https://books2read.com/u/mvWQ22

8. https://books2read.com/u/4ELe7Y

9. https://books2read.com/u/3LVPOX

10. https://books2read.com/u/bOzxKE

11. https://books2read.com/u/mKpDyd

EXPECTING MAGIC

Printed in Great Britain
by Amazon